A Witch in Time

A Witch
in Time

DISCARD

Madelyn Alt

BERKLEY PRIME CRIME, NEW YORK

THE BERKLEY PUBLISHING GROUP
Published by the Penguin Group
Penguin Group (USA) Inc.
375 Hudson Street, New York, New York 10014, USA
Penguin Group (Canada), 90 Eglinton Avenue East, Suite 700, Toronto, Ontario M4P 2Y3, Canada
(a division of Pearson Penguin Canada Inc.)
Penguin Books Ltd., 80 Strand, London WC2R 0RL, England
Penguin Group Ireland, 25 St. Stephen's Green, Dublin 2, Ireland (a division of Penguin Books Ltd.)
Penguin Group (Australia), 250 Camberwell Road, Camberwell, Victoria 3124, Australia
(a division of Pearson Australia Group Pty. Ltd.)
Penguin Books India Pvt. Ltd., 11 Community Centre, Panchsheel Park, New Delhi—110 017, India
Penguin Group (NZ), 67 Apollo Drive, Rosedale, North Shore 0632, New Zealand
(a division of Pearson New Zealand Ltd.)
Penguin Books (South Africa) (Pty.) Ltd., 24 Sturdee Avenue, Rosebank, Johannesburg 2196,
South Africa

Penguin Books Ltd., Registered Offices: 80 Strand, London WC2R 0RL, England

This book is an original publication of The Berkley Publishing Group.

This is a work of fiction. Names, characters, places, and incidents either are the product of the author's imagination or are used fictitiously, and any resemblance to actual persons, living or dead, business establishments, events, or locales is entirely coincidental. The publisher does not have any control over and does not assume any responsibility for author or third-party websites or their content.

FIRST EDITION: April 2010

Library of Congress Cataloging-in-Publication Data

Alt, Madelyn.
    A witch in time / Madelyn Alt. — 1st ed.
        p.   cm.
    ISBN 978-0-425-23261-3
1. Witches—Fiction.   2. City and town life—Indiana—Fiction.   I. Title.
    PS3601.L75W57   2010
    813'.6—dc22   2009050091

PRINTED IN THE UNITED STATES OF AMERICA

10   9   8   7   6   5   4   3   2   1

A12005970673

For Matthew and Lindsey
09-09-09
Congratulations, kiddos!
Love you madly!

The intuitive mind is a sacred gift
and the rational mind is a faithful servant.
We have created a society that honors
the servant and has forgotten the gift.

—ALBERT EINSTEIN

A Witch in Time

Chapter 1

My name is Maggie O'Neill, and I am a small-town girl.

At one time, I was loath to admit it. We all know what city people think of us out here in the ignominious sticks. I mean, I know there are instances of hickdom here and there, but honestly, it's not like it's the Dukes of Hazzard all over again. So even though some of us are monster-truck-driving, shotgun-owning, corn-growing, demolition-derby-attending, Sunday-afternoon-barbecuing kinds of people, that doesn't mean we are all country bumpkins without a shred of culture to our names . . . even if the 4H fairs do draw in more customers than all of the dusty museums in the area combined. Here we attend school programs, not Broadway shows, and for some at least, the only classical music they will ever hear comes from the middle of the football field at halftime.

To some city folk, that means we're . . . heathens.

The funny thing is, that's not really too far off the mark, depending on one's perspective.

You see, we *are* the heathens of old-time reckoning—

people of the land, whose countrified lifestyles mark the passing of the seasons in ways that many city people cannot understand.

Some of us are more heathen than others.

And I, dear friends, am a prime example.

It isn't so much that I am the epitome of an irreligious person. Call me . . . spiritual instead. Or should that be spirit-ual, hyphen intended? Because the spirits that have been hard at work in Stony Mill, Indiana, certainly seem to think they are an important part of the equation. I've lived my whole life in Stony Mill. Once upon a time I thought living here assured a certain level of safety, even if monotony was standing ever so patiently alongside, waiting for the baton pass in the Relay O' Life. The spirits seemed to have opinions about that, too.

Monotony doesn't begin to describe what we've been experiencing these last nine months. Rather the opposite, in fact.

At first it was only the sensitives who could feel the winds of change sweeping in like a summer storm through my hometown. People like my witchy boss and mentor, Felicity Dow, whose heightened senses delved into depths of perception unknown by more "normal" folk. And—surprise, surprise—people like me. As an empath—a sensitive who feels the emotions of others to the extent that they might as well be her own—I must count myself among those numbers. But after a strange collection of tragedies and calamities in town, it didn't take much sensitivity at all to realize that something was . . . different. Case in point, my perfectly perfect, if somewhat obtuse, little sister, Melanie. Mel was about as sensitive as a doorknob, and her only gift for intuition came in the form of a strong nose for gossip. Bless her heart. Yet even Mel in her expensive subdivision and ideal life had not been safe from the chaotic energies running amok in our sleepy little town.

I think it is safe to say, that trend is on the rise. Time will tell.

Welcome to my world.

My name is Maggie O'Neill, and this is my story.

August was in full swing on a late Thursday afternoon where it seemed all I had gotten done was to peer anxiously at the wall of antique clocks opposite my usual post at the sales counter. So much for being the model employee I tried so hard to be. I shook my head to clear away the mists of worry and distraction that hovered on the fringes of my mind as I rang up the purchases for what would likely be Enchantments' last customer of the day. At least I hoped it was our last. For once, I was Ready. To. Go.

"That will be thirty-nine ninety-six," I told our customer, a regular, as the numbers totaled on the cash register. It had been a long, hot day, our air-conditioning had been acting up, the HVAC crew was missing in action, and a seemingly endless period of Mercury being retrograde in the cosmos had ensured that Murphy's Law was alive and kicking. Things at the store had been chaotic at best. Add in the missing shipments; a broken crystal vase thanks to my little furry fiend—I mean, *friend*—and store kitten, Minnie; and a laptop whose hard drive suddenly stopped talking to its keyboard, forcing us all to rely on memory to locate items in our extensive inventory; and what you got in total was frazzled nerves.

All mine. Liss was, as per usual, as cool as the proverbial cucumber. My proverbial cucumbers, on the other hand, always turned out pickled.

"How do you do it?" I asked her when the customer had walked out with a gift bag packed chockfull of goodies and a smile of satisfaction on her face. The admiration coloring my tone was not for effect. I would be the first to admit that I aspired to achieve my boss's Zen approach toward life someday. It would be nice not to be affected by all of the small annoyances and frustrations some would consider a normal part of spending time on this earth.

"What's that, ducks?" Liss asked, peering at me from over her half-moon glasses as she tucked a pencil absentmindedly into the hair above her ear and pushed the Return key on the nonfunctioning laptop.

"Stay calm and cool in the face of adversity?"

Liss laughed, a lovely, merry sound that in all the months I'd known her had never yet failed to make me feel better. "I wasn't aware that we *were* facing adversity. I'll have to keep my eyes open now, won't I?"

Her unfaltering good mood stopped me in my tracks. Was I making too much of things? "You're right. I'm being overly dramatic." And I, for one, despised melodrama.

"It's just the heat getting to you, love. Now, where are those repairmen? They were supposed to be here hours ago. This old building needs some TLC."

She was right. August had been sizzling, steamy, and sultry and just plain abysmal as far as the weather went . . . not that that was unusual for this time of year. But sometimes there was a sense that we were all dancing around like grease on a forgotten griddle. You've heard of jumping from the frying pan into the fire? Yeah. Despite all of the good things that had been happening in my life of late—the most interesting of which had been the blossoming of a new and potentially promising pairing with the not-nearly-so-dark-as-everyone-thought but nevertheless dangerous-to-my-equilibrium Marcus Quinn—there was still an element of edgy uncertainty swimming around in the mix. Or was that just me, being dramatic again?

Probably.

Liss was right. What was a little hot weather in the overall scheme of things? What were a few minor annoyances? It was the town gone mad that we had to worry about.

And on that cheery note . . .

"Would you like me to wait with you for the repairmen?" I offered, although I freely admit that for once the offer was only halfheartedly made. Tonight was a scheduled off night for me, and I had made plans. Big plans. Hopeful plans.

I caught Minnie gazing at me with her luminous bi-colored eyes. I shot her a meaningful look that said, *And said plans will not require input from you, Missypants! None of your funny business.* She just blinked at me, the soul of innocence, then bent over to acrobatically lick the back of her leg.

"Oh, my dear. I wouldn't dream of keeping you. Now, now," she said, brushing away my hands as I made a move to tidy the counter. "None of that." She examined me more closely. "If I didn't know you better, I'd say you were procrastinating."

"I'm not procrastinating! I'm—" I wasn't, was I? I double-checked myself. Of course I wasn't. What was there to procrastinate about? A night of movies, munchies, and Marcus in front of the television at his house, away from the nervous energy cycling through town . . . what was there to be nervous about that?

Except the butterflies in my stomach were calling me out as a liar. Because after three weeks of exploring every facet of making out with Marcus like a teenager in the heated throes of new love, I knew that we were standing on a precipice that would change things forever, for better or for worse, and while I wanted it as much as I thought he did, there was still that edge of uncertainty about what it would mean to the relationship. What it would mean to us.

Get a grip, Maggie, I told myself. *It's not like you've never done this before.* Visions of a young Madonna flashdanced through my head, and I don't mean the beatific one.

But it really had been a while, and all the what-ifs were making me crazy.

Er.

Crazi-*er*.

Hormones. I blamed hormones. They get all out of whack when not let out of their padded cells every once in a blue moon.

"I'm not procrastinating," I repeated, ducking away from her all-seeing gaze. "I just . . . I . . . well, tonight's a big night," I finished simply, unable to find the words to explain further.

It didn't matter. Liss seemed to understand. The soft look she gave me was both compassionate and reassuring. "Deep breaths, my dear. Don't fret. Whatever is troubling you, you'll make it through with flying colors."

That was Liss for you. She always understood. She did, however, seem to be waiting expectantly for me to offer up what it was that I was so nervous about. But somehow I just couldn't. Despite the fact that I knew without a doubt that Marcus and Liss had never been the item I had originally imagined them to be, it still felt a bit like the new girlfriend comparing notes with the former. Silly, really. But there it was.

To ward off her preternatural ability to read my thoughts and moods, I bent down and picked up Minnie, who had raised herself on her hind legs and had planted her front paws against my kneecaps. (*The little minx is growing so fast!*

Sniffle . . .) She'd also been hitching her rear quarters back and forth like a hula dancer with a bad knee—in preparation for launching herself up my body, no doubt. Poor girl—foiled again! She didn't seem to mind so much. She'd closed her eyes and started to purr the moment I'd scooped her into my arms. "Well, look at you," I cooed to her. "Pretty girl."

Liss went back to fussing with the laptop. "Minnie, dear, do tell your mummy that a few well-placed red and pink candles can do much for generating a lovely romantic glow. Not that I think you'll need it, mind you," she said, switching the point of her attack to me. "Marcus seems to know what he's doing, good lad. But the Love candles are upstairs in the loft in the event you should feel the need to prime the magickal pump. So to speak."

So much for thwarting her psychic prowess. "Stop that," I said, the heat in my cheeks speaking volumes for the blush I knew must have taken root there.

"Stop what, dear?" Liss asked guilelessly.

"Stop being so good at the whole Vulcan mind meld thing. I swear, sometimes you are positively spooky." And sometimes a girl liked to keep her secrets.

"Thank you, my dear. I do try."

She didn't have to try, and I knew it. It was just a part of her, a very positive, very para-spooky part of her. One that I could only hope to emulate myself one day. It could come in handy, at that.

More and more I thought of Liss as a second mother . . . only one who was utterly unbiased save for a bighearted wish to help and a goodly dose of love. My own mother could have learned a thing or two from that. I love my mom, mind you, but Holy-Mary-Mother-of-God, that woman really knows how to push my buttons. God love her.

The Goddess, too. And all the angels and saints and protective spirits, to boot. My mother needed all the divine intervention she could get to counteract what was a majorly controlling nature.

"Come on, Minnie," I said, placing a resounding smooch on the velvety fur between her pointy ears, "let's leave Liss to fight with the computer gremlins. You and I have places to go. People to see."

Movies to watch.

Men to . . .

Come to think of it, maybe the candles would be a good idea. They certainly couldn't hurt.

"The candles are in the top right drawer in the large cabinet up in the Loft," Liss couldn't resist calling after me as I covertly made my way toward the stairs. "I dressed them myself in Goddess oil, cloves, dragon's blood, and cinnamon for that extra boost. Should be just the trick."

No use pretending I wasn't interested. I paused in my cross-store trajectory as a thought occurred to me, and turned back to face her. "Liss . . . can I ask you a question?"

"Of course, dear. You can ask anything you like."

"Well . . ." It took me a moment to find the words. It could be a sensitive subject after all. "Why is it you haven't found yourself a willing male and taken your own counsel?"

"You mean, why am I not out looking for love in all the sacred spaces?" I was relieved that she took the question for what it was—curiosity. Humor crinkled at the corners of her eyes. "What makes you think I'm depriving myself?"

I had seen the woman in action, charming every man of a certain age that she came into contact with . . . but: "That doesn't mean you have opened yourself up to love."

She smiled, and I saw a hint of wistfulness behind the pragmatism. "One does not control or influence the heart. Love happens only if or when it is meant to happen. Not before, not after."

It had been four years since her husband Geoffrey died. Perhaps it was still too soon, I mused, for her to move on in that way. The romantic in me wanted all of my girlfriends to be completely and utterly happy, and while a man should never be deemed a necessary ingredient for a girl's happiness, the fact remained that having one around sure could make life a whole lot more interesting. But maybe it would always be too soon for Liss. Maybe it just wasn't meant to be.

I was getting myself all misty. I cleared my throat. "So. Top right drawer, big cupboard."

"You're welcome."

The Loft was one of the most peace-filled places I had ever been lucky enough to experience. It was Liss who had made it that way, injecting her own personal energy into the space until the entire area sparkled with life. When the weather outside prevented her from using the circle in the forest clearing on her property just outside of Stony Mill, the Loft was where she performed many of her meditations, rituals, and spells. I myself often came up here when I needed a few minutes to clear my head, or when I just wanted to meditate and soak up the powerful atmosphere of the place. Powerful in a good way. In a way that spoke of protection, and of light working for the good of all, and of keeping out the dark. In a way that called up my own power from deep within.

Good magick.

I slid my hand along the gallery rail as I made my way toward the wall of cabinets, mostly big solid antiques. As was my habit, I circled around the center rug that marked the ritual area—to me it was sacred space, just as much as her forest glade, and not something to be crossed lightly and without regard. My deference might also have something to do with the protective Invisible Threshold wards Liss cast over the area, although as one of her inner circle, it's not as though I wasn't allowed to spend time there.

I found the candles right where she'd said I would, in a drawer clearly labeled "Candles, Red and Pink—for all romantic magickal purposes." Bingo. I selected three, a power number. Going for the big bang, without bankrupting the store for my own personal gain. I preferred to cache my romance karma, *thankyouverymuch*. Better safe than sorry.

"Might I suggest that you take a sampling of rose petals and violets from the bulk stores as well?" Liss called up the stairs, ever helpful. "Although now that I think of it, you might not want to burn it in his presence. Marcus is a smart cookie—it's not as though he doesn't know what the herbs are for. A sachet, perhaps, to tuck into your pocket?"

I decided to forgo the herbs. She was right: Marcus wasn't oblivious. And besides, while I wasn't against a little bit of pump priming, I really didn't think much of it was needed in this case. I did, however, grab a little package of dried catnip to keep the wee one well plied.

Call it insurance.

Liss was waiting for me when I returned once again to the main floor. "Or maybe some fresh fruit. Strawberries, cherries, apples are all good for love. Add in a bit of chocolate, and a savvy witch is in business." She arched a meaningful brow.

I shook my head at her persistence and grinned in spite of myself. "Good *night*, Liss."

A savvy witch also knows when to butt out. Which she did. Gracefully, of course. "Good night, ducks. And good everything else, too," she said with a mischievous twinkle in her eye.

Honestly, maybe she should rethink her stance on finding love again, I thought to myself as I gathered Minnie into her soft-sided carrier and hit the gravel parking spaces behind the store. If her current zeal for the topic was a true measure, it seemed quite possible to this armchair therapist that she was living vicariously through others as a defense against reentering the dating game for her own gain. Always a matchmaker, never a match of her own. P'raps the two of us would have to have a talk one of these days. When the time was right.

In the meantime, I had places to go . . .

And so it was with a wildly beating heart that I loaded Minnie into my aging VW Bug (early on in our partnership my dad had jokingly compared her to Stephen King's Christine due to her cantankerous and unpredictable nature, and the mostly affectionate epithet had stuck), and headed home to my basement apartment in the aging Victorian on Willow Street for a quick pit stop to freshen up before my scheduled meet-up with Marcus. My best friend, Steff, who lived upstairs, wasn't at home, but that was no surprise since she was a nurse and worked long hours.

"What do you say, Minnie?" I asked the Furry One, who blinked at me sleepily from her spot in the sun on the passenger seat. "Have a little kibble while I get dressed?"

Lifting Minnie's carrier, I made my way across the surprisingly-green-for-August-thanks-to-a-bevy-of-rainstorms lawn to the sunken entrance to my apartment. Eager to escape the steam, I let myself in, grateful for the immediate blast of cool darkness. My basement apartment wasn't exactly Home Beautimous material, but at least it was always temperate, despite the weather raging outside. I set down my things on the old dining room chair just inside the door, all except for Minnie's carrier, which I placed on the floor. Immediately she began pawing at the zippered escape hatch.

"Hold on, silly. So impatient!"

The moment she could wiggle her way out, she did, squeezing through the partly unzipped gap like a squirt of ink. Once free, she shook her head hard enough to see stars.

She blinked blankly until her vision cleared, then scampered off to the kitchen. I knew what was coming next; I stood to one side to watch the entertainment unfold. First, the industrious pawing at the food dish until it scooted right off the soft braided mat that kept the kitty dining area mess free. Next came the unrelenting flicking with hooked claws at the bottom of the door to the cupboard where I kept the kitty kibble. Finally, she hopped from the chair to the tabletop to the counter, meowed at me—loudly—and while I waited to allow her to finish what had become a nightly performance, she proceeded to knock any item within reach to the floor. Notepad, pencil, key ring. When her beady little eyes fixed on her next target, I moved in quickly.

"Whoa, whoa, whoa there, Turbo. Not the glass," I said, putting it in the sink. "I take it you want food?"

She began to purr and sauntered back and forth along the counter. And then, just to seal the deal in the event I was a little too dense to understand her meaning, she waited until I had bent down to open the cupboard before stretching out a paw and deliberately pushing the saltshaker over the edge. It missed me by inches, dousing me with a shower of salt crystals as it fell. "Hey, knock it off!"

She tilted her head quizzically to one side as if to say, *But I just did . . .*

Touché.

I scooped the crunchy kibble into her bowl and set it down on her mat. Before I could straighten again, Minnie had taken a falling leap from the counter, landing gracefully, and started crunching away happily. I only wished I could eat with that same lackadaisical absence of guilt. Instead I had to worry about the elastic on my underwear creating unsightly ripples.

You know, sometimes I think coming back as a cosseted house cat wouldn't be such a bad thing.

I watched her until I realized I was postponing the inevitable . . . What was I waiting for?

Leaving Minnie to nosh at her usual breakneck pace, I bypassed the lights blinking on my answering machine, because I knew it was bound to be nothing more pressing than the daily calls from my mom, just "checking up on me," and I really wasn't in the mood to handle her queries and complaints just yet. Instead I slipped directly into my bedroom. I'd worn ankle-cropped pants with ballet flats and a close-fitting tee to the store this morning—which was fine—but I thought maybe I'd kick things up a notch. One flirty, drapey, baby-doll cami and a pair of strappy Mary Jane peep-toes later, and I felt I'd heightened my sex appeal enormously. To this I added some earrings that sparkled and flashed when I moved my head, and then I deepened my makeup just a tad. After shaking out my hair, which had been twisted up in clips all day to keep its unruly waves from frizzing in the August steam, and running my fingers through it, I looked in the mirror to find I actually looked quite . . . good. Maybe even better than I'd intended. Hm. That was a happy surprise.

"What do you think, Min? Do I meet with your approval?"

Minnie had finished with her evening feast and was now perched, round bellied and satisfied, in the middle of my bed, watching me. She tilted her head sideways and gave me an inquisitive stare.

"Now, don't go giving me that look. Yes, I'm going out tonight. But you get to go, too—we're going to Marcus's house."

Minnie yawned, but I knew it was all an act. Pretending to be disinterested when inside that fuzzy little noggin waged schemes and daydreams of mayhem and mischief, and possibly even world domination. She perked up again the instant she saw me pick up her favorite toy, a stick-string-feather combo that would have her dancing around like a Spanish flamenco dancer, but before she could leap I popped it into a canvas tote along with her nibble treats, then cast an eye around me for anything else Minnie could possibly need.

Yet another stalling tactic on my part, and an obvious one at that.

I couldn't believe how nervous I was about tonight. It wasn't the possibility of rejection that was making me as distracted as a cat in a room full of parakeets—with Marcus, rejection had never really crossed my mind. It was the possibilities that were making me run both hot and cold today. And what possibilities they were! Because my deepest fear was that I was falling for him, fast and hard, and my track record with love hadn't been what anyone would call "exemplary." In fact, I was the poster girl for sad tales with bad endings. I had definitely been left nursing a wounded heart once or twice before. But that shouldn't be a concern with Marcus. Should it?

Hello?

Bueller?

Good grief, my sister was right. I was neurotic.

I took a deep breath. There was no reason to worry. Not this time. Things were going swimmingly with Marcus. So much so that it was easy to forget the strange events that had brought me to him. The weirdness in town. The murders. The rise in the tide of spiritual energies, light and so-not-light. My unexpected awareness of said energies, an awareness that, once acknowledged, had kept growing and growing and growing, until now it had evolved into something I didn't understand, with no clear end in sight. But none of that mattered, as long as this one thing in my life was going well.

So . . . what was I so afraid of?

Sheesh!

Minnie's placid stare seemed to echo what the voice in my head was whispering:

So? What are you waiting for?

What, indeed?

Chapter 2

Taking a deep, fortifying breath, I made myself move.

The first step is always the hardest, Margaret . . .

The voice of my conscience all too often took on the vocal stylings and attitudes of my late Grandma Cora. It wasn't something that I relished—Grandma C had always been a pragmatically stern woman of country ways and devout sensibilities, and that side of her had never failed to come across loud and clear, even as a whisper in my head. Does everyone out there have a snarky conscience? Or was I the only one?

It was because of that that I now turned a dubious eye inward. Because . . .

Since when had Grandma C *ever* been on my side?

Suspicious minds, Margaret, the soundless voice tsked.

And just what was that supposed to mean?

Only that they always find what they expect to find. Remember that.

Hm. There was something to that, actually. Deepest fears always seemed to manifest into the direst of circumstances at

the worst of times, somehow, some way. It was the biggest
reason Murphy's Law was viewed as truism with a capital
T. It was up to all of us to do our best to banish the Murph-
meister from our lives. I understood that. In theory. Practical
application proved trickier, but I was trying.

And you see Marcus as good for you, I think? the Grandma C
conscience voice prodded.

Yes. Oh, yes.

Well?

For once, Grandma C had it going on. And with her and
Liss *and* Minnie on my side, how could I resist?

Crosstown traffic was clearing by the time we ventured
past our quiet neighborhood. Not that Stony Mill rush hour
could ever compare to or compete with a larger city, but with
narrow streets and parking along the curb, safe passage could
at times be a complicated process. I cut across via the byzan-
tine residential routes, wending through subdivisions, until
I hit the sleepy older neighborhood on the outskirts that
Marcus called home. Before I got to know Marcus, I would
never have envisioned him living in a one-and-a-half-story
Craftsman-style bungalow, complete with a deep porch and
low-slung roofline. The spiky iron fence at the front might
not have matched in theory, but the river stone posts separating the sections made it work. The house was far from
modern, but it possessed a quiet dignity that felt comfortable and familiar. I loved everything about it, from the faded
linoleum in the kitchen, to the carriage barn in the rear that
had been converted into a garage-slash-motorcycle workshop,
aka the ideal Man Cave. Now *that* was what I had always
expected from my Marcus.

My Marcus. I smiled at the very thought.

I parked at the curb. *Deep breaths, Maggie my girl*, I told
myself. A quick check in the mirror I'd long ago Velcro'ed
onto the visor assured me that neither the heat nor the hu-

midity had demolished my best beauty efforts yet, though getting out of the elements would certainly help. I glanced over at Minnie and smiled.

"Here we go."

I grabbed my bag, Minnie's carrier, and the canvas tote of kitty goodies and let myself in through the front gate. It made the usual squawk of the hinges as I closed it and dropped the latch into place. The cobbled walk under my feet felt like the curving yellow brick road of Oz, leading me to . . .

"Hello, sweetness."

I felt a flush of pleasure sweep through me as I looked up to find Marcus waiting for me in the crook of the old-fashioned wooden screen door and looking nothing like the wily wizard. I stopped in my tracks at the base of the steps. Even from deep in the belly of the porch, his eyes seemed to glow in welcome. My heart did a little bounce and wobble.

Oh, yeah, I was in big trouble, all right.

I lifted my hand and gave a weak, fluttering wave. "Hi."

"I've been waiting for you."

Another wobble, and this time my stomach got into the act. *Keep your head on straight, girl*, Grandma C's voice intoned inside my head. *Nice and easy.* "You have?"

"Mm-hm."

"Oh." I was having trouble getting the gears in my brain to function. All they did was whirr. Madly.

"You going to stand down there all day?" he asked, a lilt of amusement lifting one corner of his mouth as he leaned a shoulder indolently against the inner door frame. "Or did you want me to come down there and get you?"

Well, that option did present some distinct possibilities . . .

Flustered, I cleared my throat and made a show of displaying my things as I mounted the steps. "I come with baggage."

"Do you, now. Hello, Minnie." He reached down to take them from me, setting it all inside the door, which he still held propped open with one foot, then turned back to face me. His clear blue eyes searched mine. I couldn't help wondering how much he saw there. "And *you* . . ." he said, his voice trailing off as he took my face between his hands and lowered his mouth to mine for one long, heart-stopping minute.

Big trouble.

Oh yeah.

"Hell-*ooo*, Miss O'Neill." The low croon teased my tingling lips most pleasantly.

"Hello, Mr. Quinn," I breathed back, linking my fingers together behind his neck.

"I've been waiting to do that all day."

"You have?"

"Mm-hm."

"That's funny. Me, too."

The slow curve of his lips was all I could see. Truth be told, it was all I wanted to see. Without another thought I slid my arm around his neck and kissed him soundly, pressing myself to his body tight enough that he was forced to reach behind himself to grope for the door frame with one hand to support us both. His other arm was wrapped up and between my shoulder blades, his long fingers cradling the nape of my neck. I couldn't have gotten away if I'd wanted to.

I didn't. Want to, that is.

Nervous . . . had I been nervous? How ridiculous. This was exactly what I had been hoping for. What was there to be nervous about this?

I didn't know how long it was before I drifted away from the enchantment of his mouth and back to the realization that we were standing on his front porch, displaying the full measure of our mutual fascination before God, Goddess, and the entire county. I pulled away slightly, regretfully, my hands lingering on his chest. "We should probably go inside. Someone might see."

He raised one eyebrow in amusement. "And?"

"My mother has a lot of friends."

"You ashamed of me, Maggie?"

"Of course not."

"Or are you just afraid of your mother?"

I frowned at that. I was less than three weeks away from my thirtieth birthday. A woman, full grown and in charge of her own destiny. I did not need my mother's approval for my life. On the other hand, it certainly did make life easier if the two of us weren't at loggerheads with each other.

Tricky, tricky.

"I'm not afraid of her," I told him, and I couldn't help nibbling on the inside of my lower lip. "I'm . . . wary of her web of spies, that's all."

"I see. Well, in that case, maybe you'd better come on inside." He took my hand and tugged. "I have a special way of dealing with spies and busybodies and other unwanted entities."

I knew he was just being funny, but I had seen firsthand how he dealt with unwanted entities, and in truth the experience had both frightened me and made me feel very safe in his capable hands, all at the same time. There was something deeply reassuring about his knowledge and mastery of all matters spiritual, a certainty I did not yet possess. Maybe I never would. But one thing I did know: next to Liss, Marcus made a pretty good counselor of the mysterious. Between the two of them, I was covered.

I followed him inside, privately enjoying the warmth of his hand holding mine.

"What's all this?" I asked him when my eyes had adjusted to the more shadowy interior. Unusually shadowy. I couldn't help noticing that all the curtains were drawn, and that set up in front of the big windows were what appeared to be cameras on tripods, as well as a couple of other odd-looking devices whose purposes I couldn't guess. Heavy wires, neatly bound with plastic tie wraps, snaked across the hardwood floor and down the hall toward the bedroom he used as his own private digital compound. While on his stint in the military, Marcus had served in Intelligence. Something told me he hadn't completely gotten that lifestyle out of his system.

"This? Nothing, really. Call it . . . insurance."

Marcus wasn't usually this circumspect. I peered up at him curiously. "Insurance for what? What's going on?"

He shrugged away the question. "Nothing I can't handle. Trust me on this."

I had no misgivings about his ability to handle, oh, just about anything. Without a doubt he had an innate understanding of how to handle me.

"Cameras. Wires. What's this?" I asked him, pointing to a round dishlike object.

"Just a little listening device."

"And this?" I indicated a smaller black box.

He grabbed my hand and drew me away, carefully avoiding the various tripods and trip wires. "A voice amplifier. Nothing to worry about."

Noooo, nothing to worry about here. Nothing at all . . .

"And *why* are we doing the whole James Bond thing with the neighbors?" I pressed, knowing the story had to be a good one.

"I would never spy on my neighbors without good reason," he protested as he plopped down onto the sofa and pulled me into his lap. His arms closed immediately around my waist to hold me in place.

Distractions were not going to work on me this time. No sirree . . .

"And you explain all of the devices and whatnot pointed at them, how?"

He tilted his head back on the sofa, staring thoughtfully at the ceiling for a moment. "Hm. Would you believe me if I told you that they're not directed toward the neighbors specifically?"

I glanced over my shoulder. The cameras certainly seemed to be aimed in all the pertinent directions.

He sighed, his fingers toying with one of my curls. "I take it you're probably not going to be able to just let this go."

"Doubtful."

"I suppose you're going to need an explanation."

"Possibly."

The one-word answers seemed to be working in my favor. "Well," he said, considering his options, "I suppose I was kidding myself to think that you could come over without wondering what was up."

"Probably."

"So I guess you're wanting answers."

"Mm-hm." Was that one word or two? Or none?

"You're awfully cute when you're curious," he said with a wicked grin.

It seems the one-word answers weren't working so well after all. "Stop trying to confuse me."

"Maybe I want to confuse you. Maybe"—he twirled the strand of hair around his index finger, then flicked his gaze to mine—"just maybe," he said, his voice dropping to a low murmur intended to warm a girl's blood in an instant, "that was my plan all along."

Before he could lean in to kiss me and scatter my senses to the four winds, I placed my fingertips over his lips. "Neighbors?" I prompted.

"Can't see a thing, I promise."

"But you can see them."

"Nah." He shook his head. "It's not for the neighbors, Maggie. I told you that."

"Then who *is* it for?"

"That's what I'm trying to find out."

All of this talking in circles was making my head hurt. I just looked at him, waiting patiently.

Finally he relented. "Take a peek through the view finders."

I got to my feet and walked over to one of the cameras, bending close to peer through. To my surprise, the object in view wasn't the house on the opposite side of the street. "It's pointed at the street itself," I said, frowning.

"Check another."

I did. Same story, second time around. The camera that seemed to be pointing at the neighbor's house next door was actually capturing anyone approaching the house from that direction.

"There's another camera in the dining room," Marcus told me.

The question was, why? I turned to him in bemusement.

"I think someone has been watching my place. I just wanted to see if I could catch said someone in the act. Get it on film. Try to figure out what's up."

My eyebrows lifted, and I glanced sharply toward the window. "Someone's been watching you? Why would anyone do that?"

"I don't know."

"How long has this been going on?"

"I don't know," he repeated. "A week? Two weeks? I'm not sure. I've been a little distracted lately." He winked at me.

I could relate. Boy, could I ever.

While I was up, I unzipped Minnie's carrier and set her down on the floor. "There you go, little one." She stretched and yawned, hooking her claws down to the floor as though searching for carpet to latch onto. I handed her one of her catnip mousies. "Run and play."

Obediently she picked up the tiny mouse in her mouth and darted for the nearest hidey-hole. She was almost as comfortable at Marcus's house as she was at the apartment. We'd been over often enough that Marcus had surprised us both by setting up a litter box in the laundry room and a soft kitty bed in the office window that overlooked a group of bird feeders he had installed in the yard, and by installing resident food and water dishes in the kitchen. Already Minnie thought of Marcus's place as her own.

I turned back to the living room. Still as bemused as ever, I sat down next to Marcus on the sofa. Immediately he drew my legs up over his and placed a steadying hand on my knees to hold me in place.

"Who do you think it is?" I asked him.

"Not a clue," he said. I didn't like the way his gaze slid away from mine. Why did I have a feeling that wasn't entirely the truth?

"Well, have you said anything to anyone?" I persisted. "About all this?"

"Uncle Lou and Aunt Molly know."

"I don't mean them. I meant, have you filed a report?"

His eyebrows rose. "With the police? Uh, no."

"Why not?"

The look he gave me made me realize with a start how pointless the question was, considering my ex-boyfriend Tom's role with the S.M.P.D.

"Oh. Oh, yeah." And yet the situation frustrated me. Worst of all, I knew it was entirely my fault. Not intentionally . . . but did that make a difference when someone's heart was hurting? "There has to be some route available to you. What if this turns out to be serious?"

"Hey . . . Hey." Turning, he tipped my chin up to look at

him, and my heart turned over. "It's no big deal, Maggie. I've got it covered."

"But—"

He pressed a kiss to my lips to quiet my protests. "No worries, okay?"

It was easy for him to say. He wasn't the one who was responsible for his inability to go to the police if he needed to. I was.

"So . . . what's in the bag?" he asked, purposely deflecting my concern toward another topic altogether. I understood immediately what he was doing, but since there was no easy solution to the stalker problem, I quickly decided we might as well try to forget about it. For now.

"Oh, just a few goodies for tonight."

My airy reply made his eyebrows lift in interest. A slow smile began at the corners of his mouth. "You know, this sounds promising."

"Maybe." I kept things light and teasing, though inside me the element that had perked up was far more fiery in nature.

"Hm. So are you going to show me what you've got? Or are you going to make me wait?" The blue of his eyes blazed a little hotter. "I'm not sure I'm going to be good at that."

I smirked. I couldn't help myself.

"Waiting," he supplied quickly as clarification. "I'm not great at *waiting*."

I giggled this time. I couldn't help that, either.

"I assure you," he leaned in closer, pinning me with his gaze, "I am very good at the rest of it."

Gulp. Oh. Oh my. "Glad to hear it," I whispered as the threads of our personal energies began to hum and buzz between us, searching for ways to thread together, to interlock.

"Is this a personal assessment?" I asked him. "Or one that has received acknowledgments from . . . others?"

"Rave reviews," he promised as he smoothed his palm back and forth over the curve of my hip. "Maybe you'd like to add your perspective into the mix."

"Hmm. *Maaaay*be. Tonight, you mean?"

"The thought had crossed my mind."

"Hmm," I repeated, tilting my head to consult a phantom To Do list in the sky. "I *think* I might be free . . ."

"Glad to hear it." He closed the distance in one fell swoop, capturing my mouth and my attention in one pulse-starting instant.

This was a common occurrence for us, these past few weeks, and that was something I had to admit I was quite thrilled about. I hated to compare him to Tom—that seemed unfair, somehow, mostly to Tom—but sometimes I couldn't help it. With Tom, there had always been promises of intimacy, hints of a depth of emotion, but despite a serious attraction both on his part and on mine, nothing ever seemed to . . . happen. Honestly, more had happened with Marcus in three weeks than I had ever shared with Tom. There was something sad about that. A missed opportunity to share and explore something special with another person. Or maybe I was just sad that I hadn't elicited a stronger response in him. For a while I really thought we could have had something together.

Sometimes it is hard to be wrong.

But Marcus . . . oh, yes. Kiss by kiss, touch by touch, look by look, moment by moment, he let me know how much he wanted me, and that was a very heady thing indeed. They say knowledge is power, but in a situation like this, did he hold the power? Or did I? And did that even matter when the end result promised so much fun and excitement along the way?

I think not.

And for once Minnie was playing along, not biting toes,

not burrowing in my hair, not trying to worm her fuzzy face in between his and mine. It was just me gazing up at him, slipping my hands inside his shirt collar and holding him close, and it was him, taking me along with him for a truly wonderful ride. Never had a sofa seemed so blissfully comfortable before.

"Bedroom?" His voice and breath tickled in my ear, rumbling with possibilities.

I nodded. I didn't trust my ability to speak at the moment.

Who needed rose petals and love-infused candles? Not this sometimes witchy woman.

He locked my arms around his neck and lifted me up in his arms, romance-hero style, with nary a grunt or groan to be heard. Bless the man. Nothing doused romantic fires quite as abruptly as the sudden rearing up of that ugly beast otherwise known as "Body Issues."

Kissing while walking *and* carrying the full body weight of another person *and* wending one's way between and around furniture is quite a mean feat. I am happy to report that Marcus handled all of the above most admirably. I might even say, with skill.

The bed swallowed me whole, comfy and deep. I sighed as I was pressed down into it by the delicious weight of his lean body. Kiss for kiss, touch for touch, things were progressing far better than I had even planned. It was still daylight out, the long, lazy hours before dusk would arrive, but it seemed even the stars were aligning in honor of the night, because I could swear I heard angelic trumpets sounding in my ears.

Or it could be the triumphant march of the *1812 Overture* blaring at us from the top of the dresser, over in the corner.

"No, no, no, no, no!" I muttered to myself in frustration, squeezing my eyes tight to keep my mood from dissipating like so many steamy vapors. "I changed that ringtone. Ages ago. I swear I did." Not to mention I had set my phone on vibrate.

I frowned. Actually, I pouted.

"It's mine." Marcus rolled off me with a sigh and a reluctant backward glance at my still supine body.

He grabbed the cell phone off the dresser, flipped it open, and lifted it to his mouth without looking at it. "Yeah." To me, he mouthed with a dangerous glint in his eyes, *Don't. Move.*

I wasn't going anywhere. Trust me on that.

"Hey, Liss. What's up? Maggie? Yeah, she's here." He listened for a moment. "Hold on." He held the phone out to me. "Someone's trying to get ahold of you. Sounds urgent."

Chapter 3

It wasn't too hard to come up with a list of likely suspects. Topping the chart? My loving, if overbearing mother, natch.

I could always be wrong, though.

"Oh, Maggie, I'm so glad I found you." Liss's urgent energy sizzled along the airwaves, sinking into my suddenly alert nerve endings. "Your mother has been burning up the phone lines at the store. She's quite insistent on finding you. Now, dear, I know you're, shall we say, *busy*"—I blushed at that—"but I don't think she will be willing to give up the ghost easily."

That was a given. This was my mother we were talking about. She could give any pit bull a run for its money for sheer stubbornness. "No, I'm sure she won't. I'm sorry for the trouble, Liss."

"Not to worry, ducks."

"Did she say what was so urgent?"

"Nary a whisper. But I'm picking up on family, if that helps you to clarify."

As my mom was all about family, just as much as she was about running each of their respective lives, it didn't. It could be anything.

After signing off, I turned to Marcus, who had lain back on the bed to await me. His arms were crossed behind his head, a posture that pulled the sleeves of his T-shirt tight around the bulge of his biceps. *Yum.*

I handed his phone back to him. "My mother . . ." I hesitantly began to explain.

"Call," he interjected without a moment's pause, warding off my guilt. "I'll wait."

I wished I could just ignore my mother's message, but it was a hopeless cause. There were a few things my mother was particularly good at, and extending missives was one of them. Mostly she was a master at keeping her family in check. Like a hen clucking after her chicks, she pecked us all into submission, one toe-scratched line at a time. The trick was to avoid confrontation with her entirely. Unfortunately I hadn't quite figured out how to do that.

I padded out to the living room to find my bag. It was sitting on the floor just inside the front door—right where I'd left it. I reached for the straps, missing one as I lifted, only to be surprised by Minnie rolling out of its depths in a fuzzy, sleepy ball. Laughing, I scooped her onto my lap and stroked her with one hand while I dug in my bag for my phone with the other. *Aha, gotcha.* The little display screen showed that I had three new voice mail messages. Three. That was my mother's limit. After that, all bets were off. Hence the harassment of my boss.

Sigh.

I dialed my mom's cell number—she had finally given in to the relentless advancement of technology earlier in the summer once she figured out how a cell phone would make her stalking tendencies so much simpler to execute—and waited. Two whole rings . . . she was slipping.

"Margaret Mary-Catherine O'Neill! It is about time. Where have you been, and why have you been avoiding my calls?"

"Mom. Hi."

"Don't you 'hi' me, young lady. I have been at wit's end trying to get a bead on you. Do you realize what I have gone through this afternoon?"

I didn't, actually. Wasn't that why I was calling? "Uh, sorry?" She didn't get that sometimes I didn't want to be found, and she wouldn't understand it even if I did try to explain.

"You could try a little harder than that," she complained. I could feel the disapproving little purse of her mouth growing tighter.

"I'm really, really, really, super sorry," I lied. Because I wasn't. I deserved a little quiet time with Marcus, without the threat of my overly intrusive family hovering about.

"Humph." Not her most gracious of responses, but given the purpose for her call . . . "It's Melanie," she said, referring to my heavily pregnant sister. "It's time." Her voice was a touch breathless now that I stopped to listen a little more closely. "We're all here at the hospital. Something is going on—they've shooed us out of the labor room. Only Greg is allowed in there with her. I think you should come in."

"Well, is it serious?" My mind was whirling. "Is it Mel? Or is it the baby?"

"They haven't said. Will you come?"

It was the soft quiver in her voice that time that got to me the most. Despite her sometimes overbearing nature, she was our mother, and she cared for us, deeply. I knew that. And Melanie was her favorite. "I'll be there," I told her quietly.

"Good. Oh, Margaret, be sure to stop for coffee for every-

one on the way in, won't you? We'll need four. Five counting you."

And with that, her autocratic side returned at full strength
like the force of nature it most closely resembled. My mom . . .
she really did mean well. I was sure that would make a difference. Someday.

I set both my phone and the Minmeister back down before
returning to the bedroom to break the news to Marcus. As I
walked through the doorway, I found him just fastening the
front of his jeans, and—*ohhh my*. A fresh white button-down
hung open, exposing lean muscle and a tantalizing treasure
trail of fine hair leading down to where his hands had just
been working the placket of the stiff denim. I tried very hard
not to torture myself overmuch by looking.

Yeah. Total fail.

"Where are we going?"

My gaze snapped upward guiltily. I stared at him, wondering how I was going to break it to him. "Oh, I couldn't
possibly ask you—"

"You didn't ask. I offered. Where?"

I sighed. "It's my sister. Melanie? She's at the hospital. In
labor. There might be . . . complications."

"Well, let's go."

It was sweet of him to offer, and even sweeter that he
wanted to dress to impress. But . . . "I can't ask you—" I
started to say. "I mean, it's an awful lot to ask of anyone. I
mean, who knows how long I'll be there. I mean—"

Marcus started in on buttoning his shirt, not missing a
beat. "Your family doesn't know about me, do they."

It was a statement, not a question. There was no use deny-
ing it. I ducked my head. "No," I admitted sheepishly.

"Ah." With his shirt buttoned, he stepped safely into my
circle of energy and put his hands on my arms, softly running
his fingertips up and down. "You ashamed of me, Maggie?"

I brushed aside his question, scoffing. "Of course not."

"No? Then why don't you want me to meet your family?"

It wasn't that I didn't want *him* to meet *them*. It was that I didn't want to subject him *to* them. Meeting a girlfriend's family had to be a nerve-wracking proposition at the best of times. It was a big deal—a deal breaker, in some relationships. I was a little worried about whether my family would behave. It wasn't their strong point.

"I just . . . don't want to *inflict* them on you," I admitted at last, my mouth drawing inward in a worried pucker.

I felt the gentle pressure of his thumb lifting my chin, and I braved a peek at him. The warmth in his eyes, even in the darkening room, left me wishing he had left his phone on vibrate, too. Only then we would have been risking someone actually knocking down Marcus's door.

"Maggie. Do you think they'll do something that will chase me away? Well, they won't. This event is important to your family, right?"

I nodded, even though I didn't want to.

"Then it's important to me. Because *you're* important to me."

And how could any girl find fault with that?

"What about Minnie?"

"She'll be all right here for a while. We could close her in the laundry room or bathroom for safety's sake, but I'll bet she'd rather be where she can get comfortable."

No doubt. We left her sleeping in the middle of a puddle created by a soft wool throw on the sofa. Marcus reached down and grabbed one of my bags.

The one with all the . . . goodies.

"Oh, not that one." Embarrassed, I tried to take it from him. "That's just . . . stuff. I won't need it."

Was it something in my voice that had tipped him off? His eyes lit up. "What kind of stuff?" He held the bag up just beyond my reach, the way my brother would have, growing up, when he was trying to get my goat. "What exactly do you have in here?"

"Stuff stuff." I was stretching, reaching for it with little bounces to add extra height. "Come on, we've got to go."

"Oh, all right. If you say so." He bent to set the bag down again . . . then feinted to one side and peeked inside. "Why, Maggie O'Neill, what have we here? A brazen little kit of seduction?"

If my face had turned red at all with the first tease, by now it must be scarlet. One of the downsides to having a fair complexion. The least bit of sun or embarrassment, and the whole world knew of your distress. "Maybe . . ."

"Hmm. I'm flattered." Before I could turn away and hide my face, he scooped me into his arms. "But you definitely didn't need the extra oomph. We were doing pretty well on our own, don't you think?" And he kissed me then and there just to prove it, blasting my senses with luscious heat and sensation. As my legs began to revolt, I was forced—forced, I tell you!—to hold onto him for support. Too bad we were out of time. Sigh.

On the way over, Marcus stopped by Annie-Thing Good, Annie Miller's sweet little hometown café. Not only did it have some truly diet-busting offerings that called to me every time I drove past, but Annie also served the best coffee outside of Enchantments (*a girl has to show some loyalty!*). Marcus left the truck running, and we both went inside.

The café was overrun tonight by what appeared to be mostly rowdy high schoolers, with the occasional adult couple hiding away in the corner, or at least trying to. High school . . . looking at their fresh faces and big shows of false bravado, bubbling over with excitement about every little thing, I had to wonder, had I ever been that young? And yet it was only twelve years ago that I had graduated.

How time flies.

Marcus and I stood dutifully in line for our coffees, watching Annie and her counter help run back and forth like busy bees and listening to the conversations around us. Mostly the talk seemed to center around the intricacies of the preseason football scrimmage that Stony Mill High had just lost to a neighboring rival school.

"Damn! We almost had 'em. You saw it too, right, Troy? Damn!"

"What the hell happened? Our guys were lookin' real good, then all of a sudden . . . "

"It was like something raised up in front of them, and they couldn't go anywhere. Yeah. I was like, really?"

Just another creepy day in Stony Mill proper, I'd say. If they only knew . . .

Elsewhere I overheard a familiar voice. "Jordan Everett. Who'da thought, right, Charlie? I mean, the guy had everything going for him. And after everything he went through with Amanda Roberson—"

"Don't, Tare."

"I know, but—"

"Just don't."

I turned around just in time to see Charlie Howell shoving his hands in his jeans pockets and walking off toward the bathroom, while fellow Enchantments devotee Tara Murphy stared after him in confusion. Her shoulders lifted and fell again in a soft sigh before she turned my way.

Putting my hand on Marcus's arm, I told him, "Hold the line, I'm just gonna go talk to Tara for a sec."

He lifted his gaze in the direction I'd indicated. Spotting his younger cousin in the chaos, he raised his hand. I headed her off at the pass.

"Hey, girl. I didn't see you when we walked in." It didn't take a sensitive to realize she wasn't really paying a whole lot of attention to me. "Hey. Tara. Anyone home?"

"Oh. What? Sorry, Maggie," she said. "I was just—"

"Lost in your own little world? I noticed," I teased. "Anything the matter?"

She shook her head. "No. Not really. Well . . ."

"You're not arguing with Charlie again, are you?"

"Not as such. He just . . . he got all weird just now when I mentioned Jordan Everett. You know, his old basketball rival?"

"What about him?"

"He's dead, Maggie. We heard about it at the game; the news passed around like wildfire. It just happened tonight apparently. I guess he collapsed, or it was drugs or something. No one really knows what happened for sure. He was supposed to go off to college in a couple of weeks. IU Bloomington."

"That's awful," I said, frowning. I didn't know Jordan, but I knew he'd gone through a tough time last year when his girlfriend had fallen prey to an older man on the prowl, an association that had proved fatal for both of them. Now Jordan, too, had fallen prey . . . to the curse that seemed to be plaguing Stony Mill. Or was that being overly dramatic? Tell that to his family.

Tara nodded, her dark pixie hair moving prettily around her cheeks. "He went a little wild after Amanda passed, you know. A little crazy. A lot crazy. Moody and in-your-face. I mean, he was always a little high-handed with some people, a little arrogant even . . . but he's an Everett. This was different, though. Maybe it had something to do with the crowd he'd started hanging with. Not the usual preps. Fast and dirty. Everyone thought it was a phase and pretty soon he'd be back to his usual self. Especially with college coming right around the corner. I dunno. Sad, really."

Charlie was heading back now, and Tara immediately clammed up, unwilling to press her luck. I said my good-byes to the two of them and slipped back through the crowd to Marcus's side.

"Everything all right?" he asked, his eyes on Tara.

I nodded. "There's been another death in town. A boy who the kids knew. Jordan Everett."

"That's terrible. How did it happen?"

"Don't know. Tara doesn't know either. Evidently it just happened today, in any case."

It was our turn to hit the counter next. Annie waited on us herself, as usual with the biggest, brightest smile on her face. She clearly hadn't heard about Jordan. My hippie-dippy friend and N.I.G.H.T.S. cohort, Annie was a throwback to another era with her love of loose, flowing skirts, Earth shoes, and funny T-shirts. Today's selection displayed a sassy, spindly-legged egg sporting a red leather jacket, white socks, and loafers, and wielding a wisk as a cane. Caption? "Just Beat It." Yes, it was groan worthy. It was also totally Annie.

"Hey, you two!" she shouted over the din.

"Hey!" we shouted back.

"What?"

"Hey!"

"What?!"

Shaking my head, I grabbed her notepad and pen and wrote, *6 extra large coffees, please. On our way to hospital—Mel's baby. Need sustenance.* And then as an afterthought, *Love the shirt!* I handed her back her pad.

Her freckled nose crinkled in appreciation, and she winked at me. "Thanks!" And off she scurried to fill the order with an eye on the rest of the line still queuing up behind us.

In no time at all she had brought back six giant cups of steaming, luscious-smelling coffee packed in a carrier. "Did you need anything else?" she shouted as Marcus tossed down a twenty on the counter. "Cookies? Brownies? Popovers?"

I groaned. My stomach was growling, and there was a huge piece of chocolate cake calling my name. "Don't tempt me!"

"What?!"

It was a lost cause. I had been thinking about asking whether she'd heard about the Everett boy, but with all the hubbub in the small café, she would never have heard me. Shaking my head again, I waved a good-bye, and Marcus and I swam our way to the door.

"Whew!" I said once we were again ensconced in the peace and serenity of the old truck cab.

"Whew is right. I don't know how she does it."

"I don't know, either," I said, inhaling the coffee fumes, "but I'm very glad she does. This stuff is a lifesaver."

We hit the road, arriving at Stony Mill General a scant four minutes later.

I knew from Jenna's and Courtney's births that the Labor and Delivery Department had its own private outdoor entrance for security and to make checking in easier for soon-to-be-mommies out of their minds in the throes of heavy-duty contractions, so we parked close by. Security measures required us to identify ourselves at the camera and then wait until "The Family" gave its approval for "Maggie O'Neill and guest" and we were buzzed inside. One elevator ride later and the doors opened onto a hallway adorned with a wall mural of Madonna and child in delirious swirls and happy pastel hues.

"That would be my eldest daughter and her boyfriend." My mother's voice came drifting down to us from the general vicinity of the nurses' station, just down the hall. "You might know him, actually—in an official capacity? Tom Fielding. Of the police depart . . . ment."

I could tell by the way her voice went all funny that she had caught sight of me . . . and more important, of Marcus.

She hurried toward me, her eyes fixed on Marcus the whole way. I braced myself.

"Maggie?" She transferred her attention from Marcus's lean good looks to my frazzled form. Her brows stretched high, an open inquiry that demanded an answer.

"Brought the coffee," I told her, pressing one instantly into her hand.

She ignored the coffee. I knew it was a long shot. "And *who* might this be?" she asked, inclining her head toward Marcus in a way that was surprisingly regal and demanding for a plain old small-town housewife.

I opened my mouth to answer, but before I could utter a sound Marcus stepped smoothly forward and offered his hand. "Hello. I'm Marcus. Marcus Quinn."

"Are you?" She flicked her gaze back to me. "I didn't realize you were bringing a friend, Margaret."

Marcus was now looking at me as well. I started to squirm. "Well . . . you see, Mom . . . this is Marcus. Marcus Quinn."

"Yes, he said that."

"He did? Oh, good. Well . . . Mom, you remember Marcus. He's Marian Tabor's nephew. You've met him before. Remember?"

Her smile was pained. "Of course."

"Marcus, in case you don't remember, this is my mother. Patricia O'Neill."

"A pleasure, Mrs. O'Neill. Again."

"Hm."

"Mom, what's going on with Mel?" I asked quickly. "Any news?"

Attempting to divert her attention away from me and Marcus was self-defense at its best. Anything I could do that would keep her from picking at me for the next who knew how many hours had to be worth the effort. Besides, I really did want to know.

My redirection worked, because instantly, Concerned Mom switched places with Annoyed Mom. "Melanie wasn't due until next week, but she went into full-on labor this morning. Everything seemed to be going fine for a while, but then something in the readings on one of the monitors made the nurses chase us all out of there, and they haven't been able to answer my questions since then. I've been beside myself. Your father has as well."

"I'm sure it's nothing they can't take care of," I reassured her. "Modern medicine works miracles these days. If anything looked out of whack, then I'm sure this was simply their way of ensuring a controlled environment for Mel and the baby."

"Yes, well . . ." Her gaze fell on Marcus again, and just like that, Annoyed Mom was back.

"Let's go find Dad." I grabbed Marcus and tugged him in the direction of the sign that pointed the way to the family waiting room. "Okay, now. Prepare yourself. This may not be pretty. My family . . ." I winced, thinking about it. "My mom is only the half of it. My family can get on anyone's nerves. Just let them have their say and ignore ninety percent of it, and you can't go wrong."

"Maggie, I'll be fine. Stop worrying."

Was I worried?

The door to the waiting room was closed, and I knew Mom was hot on my heels, so I took a quick, deep breath and barged on through. A blast of extra-cool, air-conditioned air hit me like a wall of ice. It was incredibly welcome after the sultry heat of the great outdoors. My dad was there, or at least I thought I recognized those big, boatlike feet in the trademark loafers with the well-worn heels, one foot balanced toes-to-heel atop the other. He was otherwise hidden behind an expanse of newspaper spread wide in front of his face. Before I could press a hand down the middle to peek overtop, I was assailed by a familiar voice emanating from around the corner of the L-shaped room.

"Hidey-ho, Miss Maggie-Oh! Come to witness the second virgin birth, have you? Oh, wait a minute. That should probably be the fourth, shouldn't it?" Grandpa Gordon's wonderfully expressive and craggy face popped into view before the rest of him—probably because he was leaning forward in his motorized scooter chair like Snoopy in vulture mode, ready and willing to swoop forth on any unsuspecting victim. His chair rolled smoothly toward me, stopping just short. He eyed Marcus up and down. "Hey now. Who's the hunkarooney?"

I leaned down and looped my arms around his neck in a loose hug, giving his leathery cheek a resounding smack. "Grandpa G, you are incorrigible and up to no good as usual, I see."

"I'm up to a lotta things your mother doesn't know about, and that's just the way I like it, missy." Grandpa G cackled, slapping his knee hard enough to jar his bones. "But you haven't said. You're going to force me to be a rude bugger and ask him myself, and you know how she hates when I do that."

"Well, I'd hate to be the one to get you in trouble with Mom," I said, giggling. "Grandpa G, meet Marcus Quinn. Marcus, this is my grandfather. You have to watch him—he's trouble with a capital T."

"Hell, honey, I invented the word," Grandpa G drawled, quite pleased with himself, as he shook Marcus's proffered hand. He sized Marcus up with a squint, not letting go. "So, what's the story with you, young feller? You courtin' my favorite granddaughter?"

I was about to clue him in that it's not called courting anymore when Marcus nodded, his expression comfortable and open as he looked my granddad square in the eye. "I certainly am, sir."

It was the strange mix of the casual seriousness of his voice, the absolute unrepentant confirmation that took me aback. Courting . . . was that what he was doing? "Courting" to me implied putting on one's best clothes and behaviors, operating on the assumption that one had to put one's best foot forward in order to captivate. Which left all of the less attractive features conveniently hidden away. What was so wrong with truth? It certainly made it easier to remember everything you put out there.

I shook my head. It was only a turn of phrase. I was being too sensitive. Probably because of all the confusion I'd gone through with Tom. Not that Tom had been intentionally trying to mislead me. I didn't think. Or maybe he was. Maybe that was the trouble all along. A sad lack of truth. Maybe if he'd been able to tell me like it was, we'd have saved ourselves a lot of trouble and heartache along the way. Or maybe if I'd been brave enough to air my own issues. Neither of us had been very . . . open to that, I don't think.

"I like this one, Maggie my girl," Grandpa G was telling me with his usual lack of a filter. "How come we are just finding out about him today? And whatever happened to that other feller you were cozying up with?"

Leave it to Grandpa G to spew a pointed question without worrying about offending. I guess when a person gets to a certain age, he figures he doesn't have a lot of time to waste, so he says whatever's on his mind. Spits it out. Cuts to the chase. Doesn't worry about upsetting the applecart, because the bulk of the apples are sad, shriveled little fruits anyway.

The door behind me snicked shut. A chill ran down my

spine, and it had nothing to do with the air-conditioning vent I'd been cooling my overheated sensibilities beneath.

"There you are, Patty. Have you met Maggie's young man yet?"

The look on my mother's face should have turned me to stone. I was surprised to find myself still drawing breath. "Yes, Dad. I met him outside. In the hall. Just a short moment ago, in fact." She sat down by my father, who still hadn't lowered the newspaper. "I was surprised, of course, but I suppose it's too much to ask these days for one's own daughter to keep her mother informed of the comings and goings of important people in her life." She sighed the long-suffering sigh she was famous for, the one that said, *If only I could get my children to listen to me, to see the guiding light of my wisdom, to hear my cautioning words and take heed.* "It's a shame, isn't it, Glenn?"

She waited for my father's response. When it wasn't forthcoming, she cleared her throat and repeated, "*Isn't* it, Glenn." Less of a question, more of a demand.

Still there was no response.

With another long-suffering sigh, she reached out a hand and peeled the widespread newspapers back at the corner. There was my dad, eyes closed behind his glasses, chin down on his chest. No wonder he hadn't said anything when I walked into the waiting room. For a moment I thought my mother was going to wake him, but at the last minute I saw a gentle smile touch the corner of her mouth and she shook her head. "Silly man. Spending half your nights puttering about that workshop of yours. Is it any wonder you fall asleep sitting up these days?"

When she turned back to me, her tone was noticeably muted. "Your dad is going to need that coffee you brought with you. Grandpa, on the other hand, might be better served with warm milk."

"Warm milk!" Grandpa G sputtered. "You trying to kill me, woman?"

"Quite the contrary," Mom countered. "I'm trying to keep you alive to see a few more of your great-grandchildren." With a meaningful sidelong glance in my direction, she continued. "Maybe *they'll* be a little bit easier on my nerves."

Evidently she hadn't been apprised of Jenna and Courtney's experiences with their *imaginary* friends . . . which of course weren't imaginary at all, as I had only recently discovered. My little nieces had been chatting with spirits from the Other Side. I wondered what my mother would say if she knew perfect Mel had been keeping secrets from her, too.

Somehow that thought made me feel a little better.

"Say," I heard Grandpa G exclaim, "that a tattoo I see there?"

I turned my attention back toward Grandpa G, who had wheeled his motorized hoverchair around and had settled into place beside Marcus. He was now poking at Marcus's bicep, where through the thin white cotton of his button-down, the dark blue outline of the stylized Celtic knot could clearly be seen. Marcus wasn't some muscle-bound he-hunk, but he had really—*really*—nice muscles where it counted and just enough definition to make any woman under the age of, oh, ninety stop and take notice. The tattoo only added to the mesmerization effect. Greatly.

"Yes, sir, it is," Marcus answered honestly, unfazed by my grandfather's bluntness.

"Got one of them myself," Grandpa G confided. "From my stint in the navy. I know what you're thinking, a land-locked old farmer like myself, in the navy? Well, that's exactly why I did it. You only get a chance to be young and foolish once in yer life. A man's gotta make the most of it." He began prying at his buttons and pulling his flannel shirt apart, ready to expose heaven only knows what.

My mother sat down beside my father and glared over at the two of them, judgment written all over her face. "Young and foolish sounds about right, but Mama always said that ugly tattoo was from when you were sowing your wild oats all over the county." I could see her eyes zooming in on Marcus's sleeve, trying to discern the dark shape beneath.

Grandpa G's face took on a decidedly impish demeanor. "Well, yeah, *this* one. But if I was to show you the one I got in the navy, those nurses up the way would be calling for security." And with the shocked horror that parted Mom's lips, he proudly peeled the flannel back to show Marcus a nondescript anchor, heavily inked, on the loose chicken skin of his shoulder. Ruefully he gazed down at the wrinkled display. "It looked a lot better back then, o'course. Jeebus, getting old is the pits. Used to be solid as a rock. Now the damn thing looks as sad as a schoolgirl trying to fill out her first bra."

Mom rose to her feet, her shoulders held stiff, and went to the wall of windows to gaze out at the deepening twilight. Though I knew I'd probably regret it, I leaned over and whispered, "So, Gramps. What's the other tat?"

He leaned in, too, but never bothered to lower his voice. "A little Polynesian girl in a grass skirt. I could make her hula and everything. The Polynesian girl, o'course. Not yer grandma." And then he cackled and smacked his knee. "Though it did used to make yer grandma get an itch, too, in her younger days, darned if it didn't!" And he laughed again, not seeming to mind a bit that my face had just gone crimson and I was furiously blinking away the images that his words had just burned into my mind.

And that was Grandpa G for you. Completely devoid of a PC filter, but somehow you still had to love him for it.

Mom's shoulders were held stiffer than ever when she turned back from the window. "Really, Dad," she admonished. "Aren't you a little old for throwing things out just for shock value?"

Grandpa G shrugged. "At my age, a little shock value might be the only thing keeping the old ticker going that day. You learn not to look down yer nose at it."

An excuse if I ever heard one. Grandpa G had never been the kind of guy to turn away from a shock-'n-awe approach to life.

Mom apparently agreed with my assessment. She crossed her arms and glared at him. "Mrs. Henderson down the street just might disagree. You scared the pants off her the other day, bursting out from behind the sheets she had on the line."

"If I'd scared the pants off of her, I'da had another reason for the old ticker to keep goin'," he quipped saucily. "And I wouldn't be lookin' down my nose at that, either."

Marcus choked, coughed, and had to pound on his chest a couple of times. "Sorry," he wheezed when he could draw breath again. "Coffee went down the wrong way."

I didn't dare catch his eye for fear of sending him into another fit of the choke-backs, but I, for one, was glad that my mom hadn't noticed that his cup of coffee was still in the carrying tray.

My mother paced over to the door to peer out into the hall. "Greg is still there with her," she fussed.

"That's a good thing. Isn't it?" My brother-in-law, family lawyer extraordinaire Greg Craven, had been known to, shall we say, let Mel handle things at the most crucial of times, so I thought it a valid question.

"Well, of course it is! But he hasn't come out to let us know how things are going, either." With nothing to see out the door, she came and sat beside my father with a restless sigh. But I couldn't help noticing that she'd left the door propped wide open. An attempt to usher in news, ASAP, perhaps?

"Well . . . they're busy in there, Mom."

"But couldn't he do at least that much? How long would it take? A minute, tops?"

Obviously she was delusional. If Greg had stepped one foot out of the labor and delivery room, my mom would have latched onto him like a leech, sucking him dry of all information until he had given his all.

"And where are the girls tonight?" I asked, again attempting to sway my mom's attention into gentler waters. The well-being of my nieces, Jenna and Courtney, ought to suffice.

"Mel's friends, Margo and Jane, are watching them," Mom said vaguely, waving away my concern. She had more important things on her mind.

Ugh. Jane Churchill I could tolerate, though I was far from convinced about the dependability of her avowals of friendship. Margo Dickerson-Craig, emphasis on the hyphen, was quite another story. One with an evil queen who liked to think the whole world revolved around her. Too bad the man in the magic mirror couldn't grow a pair and tell it like it was. If he had, that particular fairy tale could have had a happier ending.

But (and this was the important part), if the two of them had stepped up to the plate to offer their assistance at such a crucial time, more power to them. Despite our differences, especially with Margo, I would not fault them.

I just wished it could have been me. I love the girls. I do. They are sticky-sweet and wonderful, and I still felt a little guilty that Mel had decided to go the home nurse route for the last months of her problematic pregnancy rather than keep me on as her—okay, somewhat-reluctant-at-the-time, that was my fault—after-hours solution.

Especially after I had discovered the girls' . . . *gifts*. They were going to need an auntie-in-the-know to help guide their way through the murk and confusion of the other-worldly. Heaven knows Mel wasn't going to be able to help. Honestly? She was about as sensitive as a brick wall. And that was on a good day. Intuition? Mel's only demonstrated gift toward intuition seemed to be in ferreting out the secrets her friends and frenemies desperately wanted to keep hidden. At that, she was tops.

I was about to ask Mom if perhaps I should consider leaving her to the hospital vigil and heading over to Mel's to spell Margo and Jane when Mom's chin jerked up and her gaze darted left and right. She twisted in her chair. "Now where did that man go?"

Chapter 4

That man being, you guessed it, my wily grandfather, who has more tricky maneuvers than Houdini. Somehow he had managed to slip away with neither me nor my mother noticing.

"Marcus, did you see where Grandpa went?"

Marcus, who had been absorbed in trying to read the lips on the muted television mounted high on the wall, snapped to attention. "Your grandfather?" He looked first left, then right, blankly. "Well, he was right here. Um . . ."

No help whatsoever. Definitely not going to be scoring brownie points with my mom anytime this evening. She was already at the end of her rope.

"Glenn," she said, taking the newspaper out of my father's hands. "Glenn!" She rapped on the wooden arm of the chair.

"A-whuh?" My father snuffled and snorted himself into awareness. "What is it? What's wrong? Did I fall asleep?"

"You know you did," Mom accused. "Dad's gone."

My dad was still knuckling the sleep out of his eyes from underneath his old-school plastic aviator glasses. The movement knocked the glasses slightly askew, but he didn't seem to notice. It gave him a goofy appearance, like some absentminded professor. Well, he *was* a long-time accountant, so maybe that wasn't far off the mark. "Gone?" he asked, just as blank as Marcus.

"Yes, gone."

"Gone where?"

"Well, if I knew that, I wouldn't be asking you, now, would I?" my mother sniped.

If Grandpa G was anything like this conversation, he was heading south. Far south.

Poor Dad was obviously confused, and in his confusion, he wasn't at his most politically correct. "Huh . . . How'd we let that happen?"

I saw the beginnings of my mother's reaction to the poor choice of words even before she managed to open her mouth. Before the exchange could make any further southerly progress, I leapt to my feet and went over to pull Marcus to his. "Never mind, Mom. Marcus and I will pool our resources and find him. I'm sure he's close by. He can't exactly leave the premises."

"Don't be too sure about that," she countered, but she did sit back in her chair, even if she did cross her arms over herself, a sure sign that her need for control was kicking up a fuss from within. "I blame your father—he's the one who insisted on buying that godforsaken hoverchair for your grandfather."

"He needed it to get around," was all that Dad would say in his own defense. He reached for the newspaper again. *Shield's up, Cap'n!*

"He needs mobility like he needs a hole in the head," my mom muttered. "You have no idea how many times I've had to chase that man's trail up and down the street and all over town. I think he sees himself as the Mario Andretti of the senior set. And when he's not zooming down the street, draining his battery, he's stopping at Millicent Hargrove's picket fence, admiring her . . . daisies. And when it's not Millicent Hargrove—"

Obviously she was on a roll. Time for us to exit, stage left. "Okay, well, I have my cell with me. I'll text you when we find him."

"Text?" Mom's lips pressed together. "Can't you just call, Margaret? I can't understand the need for all these new what-nots these days. Text messages. Email. I've barely got voice mail figured out." She sighed. "Why can't people just call or stop by, like they've always done?—"

Before she could go off on *that* tangent, I pulled on Marcus's sleeve and backed toward the door. "I'll call, I'll call," I told her. "Back soon."

"Phew," I said as the waiting room door closed behind us. "That was a close one."

Marcus nodded, in full understanding. "Your mom is intense."

"Tell me about it. She learned from my Grandma Cora. You should feel lucky you never met *her*. Trust me. Warm and fuzzy she was not. She could have made Al Capone wet his pants."

He laughed at the visual. "Aw, she couldn't have been that bad."

He had no idea.

As I was turning away from him, I felt a ping against my right ear. "Ow," I said, lifting my hand to cover my ear. "What'd you do that for?"

"Do what?" he asked, confusion furrowing his brow.

"You know what."

"No," he said, pretending to be even more confused, "I don't. What are you talking about?"

Was he being playful? "Why did you flick my ear?"

"Maggie, I didn't do anything to your ear."

He certainly seemed serious. I just looked at him. I wanted to believe him . . . but I could still feel the firm *thwap* of the fingernail against the cartilage of my ear. "Well, you tell me what I just felt, then."

He was quiet a moment. "Could it have been just one of those things?" he asked. "You know, im—"

"I was not imagining it, Marcus. I—"

It happened again. Left ear this time. And Marcus standing there in front of me.

Frowning, I whirled around in a circle. There was no one behind me, either.

And then I heard it. The crackle of static, as though tuning in a faraway station on AM radio. Only it wasn't in the air around us. It was inside my head.

I bit my lip, listening, then tilted my head to the right the way I might if I had gotten water in it . . . even though I was hours beyond my morning shower. Nope. Didn't help.

"What's wrong?" Marcus asked, touching my shoulder.

I shook my head, and—thank goodness—the staticky sound stopped. I breathed a little easier and offered up a little smile. "Nothing. Just a little water in my ear or something. That's all."

He looked at me, unconvinced, but he didn't say anything.

I didn't know what it was or what it meant. I really didn't want to know. A part of me still worried that I was putting two and two together to make ten.

"A mountain out of a molehill."

Now that time, I know I heard it in my ear. Right inside my ear. As though the person were standing right behind me, whispering over my shoulder.

Except the voice was that of my Grandma Cora. Which

made that a distinct *im*possibility. Because Grandma C had been gone for years.

Which meant . . .

"It can't be . . ." I refused to believe it. I refused to even think it. I knew that God—if there was a God, or even a Goddess, or a Great Spirit in the Sky—had a sense of humor . . . but he would never be that much of a joker. I hoped.

Shaking my head to rid myself of any further voices, real-time or otherwise, I motioned Marcus away from the hall.

"Which way?" he asked, looking around us in all directions for some sign of my grandfather's mobile chair. He obviously hadn't heard a thing.

"It doesn't matter, really."

"Aren't we in a hurry to find your grandpa?"

I shrugged. "Not really. Where's he going to go? It's dark outside. Mom's just a worrywart. He's somewhere here in the hospital, probably making a general nuisance of himself with every young nurse he comes across."

Marcus nodded. "I could see that. He's pretty feisty for being in a wheelchair." And then he laughed. "He'd be pretty feisty out of a wheelchair, for that matter."

That was the truth.

He tilted his head this way and that, squinting at me. "That must be where you get it, then. It's certainly not from your mom." He leaned in to whisper, "I think she means to scare me, but I hate to tell her, I don't scare that easily. I'm stubborn that way. It's probably a character flaw."

I shivered, in spite of myself. A character flaw, he called it. So why did I find it so attractive?

"Because you don't listen to me, Margaret Mary-Catherine O'Neill. A man like that, he's nothing but trouble with a capital T. Mark my words. Any man who looks like a cross between a Greek statue and that Harvey Stutz who used to deliver the milk and a

whole lot more to the farm wives back in the day is not good husband material. And if he's not good husband material, why are you wasting your time?"

If I was shivering now, it was because it was most definitely my grandmother's voice, and it was most definitely not a lingering memory inside my head, come to life in a flood of guilt and self-recrimination. The sound of her voice was so real to me.

It was unnerving.

"Besides," I told Marcus, ignoring the Grandma C voice, "poor Grandpa G rarely ever gets out from under my mother's watchful eye. Better to let him have a bit of fun. How much havoc can he wreak from a wheelchair?"

A lot, as it turned out.

The pursuit of Grandpa G's trail of cheer led us from one end of the hospital to the other, from floor to floor and back again. He always seemed to be one step ahead of us, as though he had us honed in on his radar and knew exactly when to push on in order to evade capture. We finally caught up with him in the cafeteria, holding court with a couple of young student nurses in cotton scrubs giddily festooned with teddy bears and hearts. I'm not sure when the nursing profession decided that little-girl graphics were the fashion wave of the future . . . but then again, anything had to be better than white polyester pantsuits they were saddled with once upon a nightmare.

I would have recognized his cackle anywhere. I stopped short and put my hands on my hips. "Grand-*paaaaa*!"

He nearly jumped out of his skin. "Sweet Jeebus, don't do that to me, Magpie. I thought you were your mother." He held his hand to his chest. "You prit-near gave me a coronary."

Sometimes I forgot that he was not in the most pristine of health. Despite the fact he had been relegated to a wheelchair for most of my adult life, a can of oxygen strapped behind and his muscles weakening until his plaid shirts just hung on his thin body, I still saw him as he used to be (and perhaps still was in his mind)—a laughing, teasing jokester, a loving family man who refused to sugarcoat the truth, and an outrageous flirt who was all talk and no trousers . . .

"A *legend in his own mind, that man.*"

The voice again. I really wished it would stop that.

I decided then and there that just as soon as I had a quiet moment, my Guides and I were going to have a long chat about the unfairness of giving the voice of my conscience the chiding tones of my dead grandmother. I had been putting up with it for quite a while now, but enough was enough. It just wasn't right. What if I had an attack of conscience when Marcus and I were . . . when we . . . well, you know. What then?

But that was for later. Right now, top billing went to Grandpa G. I placed a firm hand on his shoulder. "Grandpa G, what are you doing down here? Mom's going nuts over, well, just about everything right now, and you decide to disappear, too?"

He just waved at me with one gnarled hand toughened by a lifetime of hard work. "Aw, you know your mom. She's just bent out of shape because she ain't in control of anything at the moment and has to wait until things sort themselves out before she can dig her meat hooks in again. And as for me, a man's gotta do his own thing every once in a while. Ain't that right, young man?" he said, prodding Marcus with that one-for-all-and-all-for-one attitude that had kept men sticking together for millennium against whatever woman stood against them.

I was neither with him nor against him in this case. I just didn't want to be the next "to do" on my mother's checklist.

"Come on, Grandpa. Back to the salt mines. I promise,

I'll try to keep you away from Mom's whip cracking as much as possible."

Grandpa G waved sadly to the young women, who had been watching our exchange with amusement, as I kept my hand on his thin shoulder to prevent another quick getaway. "See ya later, chickies. Don't be strangers, now. Any time you need a few pointers on gardening, you come see me. I'll set you straight."

"Gardening, huh?" I asked with a snort as I waited for him to pull around once the student nurses had headed for the elevators. "They're a little young for you, Gramps, don't you think?"

"No one's too young for a little gardening," he insisted, trying to pull off the innocent look . . . but I knew better.

"Uh-huh."

Grandpa G leaned back to gaze up at Marcus, who had been standing by the whole time, trying not to grin. "She talk to you this way?"

Marcus held up his hands and laughed. "I'm not getting into the middle of things, sir."

Grandpa G's mouth pursed sourly. "Coward. That means she's got you on a string." He sighed. "They all do that."

My cell phone buzzed—I had set it to vibrate, just in case my mom decided to harangue and harass. I was actually surprised she'd lasted this long.

"Hi, Mom."

"Did you find him?"

"Yes, he's right here. We found him at the cafeteria. He had a case of the munchies," I fibbed. No sense in getting Grandpa G in more trouble than he already was.

"Hm. So he didn't notice the vending machines right here in the waiting room, is that what you're telling me?"

Oops. "I think he wanted something hot." Well, that much was the truth. So to speak.

"Oh. Well, tell him he can have soup, but only if it's low sodium."

Had my "something hot" actually worked? Wow, normally she was much faster on the draw. I must have underestimated her worry for Mel. I almost felt guilty for that—maybe I should be worried more, too. "Gotcha. Listen, Mom, don't worry," I told her. "Grandpa's okay, and Mel's going to be fine. Any more news?"

"No, nothing yet." If I didn't know her as well as I did, I would have heard only the calm in her voice. But my mother was rarely this drama free. To me that meant her worry had graduated into real fear. When it came to my mother, quieter was not necessarily better.

"Well, don't worry. Mel's good—I know it." And I did. Somehow I knew, deep inside me, that all was going to be fine. More than fine. But I also knew Mom wouldn't listen to me, no matter what I said. "Have you and Dad eaten anything?"

"Hm? Oh. Well, no, I guess we didn't. We came straight here when Mel and Greg called to let us know they were on the way in and to come as soon as we could."

I glanced over to where the cafeteria workers were wiping down the area and clearing equipment. "Let me see if I can get you something from down here. They're cleaning up, but maybe they can scrounge something together."

Hanging up with Mom, I turned to Marcus and Grandpa. "Why don't the two of you head on up? I have to get Grandpa his soup, and Mom and Dad could use a little something, too."

"I'm not hungry," Grandpa G told me, a petulant scowl pinching his grizzled brow and mouth.

"Well, you're getting soup and you're going to like it, too," I told him right back, "since I had to cover for you with Mom."

"I've covered for you many a time, girly, and don't you be forgettin' it."

"Come on, Grandpa G," Marcus interrupted, not even trying to hide his smile. "Let's get you back upstairs."

Marcus stood aside for Grandpa G, but I could tell he wasn't about to let him out of his sight. Not with a meltdown from my mother threatening if my grandfather flew the coop again. The two of them headed for the hall, amiably trading jokes, while I made my way to the long cafeteria counters. It took a while to attract the attention of one of the uniformed, hairnet-sporting ladies who were in the kitchens, scrubbing lazily at the stainless steel appliances and counters and calling back and forth to each other. One of them took pity on me after hearing my explanatory tale of the baby wait and crazy family antics—"because I had a grandfather just as mischievous as yours, and I wish he was still around to make me crazy," she told me as she dished up still-warm tomato soup into two foam cups. I knew Grandpa would fuss about it being plain tomato, but beggars cannot be choosers . . . especially those who force their poor, overworked grand-daughters to shield them from the all-seeing eye devoted to keeping said beggar on the straight and narrow. My dad, I suspected, would appreciate more hearty fixin's, so I opted for the last bits of a steak and snow pea stir-fry that had been mashed unattractively but I'm certain still tastily into a gen-erous helping of yellow rice. Marcus and I hadn't eaten yet, either, but I was holding on to hopes of forgoing hospital cafeteria food completely once Mel got her show on the road, and making up for it with the tasty evening Marcus had been planning for the two of us back at his place.

But just in case, I grabbed two bags of chips (healthy, I know) and juggled with my purse as I tried to pay the lady. She looked around over her shoulder, then leaned over the counter and whispered to me, "I'd have to reopen the cash register, and it's already been counted. Just take it, hon, with my blessings."

She held out the cups of soup. Her gaze dropped to where I already held a cell phone and the cup of coffee I had carried with me throughout my search for Grandpa G.

"Oh, that won't do. Hold on a sec," she said, and disappeared back to the kitchen, reappearing moments later with a big paper bag, into which she deposited all three foam containers, the chips, several napkins, the ubiquitous plastic cutlery, and a huge handful of shrink-wrapped soda crackers for the soup. Folding the top over neatly, she slid it across the counter to me. "At least this way you'll get to where you're going without mishap," she said with a wink.

I was starting to see her as my very own Earth Angel of the evening . . . hairnet and all.

"You know my niece, don't you?"

I looked at her more closely. Suddenly the round, shiny, freckled face that had seemed familiar made more sense. "Oh my goodness. You don't mean Annie, do you?"

She giggled, delighted that I'd caught the resemblance. "Yup, my favorite niece. I thought I recognized you. I was there at the café helping out in the kitchen one day when you popped in. I sure am proud of her and what she's done with the place." She glanced down suddenly, as though embarrassed. "Well, good luck with that new baby. Hope everything goes okay for your sister." She waved at me as she disappeared back into the kitchen.

Fumbling with the lot of it, I started to follow Marcus and Grandpa. But then I remembered that there was another smaller set of elevators just behind the cafeteria that was used most often by hospital staff. If I hurried, I might be able to head the two of them off at the pass. I switched directions and walked that way instead.

Goodness, it was quiet now. At this time of the evening,

activity in the hospital really started to wind down. Patients were medded up and tucked into their beds, their doors closed and TVs turned on to their visual anesthesia of choice. The various delivery carts and patient gurneys were fewer and farther between. Nurses huddled around the center stations on every floor, catching up on paperwork and trading both gossip and information about potential patient issues. The low drone of relative inactivity should have been restful . . . but I disliked hospitals. I don't know how Steff handled working here, day after day. I had actually tried a stint as an after-hours candy striper way back in my high school days. "Tried" being the operative word. I lasted a whole two days, the second only because my mother and grandmother made me go back . . . although after the second day, which I spent hiding out in the ladies' bathroom in full meltdown mode, even they agreed that perhaps the medical field wasn't going to be my calling. The relief I felt when they gave up on the idea so quickly was monumental. I never, ever told them the real reason for my anxiety attack. Funny—I'd almost forgotten it myself. Had I stuffed it that far back into the little-used corners of my memory banks? I'd been to the hospital since then, of course, with the births of my nieces, with Grandpa's health issues, my mother's hysterectomy . . . but never alone.

Never alone, at night, in the darkened corridors, with all those . . . well, at the time, I didn't know what to call it. What to think. I only know what I felt as I walked the long halls that looked empty . . . but somehow, weren't. I knew they weren't. I knew, even though I couldn't see anything . . . and somehow that made everything worse. Hence the bathroom as hideout. For some reason it was the only place that felt safe. Strange, but true.

It did make me wonder: How much do we experience as children and teenagers that we conveniently "forget"?

Standing there with my hands full, waiting for an elevator to arrive at my level, I realized with a shock just then how very alone I was at that moment. *Crap-a-doodle-doo.* I looked back over my shoulder. The main part of the cafeteria looked very far away now, farther than it was in actuality, and the few lights left on here and there for security's sake didn't do much to dispel the pooling shadows. Beyond the windows, darkness pressed in against the glass. Everyone had gone back to their workstations, leaving me pretty much on my own here. And the elevators were not cooperating.

Come on, I thought impatiently and not a little nervously as I watched the arrival light above the closed metal doors, waiting for the *ding.*

Don't be ridiculous, Margaret. You're scaring yourself silly. Look around you. Do you see anything you need to be worrying about?

At least this time Grandma C's observation came as a thought in my head, the way it usually did, rather than a voice in my ear. Maybe that was a sign that the problem was only temporary.

And no, I didn't see anything. I probably *was* scaring myself, without reason. Whatever I used to feel here in the hospital, it didn't mean that the presences that had scared me back then were still there. Er, here.

Still, I wished I hadn't sent Marcus off ahead of me with Grandpa G. At least with Marcus I felt like I could handle whatever spirit-y stuff came my way.

Spirit, schmirit. A woman's strength comes from within. Best to come to terms with that now, my girl, while there's still time.

It was a good point, to be fair. But how did a girl truly come to terms with something that she has gone through her whole life believing was either (a) her imagination run amok, (b) nerves, (c) hormones, or (d) sheer coincidence? It required a major shift in thinking. In even existing, because suddenly, all the rules changed.

Hey, wait a minute. While there was still time for *what*? How was I supposed to come to terms with anything with threats like that hanging over my head?

Finally, the elevator doors whisked open in front of me, exposing the utilitarian carpeting, faux wood paneling, fluorescent lighting, and the usual assortment of previously cleaned stains, spills, and smudges typical of a service elevator. I stepped inside, then as the doors closed behind me, I shifted my purse and carefully adjusted the goodie-filled paper bag until I could press the correct button with my knuckle. A hum of machinery preceded the usual shift of equilibrium, and the elevator began to rise, *slooooowly*. I closed my eyes. Elevators had never been my favorite ride of choice, but it sure beat having to take an endless number of stairs. Even with all of the stray energies hanging around. If I didn't have my hands full, I'd reach into my purse for the mini atomizer of sage-rosemary-lemongrass infusion I kept around for quickie energy-clearing purposes. Liss had turned me on to the protective infusion sprays just last week when I told her that burning sage messed with my allergies as much as stray cigarette smoke . . . and I loved the sprays. They were easy to use, they smelled great, and most important, they worked just as well as a smoldering bundle of white sage in banishing the negative energies loitering around a domicile. Not to mention, the addition of lemongrass helped to refill the empty space with more positive vibes. Loved. It.

Unfortunately, there was no way I could reach it, much as I'd love to freshen up the space. I was just going to have to try to keep the yuck—both physical, by the looks of this elevator, and astral—from getting to me. *Shields uhhhh—*

The elevator . . . it wasn't moving.

Um, why wasn't the elevator moving?

I frowned, nervously looking around me. Nope, I wasn't

imagining things. It wasn't just that the elevator was moving so slowly that I couldn't feel its progress. It had stopped altogether. I glanced up at the digital number display. The screen where the floor number should show was blank. Well, that wasn't good. Murphy's Law strikes again? Or maybe Mercury Retrograde. I seemed to remember Liss mentioning something about Mercury being retrograde in its orbit within the last few weeks. That was bound to wreak havoc with electrical systems, and elevators certainly qualified. Why hadn't I paid more attention? It couldn't be a power outage—the lights were still on. Something mechanical? Oh, but wouldn't there have been a clunk or something, indicating a problem?

What's a girl to do when she's stuck in an elevator that's not moving? I tried to remember everything about elevators from all the movies I had ever seen. Not a good idea—most of the scenes I remembered involved something bad happening to the person inside said little box suspended ever so precariously from wires and pulleys. Still, as someone who didn't make a habit of riding elevators, I had little real-life experience to call upon; the movies were my only hope.

Step One: Call for help. And when it came to a knight in shining armor, only one person came to mind.

I put the bag of goodies down on the floor between my feet and dug through my purse for my cell phone, trying not to let the closed-in feeling of the elevator get to me. It was at that precise moment that the unthinkable happened.

The lights . . .

They flickered.

Once.

Twice.

And then blinked out entirely.

Oh. Holy. Jesus.

There was nothing like being alone in a small, confined

space completely devoid of even the faintest glimmer of light to make a girl realize how isolated and vulnerable she really was. The reality of my situation hit home. If it wasn't for my cell phone and the comforting glow it gave off, I might just have become a slobbering, raving puddle of goo, right then and there. Thankfully, I had just charged it at the store that afternoon.

With shaking fingers and eyes partially blinded by the brightness of the screen, the one thing standing between me and temporary insanity, I found Marcus in my list and clicked Send.

"Hey, you," he said through the phone speaker. "I thought we'd lost you."

I could have sagged with relief at the wonderfully reassuring sound of his voice . . . or, I could have if I didn't already question the number of germs I would be exposed to on the worn carpet. "Marcus, what's going on out there?"

He must have heard the uncertainty in my voice, because his energy shifted and became still, the change discernible even over the airwaves. "What do you mean, out there? What's wrong?"

"What's wrong?" I couldn't hold back a shaky laugh; it just shuddered out of me. "Well, I thought being stuck in an elevator was bad enough, but I have to admit, the power failure really topped it."

"Stuck in a . . . Wait, what power failure?"

Was it my imagination, or were the shadows shifting around me?

Distracted but hoping for the best, I threw up my shields and contracted them into a tight, tight mesh. "What do you mean, 'what power failure'?" I answered with an echo of my own, a little low on the patience meter. "Are you telling me you have lights out there?"

"They haven't even blinked. Where are you?"

"In an elevator. Didn't I just say that?" *Steady, girl. No need to panic.*

"Okay, okay. No worries, you hear me?" He paused, and I could hear a note of humor creep into his voice. "I, uh, would say don't move, but I don't guess that's going to be a problem."

I laughed in spite of myself, covering my mouth with my hand before the laugh could turn into a gibber of fear. Before I thought to clarify that I was using the rear set of elevators and not the main bank out front, Marcus had clicked off. I redialed his number, but instead of Marcus I received that singularly infuriating canned message that my call could not be completed at this time. Ah, well. There couldn't be that many elevators malfunctioning. It should be fairly obvious. Just a matter of time.

Right?

What I needed was a distraction.

Marshall, I thought. My handsome big brother was a happy resident of the Big Apple, having moved out there years ago—I suspected it had just as much to do with living his life away from my mother's watchful eye as it did leaving sleepy Stony Mill for the hustle and bustle of life in the fast lane. As such, Marshall was now an elevator expert in my book.

I clicked his number in my contact list and waited while the phone rang. Hurray, cell phone reception intact.

"Hey, sis. What's up?"

I could have melted with relief that he'd actually picked up the phone. "Well, me actually. I'm stuck in an elevator."

His laughed burst into the phone. "You're what?"

"Stuck in an elevator."

"In Stony Mill?" He laughed again, even harder. "I mean,

what are the odds? Do you *know* the last time I got stuck in an elevator?"

"Yeah, yeah, very funny. This is serious, Marshall. What do I do?"

"Well, hell, I don't know. Is it a power outage?"

"Yes. No. I don't know exactly."

"Hm. All right, so I give. Where *are* you, Mags?"

"At the hospital, where else?" He should have known that. Was there another elevator in Stony Mill? I didn't think so. And no, the grain elevator didn't count.

There was a pregnant pause on the other end of the air-waves. "The hospital? Are Mom and Dad all right? Grandpa G? What are you doing at the hospital?"

"Marsh—it's Mel. She's having the baby."

"Oh. Well, that's a relief." A pause. "Again?"

If that was an example of how far removed he was from our exciting little lives out here in farm country, then I would say it was a pretty good bet that he never intended to come back. "You're just lucky it's me calling you," I told him. "It could be Mom giving you the news. And you know what subject would come up straight after that."

"Yeah. *'And when are you going to get around to finding a nice girl to settle down with?'*" he falsetto'ed in an eerie representation of our mother's voice. "Thanks for the heads-up. I'll be sure not to pick up the phone until she gets it out of her system. Again."

"Good thinking. Now, about this elevator . . ." I reminded him.

He laughed. I sighed. I suppose it was a good thing someone could see the humor in the situation.

"Sorry," he said, only I knew that he wasn't, really. "Well, jeez, Maggie, I don't know. Is there an emergency button?"

One big, bright red plastic button at the bottom of the button panel. Check. "Yes."

"You could try that."

Hm. In movies, any big red button, when pushed, made a horrific, earsplitting clamor. "There are people sleeping, Marsh."

"Well, okay. I mean, if you *want* to spend the night on the floor of the elevator until someone figures out that it's not running . . ."

I glanced down at the floor. Ew. "They would miss me long before that could happen," I said confidently. "Besides, my boyfriend's on it. I called him first."

"Oh, well hey. Why didn't you say so? You've got everything under control. Just a matter of time."

I could hear from the unspoken undercurrent in Marshall's voice that I was losing his interest. "Did I catch you at a bad time?"

"Who, me? Nope. Not at all. Just . . . just got out of the shower here and I'm dripping all over the floor, that's all."

"All right. I guess you can't help me. Thanks anyway. Go dry off."

"'Kay. Talk to you later, sis. Oh, and let me know how goes it with Mel."

He hung up so fast I didn't even get to say the word "good-bye." So much for big brother as distraction. Or even elevator expert.

I was about to try Marcus again when my phone buzzed in my hand with a new text message. From Marshall, I discovered when I clicked through the menus to read it. "Almost there, darling . . . Meet me at the elevators. Can't wait."

Oh-ho-ho. Darling?!

Marshall, Marshall, Marshall. Someone has a leetle 'splainin' to do.

Smirking at the misrouted message in spite of my momentarily forgotten duress, I texted back: *Would be happy to meet you at the elevators, darling, if I wasn't currently stuck inside one. Can't wait to hear about this one, BTW. Much love, Maggie.*

I wondered if my mother knew about Darling.

I would bet . . . not.

Good leverage, that.

Chapter 5

I was tempted to leave my phone open as a makeshift flashlight to chase away the shadows that felt as though they were closing in on me . . . but then caution started waving at me from the sidelines. What if it took longer than just a few minutes for them to first find me and then get me out? I didn't even know what floor I was on. Or even whether I was on any *one* floor at all. Who knew how long it might take? Maybe I'd better take caution's advice and conserve battery power, just in case. Only use it if I needed to.

It was just a little bit of darkness after all.

In a completely unfamiliar, closed-in space.

It wasn't that I was claustrophobic. It wasn't even that I was afraid of the dark. A year ago, I would probably have been able to talk myself out of any niggling fear that might crop up in a similar situation. But now . . .

It was more the absolute certainty I felt that there was activity here—spirit activity—that had me on edge. With years and years of accumulated people energy, who knew how many traumatic passings within these walls, and potential unfinished business around every corner, was it any wonder that others still walked these halls? I felt it here, in the elevator with me, too. Not any one inquisitive or watchful spirit in particular, but that insidious buzz of stray vibrations along my nerve endings, just skimming along the surface.

For me, hospitals were little better than funeral homes, or cemeteries.

And there I was, alone, without a flashlight.

Except . . . ooh!

I had nearly forgotten the slick little LED light I kept attached to my key ring. With a cry of triumph, I dug it out of my handbag, and fumbled around with the keys until I found the right attachment. With a flick of the miniature Perma-On switch, the tiniest brilliant white light came to life at my fingertips. Its glow didn't go far, and it cast strange shadows all around me, but it was at least reassuring to know that I could have a little light and not worry about not being able to contact the world outside of this elevator car because of a dead cell phone battery.

With a sigh that was an uneasy mix of nervousness and boredom, I scooted the paper sack full of food over to one wall to keep it from being tripped over in the event that they should get the doors open before they figured out the power disturbance. The only thing for me to do at this point was to settle in for what I hoped was my *very* imminent rescue. I leaned against the handrail on the back wall—standing, of course.

I don't know how long I had been there when I first heard the voices.

"Are you sure she doesn't realize . . ."

"Don't worry, I've taken care of everything."

Two male voices, low in pitch and faint, as though they were traveling a great distance. I supposed that made sense, given that they were passing through layers of metal and paneling and who knew what else. Most definitely they were not of the paranormal variety, thank goodness.

"Hello!" I shouted, hoping to make my voice carry through the door. "Hello?"

The voices continued on as though I hadn't made a peep. I didn't understand. Why could I hear them but they not hear me?

"What if she suspects—"

I frowned as the words drifted down to me as through a tube, hollow and somewhat muffled, though still discernible. Something about them made me instantly bite my tongue. Gosh, maybe it was the faintly threatening tone to the conversation. What if she suspects? Suspects what? I leaned forward and pressed my ear to the crack in the metal door. *Come on*, I thought, *don't mind me. I'm not here. Keep going, keep talking . . .*

"No way. No way she'll ever suspect. Not until it's too late."

Too late? Too late for what? I didn't like the sound of this at all. Where were these voices coming from? Were they right outside the closed elevator on whatever floor I was on? I backed away, suddenly nervous. What if the doors opened and they saw me there, eavesdropping on their little . . . conversation?

"It's in the bag. Trust me. The trick is to get her out of the way for a while . . ."

"And then . . ."

"BOOM."

Um, forgive me for saying this, but . . . That. Sounded. Awfully. Final.

I stood up a little straighter, scarcely daring to breathe for fear I'd miss something.

"I'll have it all arranged. And then we strike. She won't know what hit her."

"*When?*"

I found myself nodding feverishly—yes, but when? When?

But before they could say anything else, the lights flashed and blinked their way on in the elevator, and with a sudden lurch and the whirr of motors, the world beneath my feet shifted. It should have been a moment for rejoicing, but instead I found myself cursing old Murphy and his ridiculously bad timing. I'd made it this far in the lonely darkness; another couple of minutes of trying to decide what was brewing between the two strangers would not have killed me, and I was worried about what it might mean.

What could they have been talking about? They were up to no good, that was for sure.

Before I could even think to start hitting all of the rest of the floor buttons, I had already arrived at Labor and Delivery, and the doors were opening.

"There you are!" Marcus exclaimed, the relief on his face evident. "There were two elevators malfunctioning. It was a fifty-fifty shot, and wouldn't you know it? The maintenance guy got the wrong one opened first, and then he got called away because they had an urgent need for blood from universal donors, lucky guy, and— *Whoa*!" he yelped as I yanked him inside the elevator with me and slammed my palm against the red button that closed the doors before their usual wait time was over. "You know, if you'd wanted some alone time that much, all you had to do was say so," he quipped, backing me up to the elevator wall and moving in to nip playfully at my neck. "I'm more than happy to oblige."

For once, his flirtation didn't faze me. Impatient, I brushed him away. "Shh." I pressed my ear tightly to the closed crack in the door.

Marcus lifted his brows ever so slightly. "Maggie . . . what are you doing?" he asked in the slow, exceedingly patient way a person might address someone who had suddenly gone off the deep end. "Don't you want to select a floor?"

I waved my hand at him in a shushing gesture. "Shh! I'm trying to see if I can hear them. Oh, I hope they haven't disappeared."

"Who?"

"Shh!"

"Okay, okay. Shushing."

I listened, hard, pinching my eyes and straining with the effort to hear the voices that had carried to me before on the wings of . . . what? Fate? Kismet? Or just plain bad luck?

"Maggie." When I didn't answer right away, Marcus tried again more insistently, tugging at the hem of my blouse. "Maggie? Hey, what's going on?"

Frustrated, I eased back away from the closed door. "I think they've gone," I wailed. "I can't hear a thing. Damn. Damn, damn, damn. Maybe we should go down a few floors and try again."

Marcus turned me toward him and put his hands, warm and soothing, on my shoulders. "Who has gone?" he prompted.

"I don't know who. I don't know!" I shook my head in frustration. Of course they'd gone. Clearly my questionable luck of the evening was holding steady.

"Shh, shh." He pressed a kiss to my forehead, his lips remaining in place until the strength and reassurance they at once conveyed pulsed through me in a calming wave. "I think you'd better tell me what happened. What has you so worked up, hm?" He cast an eye around us in the closed elevator. "I think I'd prefer another spot, though."

So would I, now that I realized there was no chance of discovering the identity of the two men who had been so blithely discussing heaven knows what.

And that was partly the trouble, and the reason I wanted so desperately to understand. I didn't know what they were talking about, and yet it had me worried. Was that so unreasonable? After all the cumulative . . . experiences of the last ten months, I think I had earned the right to be wary.

Marcus punched the button that opened the doors and led me by the hand out onto the Labor and Delivery floor to a quiet grouping of comfy chairs at the end of the hall—away from the waiting room that held my mother, father, and grandfather, thank goodness. I needed a breather. "Okay. Now. Tell me. Beginning to end. What's going on?"

It all came out in a rush, the conversation I'd overheard and the sinister tone of it. Marcus was frowning as I finished recapping the tale.

"And you don't know where the two men were speaking from?" he asked. I was glad that my hands were still held sheltered within his, because mine were trembling and I couldn't make them stop.

I shook my head. "No. I have no idea. I don't know if they were on the same floor that the elevator was stuck on or whether their voices were carrying from some other floor. I just don't know."

"But you're worried."

"Why wouldn't I be? With everything that the two of them said? That was not a normal conversation to be having, Marcus."

But my lovely new boyfriend seemed all of a sudden determined to play devil's advocate as he hedged, "I can see how upset you are. And in light of everything else that was going on at the time I can see how it would have sounded bad. Suspect, even. Come on, Maggie." He playfully joggled my hand around in an attempt to get me to loosen up. "Don't you think you're getting yourself all worked up for nothing? You have absolutely nothing to go on here. Did they really say anything at all? If you had a chance to think about it, you would see that it could feasibly be, and probably is, nothing to worry about."

I looked at him, wanting to believe. Was I making too much of nothing? And yet, what if this one conversation was just the tip of the iceberg for something truly horrible? Something preventable? "But what if it's *not* nothing?"

It wasn't a comfortable question. But then, it wasn't a comfortable scenario. He took his time formulating his next words. "You're here for your sister—who is still having trouble; your brother-in-law just popped out to tell us—and even if what you overheard was a true threat, there is nothing that you can do about it. You wouldn't have any way of recognizing the two voices. You don't know where they were coming from. You don't know who they were talking about. You said yourself you don't even know what floor your elevator was stuck on. Why don't we go back to the waiting room with the rest of your family and try to forget about it, okay? You'll feel better."

They were all good points. I let him pull me up to my feet, and I let him lead me back down the hall toward the waiting room and my family. Maybe I even let myself be convinced.

Mountain out of a molehill, Margaret . . .

Yeah, I know, I know. Thanks, Grandma C.

Of course, some molehills are bigger than others. Remember that.

Now what was that supposed to mean? Would it be too much to request that the voices of conscience *didn't* resort to cryptic platitudes when the going got tough? I ask you.

"There you are!" My mother didn't miss a beat when Marcus nudged me through the waiting room door. "We've been looking all over for you. Your grandfather is starving to death. Anything you might have gotten us is bound to be ice cold by now."

In times of great stress, my mom liked her hyperbole. A lot.

I held out the paper sack. "Didn't Marcus tell you?"

"About the elevator? Yes, of course. But you would think they could have hurried up about the whole thing. We do have a lot going on right now, and we needed you." She resolutely did not accept the bag.

I glanced over at Marcus, who just shrugged, the expression on his face carefully neutral.

Sighing, I let my arm fall back by my side, and I turned toward the kitchenette the hospital so thoughtfully provided to those families holding vigil for their impending arrivals. "I'll just heat things up for you."

"Leave the girl alone, Patty," I heard Grandpa G grumble at her behind my back. "It's not like she meant to get stuck in that there elevator."

My mother spluttered and fussed her way into silence, but not entirely willingly. I had a feeling it was only Marcus's presence that was keeping her inner bitch at bay.

Still, she couldn't help muttering when I presented her and Grandpa with their reheated soup. "Tomato?"

"I like tomato," Grandpa G offered. Bless his helpful little heart. It almost made me sorry for forcing the bland selection upon him, even though I had known it wouldn't be his first choice. Almost. After all, Grandpa G was the whole reason I had gone down to the cafeteria in the first place, which had eventually led to my elevator fiasco. "Ooh, and crackers, too!" he added with a wink at me as he snatched them from my outstretched hand.

"Yer welcome," he whispered to me, looking pleased as punch with himself as I moved past him back to the microwave.

My dad blinked as I handed him the foam container of now-cold pseudo-Chinese over the top of his still outspread newspaper. "For me? You didn't have to do that . . . but I am awfully hungry. Thanks, hon."

"You know what would be good with this?" Mom had apparently gotten over her momentary annoyance. "More coffee."

Tomato soup and coffee? The very thought turned my stomach, but always the compliant daughter—well, almost always—I got to my feet, ready to serve.

"I'll get it," Marcus said, staying me with his outspread hand before I could make a move. "Can't have you getting swallowed up by another elevator."

I smiled at him, grateful and relieved not to have to brave the now dimly lit halls again. As if I needed another reason to be happily enamored of him. I sighed a contented sigh and instead found my own still-full cup of coffee and went to warm it up in the microwave, just to have something to do that did not involve sitting across from my mother, waiting for my sister to pop.

The door to the waiting room opened just as Marcus reached for it. He stood aside, and Mom leapt to her feet in anticipation. Dad and Grandpa G, on the other hand, were too busy noshing on their dinners to notice. But instead of Mel's husband Greg walking through to let us know our vigil had come to an end, another family filed into the room to join us in a vigil of their own.

Marcus did a double take. "Joyce! Harold! What are you two doing here?"

Chapter 6

The presumed Harold, a tall, barrel-chested man in a plaid cotton shirt, his stomach out to there over a pair of khakis, held out a hand to Marcus. "Hey there, son. Good to see you. It's been a while." As Marcus enveloped the much shorter, even rounder silver-haired wife into a friendly hug, Harold continued. "We're here with Harry Jr. and his wife. The baby's comin' a little early, it seems."

Joyce nodded, her eyes worried but her face stoic. "It'll be fine. Just a matter of time now."

Harold looked over at Marcus. "But what are you doing here? Did I miss some news of some sort? Your Uncle Lou and Aunt Molly been holdin' out on me?"

Marcus laughed, holding up his hands in a keep-away gesture. "Whoa there. Nope, no way, no news on my end. I'm here in a purely supportive mode." He turned to one side and swept an arm wide to indicate me. "I'd like you to meet someone. My girl, Maggie O'Neill. Oh, and her parents, Glenn and Patricia, and her grandpa, Gordon. Maggie, everyone, these two fine folks are Harold and Joyce Watkins, old friends of my Uncle Lou."

Grandpa G stopped ladling his cracker-laden soup into his mouth long enough to wave a spoon at the newcomers. My mother and father nodded a hello, although I couldn't help noticing my mom deep breathing again at the words "my girl." Oh well. She'd get used to it.

"Well, it's sure a pleasure to meet you all," Harold Watkins said. "Looks like we're in the same boat tonight, eh?"

My mom took the helm of that vessel. "It's my daughter, Melanie," she confided. "She's in with her third tonight, and . . . well, to tell you the truth, we're not quite sure how it's going. It's been very quiet, and I'm not ashamed to say that's making me nervous."

"Oh dear," Joyce Watkins said, coming over and plopping her plump self down on the loveseat beside my mother, her round face going all soft with understanding. She took Mom's hand in her own and patted reassuringly. "Don't you worry. Everything will be all right, I'm sure of it. The good Lord sends his angels down from on high to watch over all the newborn babies and their mommies at times like this. All we can do is leave the details up to him. No more, no less."

My mom just looked at her, and for a moment I worried about what reaction her pause for breath was hiding. But in the next she heaved a sigh of resignation and bowed her head, nodding shamefacedly. "You're right. You're so right. The Lord giveth, and the Lord taketh away. How could I forget that?"

I cringed, wishing she hadn't gone for the giveth-and-taketh speech tonight. Not after the town had just lost another young man in Jordan Everett. Not after what I'd overheard in the elevator. I exchanged a glance with Marcus.

Don't worry, he mouthed from behind my mother's back. Aloud he said, "Excuse me, I'm off to get coffee. Harold, Joyce, can I offer you some?"

"Oh!" Joyce said, beaming. "That would be lovely. Thank you, dear."

"Need some help?" Harold asked.

The two of them headed off, and my mom and Joyce quickly got down to the business of comparing motherly and grandmotherly notes. When I saw the wallets come out, fat to bursting with photos, I had to smile. Fast friends with similar tastes, they gabbed, they oohed, they compared notes, they conferred.

"Hot damn!" Grandpa G's outburst was so sudden it scared us all. Not only that, but he was wriggling around so much in his hoverchair that I worried for a moment he might flop right out like a fish. "Hot damn, didja see that? That boy's got talent up the wazoo. Socked the ball right outta there. Right outta the damn park!" His thin body quivered within the folds of flannel and denim overalls that were his daily fashion faux pas.

"Dad!" Mom exclaimed.

Grandpa looked away from the screen with his brow furrowed, as though he didn't understand what the fuss was about. "What? Well, he did. Right out of the damn park. What?"

My mom sighed, her brows knitted together, face like thunder. "Men," she muttered under her breath to her new-found BFF.

Mrs. Watkins smiled politely, but the crinkles at the edges of her eyes betrayed the humor she saw in Grandpa's behavior.

Trying to forget her exasperation, Mom got back to business. "Now, Melanie is my youngest daughter. Neither my

son nor my eldest daughter"—pointed look in my direction—
"have found their special someones yet. I keep telling Maggie
here that she's not getting any younger, but"—meaningful
sidelong glance—"you know how well parents are listened
to these days."

"Oh, yes. Yes. I suppose that comes with life and experience, though. Our son was the same way, you know. Married
so young, and his bride even younger, but they waited to add
a child into the mix, and you know, I think waiting was
the best thing they could have done . . . even though my
grandma clock had been ticking at warp speed all along."
She reached over and patted my mother's fat wallet. "But you
have such lovely granddaughters to be proud of. The others
will come along in time, I think," she said with a kindly side
wink in my direction.

I was especially glad that Marcus had been out for this
particular conversation. Nothing like a little baby pressure
in the early days of a relationship to scare a guy away forever. Now I was really wishing I had somehow managed to
convince him that he didn't *have* to accompany me to the
hospital. I alone knew the danger. He couldn't possibly have
understood the force of nature that was my loving mother,
and I was worried that before the night was over, he would
be finding out.

*Oh, I don't know, Margaret. It's a good test of a man's
character . . . best to know these things at the onset.*

And why did everyone, my conscience included, think
that I was ready for children right here, right now, anyway?
I mean, yes, someday, I would like a family. I was pretty sure
about that. I might even want the typical, picket-fence scenario, and although I wasn't completely sold on the existence of fairy-tale endings, I was definitely willing to consider
the possibilities. But I think the thing that scared me the

most about the prospect of children of my own was this: Over the years, I had watched my mother put all of us before her in every single aspect of her life. That wasn't so much the problem—eventually I had decided that was just an inherent part of being a mom. What really worried me was the way her life had eventually stopped being about herself so entirely that there no longer seemed to be a "Patty" at all. I wondered, sometimes, whether she even remembered who she had been before the three of us came along. And now with us out of the house and my father and grandfather not playing nice with her need for absolute dominion, I had a feeling she was looking to us for new and improved ways of filling the gap.

My mother was still waxing eloquent about how terrible it was that adult children should have so many priorities claiming their attention these days. She didn't seem to notice that her new friend seemed to be waiting for the right moment to jump in. Sensing an appropriate pause at last, Joyce Watkins leaned in confidentially.

"You know, I'm as guilty as the next mother, wanting grandchildren, and the sooner the better. The good Lord knows, I pushed and prodded my son and his wife for far too long, to my everlasting shame. I don't know what I was thinking. Just me being selfish, I guess. I didn't mean to cause any trouble for them. He's my only child, you see. Harold and I never were able to have another. Not for lack of trying." *Oy.* I for one really didn't need that visual, but . . . "So you see, grandchildren, the more the merrier, the quicker the better, seemed to be the perfect solution. In the end, though, I think the constant nagging did the two of them more harm than good."

That decided things. Joyce Watkins was my new best friend.

Mom pulled her chin in and gazed at her over her thin gold frames and bifocals, obviously unconvinced. "Do you?"

Joyce nodded. "For a while there, I think they might even have been close to separating. Maybe even breaking up entirely. And that right there, that was my wake-up call. I don't think I ever would have forgiven myself if I had been the cause of that. I really don't."

"What happened?" my mother asked.

"I don't know, really. It was touch and go there between them for quite some time. Neither of them confided in me, but a mother can tell these things. Could have cut the tension with an old butter knife. It's not so hard to read between the lines. There was a shadow that came over their relationship. It hung over them, even over their home. Oh, that probably sounds melodramatic, doesn't it? Just a silly woman's musings."

"No," my mother said in a quiet voice. "No, I think I know what you mean."

Joyce nodded. "It's a mother's curse and blessing, isn't it, being so close to your child that you can just tell when something is wrong. Something changed between them." And then she brightened. "But there's a happy ending. Because, like the flick of a light switch, all of a sudden it was over and done with, everything seemed completely better, and just like that, she was pregnant and they were happy. So happy. And just in time, too. You see, Harold—well, with his heart condition, things are touch and go. One never knows . . . and I so want him to be around to know his grandchild."

By now poor Joyce had tears in her eyes. She dug in her purse, sifting through the contents, but her eyes were overflowing the banks. My mom, efficient as ever, reached with military precision into her purse, located a clean tissue, and pressed it into Joyce's hand.

"Oh! Thank you." She applied the tissue liberally, then

blew her nose until it squeaked. "Anyway, as you see. A happy ending. This baby is a godsend, truly."

I had heard the deeper meaning in Joyce Watkins's tale, but I'm not sure my mom had picked up on the messages Joyce was sending out.

"Ah, yes. All babies are gifts from God."

Happily now, the two middle-aged grandmothers—well, a grandmother and a very-shortly-to-be-grandmother— smiled at each other.

For a few moments we all sat together quietly: Dad reading the paper again after having finished his stir-fry, Mom and Joyce bolstering each other through a moment of shared experience, Grandpa G muttering under his breath about fools and tools as he changed the channel over to the local news. I caught a quick glimpse of an interview with Chief Boggs, who was lamenting the rise in crime and the need for a budget increase, declaring, "What we have here, folks, is an epidemic; some might say, of Biblical proportions," but then Grandpa clicked on. I went back to what I had been doing: using the façade of a fashion magazine to hide the fact that I was meditating . . . or trying to. I finally gave up when Marcus and Harold returned with fresh coffee—hot, yes, but fairly disgusting—and sat down with us, passing the time with chitchat.

Restless, I stood up. Grandpa G had been looking bored to tears and glum now that his favorite team had lost the game after all the excitement. "Grandpa G, how'd you like to go get some air?"

His watery blue eyes lit up in an instant.

Marcus stood up as well, quietly stating his intention to accompany me wherever, whenever. That warmed my heart, too.

"Just be sure to keep him away from the snack machines," my mother interjected with an imperious wave of her hand.

Grandpa's grizzled face fell just a bit. He muttered under his breath as I manually steered his chair toward the door. "Spoilsport."

"And for heaven's sake, don't let him out of your sight for a minute!" she called after us as the door closed with a solid *snick*.

"That woman is going to be the death of me yet," Grandpa G grumbled, crossing his arms over his chest. "Don't do this, don't eat that, don't breathe, don't think, don't, don't, don't."

I ruffled his sparse silvery hair. "She loves you and wants you to take care of yourself."

He leaned back and arched an eyebrow up at me over his shoulder. "I suppose that's what you tell yourself every time she gets a little high-handed with you, is it, missy?"

I laughed. "Well . . . maybe not. But it's probably true."

"Where should we go?" Marcus asked.

But before we could go anywhere, the doors to one of the labor rooms down the hall opened. Through the doors backed a man suited up in blue-green surgical scrubs, his surgical cap still in place but his face mask pulled down under his chin. He was a nondescript man in every way except for one: the light of deep, utter, profound joy that was etched into the sun-worn lines of his face as he gazed down into the little bundle he held in his big hands. It was that expression that stopped me in my tracks and compelled, no, *dared* me to look. My heart started to beat faster, and my chest squeezed tight. He scarcely noticed us as we stepped out of the way so that he could reach the family waiting room. He knocked on the window and held up his little bundle, backing up in self-defense as Joyce came hurtling through the door, her face aglow like a candle. Harold followed at a slightly more measured pace.

"Mom. Dad. I have a son," the man announced, awe reverberating through his voice. "Can you believe it? This is my son!"

There is something about a moment of purest joy that commands the attention of those fortunate enough to witness it, even from the sidelines. Neither Marcus nor I nor even Grandpa moved. We all just stood by with silly little grins on our faces, watching the scene unfold.

"*Ohh!* Let me have a look at the little bean sprout!" Joyce squealed like a pro. A professional grandmother, that is, with her smile on high beams and her hands making the universal "gimme, gimme" gesture.

"That was certainly fast," I heard my mother say as she came to the doorway to see what all the ruckus was about. "Bless her heart."

"I'm sure your new grandbaby will be along any second now," Joyce said reassuringly in between cooing in delight over the tightly wrapped newborn in her arms. "Just look at you, little man, how precious you are. Have you ever *seen* anything so precious, Harold? Oh, he looks just like you, Junior. Don't you think, Harold?"

New Grandpa Harold looked down over her shoulder at the baby. "Naw, he's got a whole headful of his mother's dark hair, and he has her dark eyes, too."

"Oh, but *around* the eyes, dear. And the nose. And the little mouth."

Clearly she was too enraptured to remember that newborns rarely resembled anything more than each other, with the same button nose, swollen eyes, and rosebud mouth that every other newborn baby sported. Grandmotherly love. It was a wonderful thing. She began pulling the blanket away, exposing tiny, pink flailing arms with the most perfect little fists. Awing again, she took one between her thumb and forefinger. "Would you look at this? Have you ever seen anything more exquisite? Oh! There's something he did get from his mother," she said, rolling his armband around. "His blood type. Junior's is A positive. But that doesn't matter, does it?" she cooed, tucking arms and fists back inside the warm flannel. "No, that doesn't matter at all."

Somewhat less tolerant of all the baby mush, Grandpa G was starting to get restless, so Marcus and I tiptoed away, closed the door to the waiting room and, smiling, pushed Grandpa toward the bank of elevators.

"You don't have to push me around," Grandpa grumbled. "This is a fully operational hoverchair, you know."

"You could just enjoy the attention," I told him.

"I'd enjoy it more if it came with one of them there chocolate chip cookies I saw in the machine downstairs when your hunky man here pushed me on past."

"They're not even good chocolate chip cookies."

"But they are cookies," he said with a wink and a cackle.

"Oh, Grandpa."

We veered off into the little hallway that led to the main elevators (*not* the service elevators—I wasn't going anywhere near those anytime soon), and I reached around Grandpa to push the call button. As I turned back to warn him about the addictive evils of cookies, I was startled to find a face looking out at us through the narrow pane of glass set into the stairwell door behind us. A young man with dark curls that flopped down over his forehead and dark eyes that burned into mine.

My breath caught and my hand flew to my throat.

"What's the matter?" Marcus turned around to see what I was looking at. He saw the man just as he backed away. The man seemed to catch his gaze with a slight nod, and then I saw a flash of movement deeper within the stairwell as he retreated.

Marcus gasped. Dramatically. His reaction made me clutch at him and press my body up against his side. "Did you see him, too? What? Oh, jeez . . ."

For a moment, I honestly believed his reaction was true . . . and then he dissolved into laughter, and I thought I was going to have to smack him. "The look on your face!" he gasped, only this time with half-suppressed laughter.

"Yeah, yeah, very funny," I sniffed, pouting.

He grinned. "Sorry. It was just the maintenance guy, Maggie. Probably checking on the elevators, after all the trouble."

"Oh, the maintenance guy." I felt a little silly. "You mean the one who fixed it earlier?"

"The one and the same."

Okay, so I was feeling a lot silly. I couldn't help being jumpy. It is just something that happens to me whenever I'm startled. Humph.

"Yeah, yeah, less yakking, more snacking," Grandpa sassed, switching on the power to his hoverchair and maneuvering into the now-open elevator, leaving me to hurriedly get on myself or risk the doors closing with Marcus and me left out entirely. The door tried to close on Marcus, but he held his hand up and—now, I know I'm an imaginative person, but I know I did not imagine this—well before the rubber bumper got to his hand, it reversed. No, the heavy metal door was *repelled* back as though by some invisible force, allowing him to walk through unimpeded.

I gaped at him.

"What?" he asked, all innocence.

I couldn't ask him how he did it—not in front of Grandpa G with his big ears all cocked and primed. But let me get Marcus alone for a minute and that would be another story. And I for one couldn't wait to hear it.

Down on the main level, we found Grandpa his cookies, then took him for a stroll outside beneath the grand colonnade that had been added to the front of the hospital with the last big-dollar renovation to give it a progressive, trust-Us-with-your-health appeal. The heat of the day was still oppressively present even though the sun had finally sunk to its resting place for the night. If anything, it somehow felt even hotter, as though there were some sort of invisible shield over the town, holding the heat in place beneath the starry evening sky. "Hot," "damp," and "cloying" were all words that came to mind. Not to mention the mosquitoes. Grandpa seemed impervious to both the heat and the needle-nosed varmints, but even Marcus seemed to be getting tired of fending off their persistent dive-bombings.

By then it was nearly midnight, so my dreams of time alone with Marcus this evening had fallen by the wayside. And still no baby from Mel. Girl had better get her baby mama move on.

We were about to head back in when my cell phone rang in my purse. *Mom*, the front screen read. I scrambled to flip it open. "Hello?"

"Maggie, it's time! They've taken her into surgery for a C-section." She was hyperventilating, her breath puffing excitedly against the mouthpiece.

I looked at Marcus. "It's time. Mel's being taken into surgery." Grandpa just yawned. "We'll be right there, Mom." And no stopping for coffee this time!

Marcus took over pushing Grandpa's chair—Grandpa whooped like a boy as we rounded the first speedy corner—and we hightailed it for the elevators for what felt like the umpteenth time of the night. We had just made it back to the waiting room when Greg burst through the door, still covered in the head-to-toe scrubs he'd hurriedly donned before heading into surgery with Mel.

It was the first I'd seen of him since walking through the hospital doors, hours ago now, and who knows how long he had been there with Mel, but somehow overall he managed to appear the same pristine, well-kempt man he always was. He didn't even have a five o'clock shadow—how did he do that? The only sign of his lengthy bedside watch was the cobweb of red veins in his eyes and a slight tic at his left temple. He was a handsome guy, though not really to my taste as his style leaned a little too far in the direction of male elegance, which in some men tends to come off as . . . effeminate . . . but Mel didn't seem to mind, and I supposed it was part and parcel of the controlled, by-the-rules "legal ease" (*heh!*) necessary in order to command respect and influence in the courtroom.

Greg's mouth opened, closed, then opened again, but still mustered no voice. Bewilderment swam in his pale eyes.

"Well?" Mom demanded, ending on a shrill note in the urgency of her own need to know.

"T—" Greg choked, then coughed.

"I'm sorry, dear, what was that?"

"T—" Greg tried again.

Mom's patience left her. "Oh, for goodness' sake, Greg, get it together!"

"Twins!" he exploded at last.

Chapter 7

With the expulsion of the word, his strength seemed to leave him, along with his equilibrium. He staggered slightly on his feet, then dropped heavily into the nearest seat, looking stunned.

"*What?!*" Mom cried. "What do you mean, twins?"

My mouth had fallen open. "Oh my gosh."

"Hot damn, son!" Grandpa said, shaking his head in admiration. He reached over and poked Greg in the shoulder with a gnarled finger. "How on earth didja do that? Didn't think you had it in you. I mean, look at you. Did any of you think he had it in him?"

Leave it to Grandpa G.

Dad looked at least as stunned as Greg, but his surprise dissipated faster. "Well, that's just wonderful news," he said. Mom burst into tears, and he put his arm around her, rubbing her shoulder. "Isn't it wonderful, dear?"

Mom nodded. "Wonderful."

"Well, don't just sit there!" I told him. "We need details.

How is Mel doing? The babies? Are they girls? Boys? One of each? And most importantly, how did this happen?" Marcus arched a dark eyebrow at me, his blue eyes sparkling with humor. "Well, I know *how* it happened," I amended quickly, blushing, "but how on earth did she not know about it?"

Greg just shrugged, at a loss. "I can't explain it. A miracle of modern medicine, I guess."

Some kind of miracle, that was for sure. Mel had received the works as far as medical care went—the best OB/GYN, ultrasounds, vitamins, the best home care when she had experienced problems with her pregnancy . . .

Hey, wait a minute.

I was no expert—obviously, since I'd never actually gone the pregnancy route myself—but weren't ultrasounds fairly foolproof these days? I'd heard they actually have imagery so high res that you could see actual faces and details in 3-D.

"Anyway, Mel is fine. She was awake through the whole thing. Doc is stitching her up, and the babies—both girls, by the way, Mel has already named them Sophie June and Isabella Rose—are being run through the battery of tests, but I wanted to make sure you all knew. They're fine, too. Now I'm going to go call my parents in Arizona, and then I have to get back in there or Mel will have my hide."

My mom was beaming, her earlier anxiety for her youngest and most favorite daughter forgotten in light of the relief of Greg's news. In a moment of sheer grandmotherly pride, she threw herself into my dad's arms and bounced—*bounced!*—up and down on her tiptoes. I couldn't remember the last time she had done anything so uninhibited. "Did you hear that?" she asked, leaning back in his arms and touching his face in a way so intimate that it almost made me feel guilty for watching. "Did you hear? *Twin girls!*"

Dad grinned right back at her, years stripped away from

his face in the process. In that moment, I could see the young married couple in the two of them. "Two at once. Who would have thunk it?"

He kissed her several times on her cheek, over and over again until she chuckled.

"Now, stop that, Glenn, before you embarrass Mr. Quinn."

"Mr. Quinn?" Grandpa G squawked in protest. "What do *I* look like, chopped liver?"

Even Marcus was swept up in the glow of the enthusiasm and excitement surrounding us. "I would never have thought your sister was expecting twins. She looked so petite when you introduced us last month. You know, you two don't look like each other much at all."

Now, I know he didn't mean for that to sound the way that it came off, but it still stung. Yes, Mel was my tiny and perfect sister. Yes, she was built like a fashion model, even while pregnant, whereas I resembled a more sturdily built model . . . like a boxy Model T Ford. But every once in a while, it might be nice not to be constantly reminded of that fact.

He saw my face fall, and backtracked immediately. "I mean, your hair is darker, like the color of honey, or whiskey"—he leaned closer to whisper in my ear—"and you are definitely curvier." His voice made a purr of the first part of the word; it sent a shiver zipping along my spine. "Which, in case I never mentioned it, I happen to really enjoy about you."

I blushed again as I saw my mother's eyes alight on the two of us, but this time I didn't let it affect me quite as much. After all, she knew about Marcus now. Later there would be time for questions about what happened to Tom and why we were no longer seeing each other, but for now she knew as much as she needed to know, and she was just preoccupied enough to let me be. For a time.

And I, for one, was determined to enjoy my momentary peace.

Mom was itching to go way before the nurse came in to say that Mel was resting peacefully, but that we could all go and look in on her if we wished.

"Patient registration is fairly light here today," the red-headed nurse told Mom, "so we've put her in a room without a roomie. With her having had twins, I, uh, really didn't think she'd complain about that.

"Of course," the nurse continued, "she'll be staying with us for at least four days. As long as her recovery goes as planned, she should be released then."

"That long?" my mom asked, the frown between her brows returning. "Is anything wrong? She was never held that long before."

The nurse explained, "It's the C-section. Her previous pregnancies were via natural childbirth, if I'm not mistaken. You see, there are more chances for complications following a Cesarean. The lengthier stay helps us to ward off the risks involved with a Cesarean birth. All of this would have been explained to Mrs. Craven by her doctor during her primary care visits. And of course, seeing as how the babies were multiples and they were a little bit underweight—that daughter of yours has a teeny-tiny uterus, I would never have pegged her for a twins mom—well, we're going to want to make absolutely certain they are starting to gain before we let them go."

I could have gone without hearing about my sister's delicate inner beauty, but that was just me.

My mother's concern had only increased with the nurse's explanation. "Is anything . . . *wrong* with them? Something you haven't told us?"

"No, no. Certainly there is always room for concern with a lower-birth-weight infant. But your grandchildren are only marginally under that, and both scored high enough on their Apgars. Lucky for your daughter, she went nearly full term, almost all the way to her scheduled C-section. The longer in utero, the stronger the babies' lungs. Now, I'm not allowed to give you any guarantees, but I'd say the odds are pretty good they'll be going home with their mama. But mind you, you didn't hear that from me," she said with a wink.

"Which room is hers?" I asked.

"Twelve twenty-three. Down the hall to the T, then turn left. It's going to be a pretty quiet stay for her; there are only two other new mommies on the whole floor tonight." She wandered down the hall on silent rubber soles, gazing at the chart she held on one arm as she scribbled away.

We all filed down the corridor, with a sleepy Grandpa G taking up the middle position. Marcus took my hand and squeezed it. "How are you holding up?" he murmured.

I squeezed back and smiled at him. "Good. Better than Mel, I'll bet, despite her teeny-tiny uterus."

He laughed. "Are you sure you don't mean '*Thanks to* her teeny-tiny uterus'? Because I'll bet right now she's going to be admiring your figure and wishing she had it."

"You don't know Mel. Give her a couple of weeks and she'll be strutting her stuff, back into her pre-preggo jeans, complete with prominent hip bones."

Sigh.

"Hm. Just the way she's put together, I guess. By the way, I hope this doesn't offend you, but . . ." He leaned in and whispered, "I'm not certain I'm comfortable discussing your sister's parts with you. Or with anyone else, for that matter."

I hugged into his arm. "Oh good. I was a little worried for a minute there. I mean, what does that say when your guy *is* comfortable discussing things like that?"

He just grinned.

The door to room 1223 was standing ajar, so we tiptoed inside, peering around the edge of the door as we did. The dim fluorescent over the bed was switched on, casting the room in an eerie half light. Mel was in the bed, tucked in tightly up to her armpits, face wan and pale, blond hair tousled, if not outright mussed, and IV tubes taped along her arm to their connection points in her hand and wrist. I glanced discreetly down at her belly. Just as I suspected. It was rounded, yes, and big by Mel's standards, but most women would sell their husbands to look even that slim.

Sigh. Again.

Greg waved at us from a lounging recliner in the corner. The poor guy. I could almost feel sorry for him. He looked nearly as wiped out as Mel did.

And there, to the right of Mel's bed, were two glass bassinets.

"Oooooh, let me see them!" my mother whisper-squealed. How she managed the two effects together, I cannot understand. And then she half tiptoed, half pranced across the floor, looking like some manic ballerina elf and not the middle-aged grandmother that she was. "Oh, look at the little darlings. They're so tiny!"

The four of us, minus Grandpa, crowded around the bassinets. "Tiny" was just not strong enough a word. "Diminutive," certainly. "Lilliputian" might have worked, if only to drive the point home. They were the smallest human beings I had ever laid eyes on. With their legs and arms swaddled up toward their chests, they couldn't have stretched more than a foot from stem to stern. Their tiny heads were roughly the size of large oranges. They almost didn't look real, except they were too exquisite not to be.

I looked over at Greg. "Are they sure it's safe for them to be in here, away from the nurses, if they're under observation?"

He used his head to silently indicate the monitors that were tracking their every breath and heartbeat.

Her expression rapt, Mom was obviously itching to get her hands on one, but somehow she resisted picking them up, instead satisfying herself with stroking along a cheek with the back of her index finger. I felt a tug, unexpected and incredibly strong, somewhere around the general vicinity of my heart as even in the midst of a dream the baby turned its face toward the touch and a small, delicate mouth opened.

"Have you ever seen anything quite so perfect?" she cooed, as close to melting as I had ever seen her.

"Well . . . Jenna and Courtie were both very adorable babies," I hedged magnanimously.

"Well, of *course* they were adorable. All babies are adorable. But . . . two at the same time . . . and so small . . . !"

She really was melting. Not Wicked-Witch-of-the-West, bucket-of-water, flowing-back-into-the-ground-from-whence-she-came melting, but still completely all consuming. It made me wonder if that's how she had been when she had given birth to each of the three of us older O'Neills. Or was becoming a grandmother remodeling her emotional sensibilities?

"I just want to get my hands on them . . ." Mom sighed.

But she wouldn't, not yet. They were sleeping off the trauma of their arrival to this strange new place, and Mel needed her rest, too. It would be almost criminal to wake them up now. Besides, Greg was shooting daggers at her for even mentioning the possibility of picking them up. Something told me the new papa was stressing, big time.

"What's the matter, Greg?" I asked him, quirking a smile.

He just shook his head, then stood up. "I gotta go. I'm beat. Someone tell Mel for me, would you? I have court in the morning."

I froze, not knowing what to say. He couldn't be bailing on Mel so soon after delivering, could he? Husbands just didn't do that these days. We weren't exactly living in the old-school, Donna Reed version of reality, where the man was encouraged to do his thing while the woman just sucked it up with a smile. Not only that, but Greg actually sounded . . . pissy. And I couldn't see why. Was it postpartum letdown, man style? Surely there hadn't even been time for that. The babies were just now here, for heaven's sake. Time for him to take a quick step back, take a few deep breaths, and get himself in the right headspace for new-and-improved daddyhood. In my not so humble opinion, that is.

Mom scarcely noticed him leaving, but I saw the scowl settle into the furrows on my usually mild-mannered dad's forehead. Greg saw them, too. He made some bland excuse of a mumbled apology, but that didn't stop him from leaving, pronto.

And why was it that Mel chose that very moment to wake up from her sedative-induced slumber?

"Hm . . . mm . . . wh . . . rz . . . grg?" she muttered.

Mom leaned down over her and kissed her on the forehead, then smoothed her hair away from her face. "What was that, Melanie dear?"

"Grg. Whrz. Grg?"

Mom still looked confused, but I had been there many a time when Mel had come home from high school parties three sheets to the wind and unable to get her tongue to function like a normal human being's, so I had a better grasp of her tendency toward twisted linguistics. "I think she's asking where Greg is," I told Mom.

"Oh. Well, Melanie, darling, he had to go home. He has to work in the morning. He wanted us to tell you."

"Greg?"

"Yes, dear. Hooooooome." She stretched out the word as if doing so would somehow make it easier for Mel to grasp the concept. It was the same method used the world over when dealing with a person who was exceptionally slow-witted. Which by definition, at least at present, Mel was.

"Dideeseethuhbabeeeeez?"

Slightly clearer. No translation required this time. "Yes, dear. He saw them."

Mel sighed, happy. "Pretteeebabeeegrlz."

At least she remembered that much. Greg had mentioned she'd been awake for the delivery. She'd even been coherent enough to name the babies. No one would ever guess that at this particular moment in time. The meds they had her on must be crazy strong.

"That's right. Pretty girls. Just like their mama." Mom stroked her hair back from her forehead again, the light in her eyes so soft and tender that I felt a pang, sharp as an arrow in my heart. Was it wrong of me to hope that at some point in my life she had looked at me that way? She must have, mustn't she? I just wished I could remember it.

"Why don't you rest now, Melanie. Just close your eyes and rest."

Mel didn't need to be told twice. Not being all the way there to begin with made it easy. Her eyelids dropped like a shot. "'Kay. Bye."

And over and out.

"Are you going to stay?" I asked Mom. She had moved back to the bassinets and was hovering there. "Someone should stay."

She tore her gaze from her newest granddaughters as my father moved forward behind her to put his hand on her shoulder, and reluctantly shook her head. A nod toward the corner gave the reason why: Grandpa G had parked his chair there in an attempt to be out of the way of traffic and had promptly nodded off. That would explain the distinct lack of wisecrackery.

"I'll stay."

The words came out of my mouth before I even realized they were in my head, searching for a way out.

My mom turned and looked at me, her reaction sheer surprise. "You will?"

I would? "Um, yeah. If that's okay. I mean, if you'd rather . . ." I risked a glance at Marcus, but he was smiling and shaking his head in a completely indulgent way. Whew. But we'd both known it was probably too late now for any plans we'd made anyway.

"Well, if you don't mind staying," Mom said slowly, searching my face and eyes as though trying to make out what alien race had taken over her eldest daughter, "it would be easier for me. Grandpa has to have his medicines in the morning, and your dad never gets them right."

She did, however, pause to take a few digital pics of the wee ones. "So the girls can see their new baby sisters—I'll stop by to see them in the morning before coming here."

Marcus waited until my parents had steered a spent Grandpa G out the door and up the hall before he came up behind me as I stood over the bassinets myself, gazing down softly at my new nieces in all their angelic glory. He wrapped his arms around my waist and rested his chin on my shoulder and held me a moment. "Pretty amazing, babies."

"Yeah."

"You ever want one?"

"Someday. Maybe more than one. I'm not sure." More moments like this, and I had a funny feeling I could psych myself up to that state of mind pretty quickly. But it was better that he didn't know that. "You?"

"Someday." He kissed the top of my head. "You going to

be okay if I go home? Minnie is bound to be needing some affection by now, I think."

Minnie! In all the excitement, I had forgotten that she was still at his house. "Is it all right if she stays with you tonight?" I asked.

"Well, she'll make a poor substitute for you, but I guess she'll have to do."

His quiet statement sent a shock wave of awareness straight through me. It seemed so long since we had fallen into his bed, only to have our plans for an evening of getting to know each other really, really well fall through because of Mel's impeccable timing and my mother's seemingly arcane ability to track me down wherever, whenever. I turned my head, ever so slightly, and he was there, waiting for me. Our lips met, blended.

"I wish things had turned out differently tonight," I whispered on a sigh when it ended.

"There will be another time. Lots more other times," he promised. "Right now it's time for you to enjoy an intimate moment with your family. That's important, too. I'll still be here. There's time enough for everything."

Time. A girl could get caught up in it, if she wasn't careful. Me, I just wanted more of it.

Checking first to make sure Mel was still asleep, I grabbed him by the collar and pulled him back for just One. More. Taste.

"*Mm,*" he breathed against my lips, brushing his own along mine in a gentle but somehow completely enthralling caress, "you keep doing that and I'm going to have to think a little bit harder about sharing you in the future."

"Oh good. Then that makes two of us."

Reluctantly I released my grip and eased out of the enveloping warmth of his energy. "I'll see you tomorrow, then?" I asked.

His blue eyes glowed at me through the semidarkness. "Mm-hm. Most definitely."

Yay! Now that was definitely a cause for rejoicing.

When he was gone, I stood there a moment, my arms hugging around my waist, smiling to myself and basking in the glow of happy.

"Well, that is certainly a step forward."

Melanie had opened her eyes, having managed, apparently, to drift out of the chemically induced slumber that only moments before had seemed to hold her in its sway. She'd obviously reacquired some of her heretofore misplaced speech capabilities as well.

Embarrassed, I dropped my arms. "Well, what a time for you to wake up and regain your senses."

"Touché." She shifted in her bed and winced. "Ow."

"Hurts?"

"Yeah. Like a bitch."

Yeah, I could see that. "Shall I call the nurse?"

She shook her head. "Where's Greg?"

She didn't remember the conversation she'd had with Mom just a little while ago. "He had to go home. He had work in the morning."

Mel frowned and closed her eyes, her lips tightening. "Hm."

My offer to stay with her had come out of the blue, and I really didn't quite know what I could do for her . . . but I was there for the duration, so I decided I would make the best of it. "The babies are beautiful."

That brought a tiny smile. "Thanks."

"But then, so are Jenna and Courtney."

"Of course. This is the one thing I'm good at."

There was a sadness to her words that I didn't expect and wasn't really comfortable with. My always confident little sister wasn't allowed to feel vulnerable. But then, maybe that was her weariness talking. There were shadowy smudges under her eyes, and there was a fragility to her that I wasn't used to seeing. "Don't be silly. You're good at lots of things."

"Am I?" She fell silent a moment, running a hand gently over the blankets covering her tiny mound of a stomach. When she spoke again, it was with a change of subject. "I like your guy. Marcus. I keep meaning to tell you that. It was very kind of him to come out to my house like that when he didn't know me from Adam and try to help. Not every man is willing to help out a stranger. Some can't even be bothered with their own families."

I felt a hint of discontent beneath her words. It made my intuitive senses tingle. "Thanks. I like him, too."

"How did Mom take it? I assume she's figured it out."

"Yeah. And I don't know. I should probably feel lucky that she was more concerned with what was going on with you than to spend all her time worrying about me." That was almost certainly an understatement. "Mel . . . something the nurse said had me wondering. You . . . did you know that you were going to have to have a C-section? She made it sound like it had been scheduled and that you'd almost made it, only to go into labor." Or maybe I was the only one in the family who hadn't been apprised of her delivery intentions. That was a possibility, actually. Odd girl out, and all that.

"What? No. No, of course not."

"I mean, I know with complications C-sections are sometimes a safer bet, but last I knew it was business as usual. And the babies," I continued on as another question reared its head. "You didn't know that you were carrying twins, did you? I mean, Greg looked pretty surprised."

She huffed out a sigh and ran her hand back over her hair, threading her fingers through and plucking at her blond bangs over and over. "I don't know why you're asking me all these questions," she pouted. "I've been through an awful lot tonight."

"I know, but . . . I guess I was just curious."

She stared at the light over the bed for a moment. "You know, I am feeling tired after all. I think I'll just close my eyes a little while, if you don't mind."

Why did I get the feeling she was playing the avoidance game with me? But I let her close her eyes, and I let her pretend to sleep until the dream god Morpheus came to carry her away. There was time enough for questions later, when she couldn't throw up a red flag of caution to warn me away. She couldn't avoid me forever. Because the more that I thought about everything, the more certain I was that there was something she was hiding, or trying to hide, from me. And when Mel didn't just come right out and spill whatever was on her mind, that was a pretty good indication that whatever it was, was serious.

Chapter 8

I spent part of the night in the fake leather recliner in the corner. It wasn't the most comfortable place to sleep, but it was just for one night, I told myself. One night that I wasn't going to be sleeping much anyway, because . . . well . . . there were babies to hold and coo over!

I was an old pro at being an auntie. I had been one of the first to hold Jenna after Greg had managed to get stuck at the airport in Chicago during one of the worst snowstorms the Windy City had seen in a decade. I had been present and accounted for at Courtney's birth, too, and had done my share of babysitting and girls' afternoons out over the years. Even if my mom had not asked me to come to the hospital this time around, I would have been hard-pressed to stay away . . . although I might at least have taken the opportunity to share a little quiet interlude with Marcus first, if you know what I mean.

I had many reasons for wanting to be the one to stay tonight, and not the least of them was the sweet little things that awoke right on schedule around two in the morning, making mewling sounds from within the flannel blankets that swaddled them into compact little bundles. Mel had never been into breastfeeding and had made her preferences known in her chart, so there was no reason to wake her when she was still feeling the effects of the anesthesia. She would wake up soon enough, ready and eager to see her little girls, but for now I was there. A fuzzily permed and somewhat chubby nurse brought bottles of formula, tsking none too softly to herself over young mothers who did not appreciate the finer aspects of breastfeeding. She handed me a miniature bottle and a babe, made sure I knew what I was doing, then took over with the second baby. If I knew what I was doing, then I'm not sure what kind of super-expert that made her, because before I knew it she had fed, burped, changed the diaper of, and then reswaddled the baby in the same amount of time it took for me to get the first to drink even half an ounce.

"I'll just take this little peanut down to check her stats. How'z about, Auntie, you bring that one down to the nursery when she's finished so I can get her, too, and we'll see if the doctor has added anything to the charts for them or for Mom here."

She whisked the baby away, leaving me alone with a sleeping Mel and a second baby girl not nearly as interested in eating as she was in peering up at me from beneath her little hand-knitted pompon cap with eyes swollen from the drops all newborns are given. I couldn't help staring back into the dark blue eyes and noting the exquisite detail of tiny blond lashes, the fine wisp of golden eyebrows, the button nose that all babies seemed to have, and the painfully perfect bow of pink lips. So. Incredibly. Beautiful.

All babies are beautiful, I kept telling myself. And that was true. So why, why, *why* was I fighting the baby wants right now in a big way? Every time I looked down at this little one, I felt a tiny, unmistakable tug at my heart, and an expanding warmth. It felt a little bit like the first flush of love. Yeah, that was probably it. Because it most certainly did not have anything to do with the jump-starting of my biological clock. That was nothing more than a myth that women of all ages continued to spin to justify their sudden decisions for wanting to get married and settle down into that white-picket-fence lifestyle.

Not that there was anything wrong with that. But I was far too young.

Far.

And more than that, I reminded myself as I leaned down to kiss the little pumpkin in my arms on the forehead and breathe in the baby smell of her while my heart did flip-flops in my chest, at present I was just flat-out ill-equipped for the job. Having a family required several things—a stable relationship, a padded nest egg, a fabulous medical insurance plan—none of which I could lay claim to at present. Now was most definitely not the time for me to start going all broody and weird.

And talk about a guaranteed intimacy killer in a new relationship. One hint of the my-biological-clock-is-ticking discussion, and a girl could kiss almost every new-to-her boyfriend good-bye. Marcus was special, but that was asking a lot, even for him.

For the umpteenth time that night, I cursed Mel and her ridiculously bad timing.

And as for this new "feeling," which at least was one thing I could count as having nothing to do with the metaphysical: No, no, no, no, and most definitely, *no*.

The baby girl in my arms sighed in the midst of half-heartedly nursing her bottle, smiled, and then fell asleep, looking angelic as all get-out.

The universe was so not playing fair.

Since she wasn't likely to finish eating anytime soon, there was nothing left to do but to relinquish her to the nursing staff, as requested.

Holding her carefully, I set her in the bassinet and made sure the blankets hadn't come untucked. Then, after checking to be sure Mel really *was* sleeping and not just pretending this time, I wheeled the cart *slowly* out the door and down the hall, past doors swung wide on their hinges, past rooms that were mostly devoid of occupants. The sound of the wheels on the ceramic tiles made me cringe, but it didn't seem to bother the cart's only passenger. We passed one room whose door was mostly closed—inside the room, the shifting light patterns suggested that the TV was on, but no sound came from within. Muted, probably.

The nursery had several lamps switched on, but maybe that didn't bother sleeping babies as much as it did adults. Though right now, the only babies present were the twins. I had almost forgotten how few maternity patients there were tonight. Looks like it hadn't gotten any busier, either.

The frizzy-haired nurse glanced up from the paperback romance she had been engrossed in, and started to get to her feet. "All finished?"

I held up the bottle, which had an ounce of formula left. "Not as such. Though I doubt you'll get her to take any more." It had started out with only two ounces in it as it was.

The nurse didn't appear fazed by this. "Not all of them want a full meal on their first night in God's country."

"Not even the breastfed ones?" I asked, only slightly teasing.

"Not even the breastfed babes," she admitted. "Sometimes it takes them a day or two to get a fire in their belly."

She rolled the cart in beside the other. As though they each sensed the other's presence, two precious faces turned and angled gently toward each other in their sleep.

I had never seen anything so wonderfully stirring in my life.

The nurse noticed, too. "Aw, look at that. Aren't they the cutest little things?"

"Do all twins do that?" I asked her.

She nodded. "Funnily enough, they do. It's like they have this invisible radar for each other. Twindar." After another moment, she chuckled and shook her head. "Look at me. As though I hadn't seen babies every work night for the last twenty-two years. You'd think I was a newbie, wouldn'tcha, at this rate. Moonin' over every pretty baby that crossed my path. Now," she said, all business again, "let me take this one off your hands, and why don't you head back to your sister's room to get a little shut-eye. I'll bet you're not used to staying up all night with babies."

I shook my head, smiling. "I guess not."

"My guess is, your sister is out for the rest of the night—most C-section mommies have enough anesthesia and pain meds in them to keep them in and out of la-la land for a good little while. You might as well get some rest, too."

It had been a long day, and it was proving to be a long night. And she was right—I wasn't used to this. A little catnap was starting to sound like a pretty good idea.

Heading back toward Mel's room, my weariness descended on me like a weight pressing down from above. Every step felt harder to manage. Yawning, I rounded the corner, thinking about how good sleep was going to feel.

Someone had laid out a stack of flat sheets and a couple of soft blankets on the love seat in Mel's room. Mel herself had not budged—she was still flat on her back, as out of it now as she had been when I had left the room moments before. Moving quickly, I threw a sheet over the recliner and then collapsed on it, leaning back as far as the chair would allow. *Ahh.* Bliss. From a supine position, I flung the first blanket outward, using my feet to maneuver the lower part into position as best I could. *There.* The second blanket could wait, because for now I could feel unconsciousness calling me into oblivion with its siren song of black nothingness, and I sank toward it, willingly. Eagerly.

I don't know how long I had been out when I opened my eyes, not quite awake but no longer quite asleep either. It took me a good, long moment for my foggy brain to process the strange room I found myself in, and why. For some reason it seemed a sound must have awakened me. At first I thought it must have been the nurse returning the babies to the room. I sat up straighter in the recliner and forced my eyes open wider, blinking away the sleep dust that made me want to close them again. But a glance around the room showed no babies, no bassinets. Perhaps it had been Mel, I thought then. But Mel slumbered on, her mouth falling open ever so indelicately in the depths of it.

Baffled, I let my eyelids drift closed again, grateful to subdue the sandpaper-grit monsters that had launched a sneak attack the moment they had sprung open.

Voices.

And no, not the in-my-head kind. (And as a side note, why did it have to sound so bad when I put it like that? I ask you.)

I kept my eyes closed, as though the very act would allow me to focus harder, hear better.

But no matter how hard I tried, I couldn't hear the words, not even the tone. Only a steady drone, varying in pitch.

One thing I did hear, moments later, was a door opening on pneumatic hinges as the pull latch released, followed by a low voice. Female. The sibilant hiss of it settled in my bones, even though the words remained unintelligible. Someone was not happy.

The woman's voice was raised. "Get away from him. Get away from me. And don't come back here, you hear me? Don't. Come. Back. Please. Just don't."

"You're being a bitch, you know that?"

"And I don't have a right to? God. I can't believe I ever . . ."

"You don't have to worry—I gotta go out of town for a while."

"Yeah, I heard about the kid. Nice."

"Yeah. They'll want to know where he got it. I don't want to be around while they ask questions."

"He was eighteen years old. Eighteen."

"Hey, he was an adult. He made his own choices."

"Don't we all."

"—not my fault—"

"Then why are you leaving town?"

"Hey, he came to me with a problem. I helped him."

"Never mind. I don't want to know. I'm glad you're going. Why don't you stay away, while you're at it. Stay away and leave us alone."

"But when I get back . . . we'll talk."

"Don't threaten me."

Curiosity got the better of me. Carefully, I slipped from beneath the blanket that was covering my legs, and being careful not to trip in its entwining folds, I tiptoed over to the door to the hall. I had left Mel's door ajar earlier—in the event the nurse brought the twins back to the room, I wanted to be sure she wouldn't accidentally wake Mel—so it wasn't hard for me to shift into place so that I could look through the crack in the door and have a narrow but clear view of the corridor . . . which meant I also had a clear view of the man who skulked out of a room down the way. Yes, skulked, in every sense of the word, stopping at the intersection of the two patient corridors in order to peer around the corner. He paused as a page came over the intercom system:

"Tony Nunzio, dial 212. Tony Nunzio, 212."

He took his cell phone from a clip on his belt and punched a few buttons. Then, instead of making his way down past the nurses' station, I watched him dart toward the service elevators—the very ones that had held me captive earlier in the evening.

It was the same man I had seen looking out of the stair-well when Marcus and I had taken Grandpa G out to burn off some energy. Dark hair that waved just so with wayward curls, sort of attractive in a rough-and-ready kind of way. In his nondescript navy blue uniform and soft-soled shoes, he had certainly dressed the part for some quiet, behind-the-scenes subterfuge. But why the James Bond routine in the first place?

Curiouser and curiouser.

Never you mind, Margaret Mary-Catherine O'Neill. Sometimes, keeping one's nose parked in one's own business is the only safe bet.

Safe, sure. But how boring.

Fun times on the maternity floor.

But with the man and the peculiar situation gone, the energy on the floor returned to normal, and with it my own energy also ebbed. Yawning widely, I made my way back to my roost in the recliner and settled in. I was out—again—before I could even finish leaning back and locking the chair into position.

* * *

Morning came all too soon when I awoke with a start to a presence in the room—the early-bird arrival of Mel's OB/GYN.

"Hello there," said a tall, thin, middle-aged man with a surprisingly full head of hair and an equally full goatee. "Did I interrupt your sleep?"

I rubbed the sleep from my eyes and blinked a few times. "Not at all. I always look like this when I'm awake."

He laughed. "I'm Dr. Jonas, Mrs. Craven's physician. Hope I didn't surprise you, but I do my rounds right after breakfast, before I head into my office." His warm brown eyes sparkled merrily. "Babies and happy moms. It's the best way to start the day."

"And sleep-deprived older sisters," I said, stifling a yawn. "Let us not forget those."

He nodded. "Sleep deprivation is nothing to be sneezed at. Look at the bright side. You get to go home without a little one—or two, as in Mrs. Craven's case—to keep you from sleeping tonight."

He was right. And what was a little sleep deprivation between sisters, anyway? "So, did the twins surprise you as much as they surprised the rest of us?"

He looked at me oddly. "Hardly. Surprises are rare these days." A pause. "Didn't you know?"

I shrugged, not wanting to rat Mel out. Yet. "Our family is . . . *weirdly secretive* at times. That might just be one of those things someone conveniently forgot to mention to me."

"Ah," he said. "I understand."

It was a good thing he did, because I wasn't at all certain that I did. How the hell could Mel know but not tell us? And she had to have known. The nurse said that a C-section had originally been scheduled for next week, but Mel had gone into labor early. The doctor knew about the twins. Mel couldn't have been unaware.

"Her toxemia worried us all—is that going to continue to be a problem?"

"No. I've explained all of this to Mrs. Craven. Issues with pregnancies often crop up when you're carrying multiples. It was just one of those things you have to deal with."

"Are you two finished chatting?"

We both turned to find Mel frowning grumpily. Someone had awakened from her drug-induced hibernation with a burr up her—I mean, *in* her paw. Well, if she was going to be cranky, at least I knew she was going to be all right.

"Good morning, Mrs. Craven. How are we feeling this morning?"

Melanie frowned even harder and crossed her arms over her, then winced as the movement brought her pain. "I've just been cut open left, right, upside down, and sideways. How would *you* be feeling?" Then she relented. "I'm okay. I'm not too proud to admit, I've been better. Where are the babies?"

"How about if I go tell the nurses you're ready for them while the doctor checks you over?" I offered.

You see, I knew my limitations. Her doctor would be checking her incision, and there was no way in Hades my stomach—not to mention my flagging equilibrium—would stand for that. It wasn't the blood so much. Just the possibility of someone going through pain—I was almost guaranteed to lose it. My mom and my grandmother used to accuse me of just being dramatic, but they didn't feel what I felt. As an empath who tended to pick up the pain and stray energies of others, I simply was not cut out to be a nurse. No way, no how.

Mel glanced my way. "Have you been here all night?"

I nodded.

"Greg?"

She must have really been out of it last night. But, she

had the mother of all excuses. *Ba-dum-bump.* As in baby bump. Double *ba-dum-bump.* Literally. Oh, I slay me. "He had to work today," I told her yet again. "And he went to be with the girls. I'm sure he'll call you before long."

"Hm," was her only response. Again.

Dr. Jonas started peeling back the bedding, so I high-tailed it toward the door.

"Maggie?"

Cringing and hoping against hope that she wasn't going to ask me to stay there with her for moral support through the doctor's exam, I paused with my hand on the pull latch. "Yeah?"

"Thanks."

It was so brief and so sudden, I almost didn't recognize it for what it was: a rare show of gratitude from my baby sister. And just as it had when we were little girls, before she grew up to claim the entitlement issues of a princess in the making, it melted my heart. "Anytime," I told her. "By the way, Mom will be in shortly. I'm going to have to head into work myself, but I'll stop by at lunch, okay?"

And then there would be time to ask some of those questions that had cropped up. Like why no one except the doctor and nurses appeared to be aware that she would be having twins. And a C-section. That seems like an important bit of information to have, in my eyes.

"'Kay," she said with the faintest of waves. "See you later."

I closed the door behind me, almost—*almost*—wishing I had the wherewithal to stay.

Just one peek at the wee ones before I left . . .

As I headed back up the hall, distant memories of the night before flickered into my consciousness. I had been half out of my mind with sleep, but I knew I had not just dreamed it. I slowed as I walked past the door that the mystery man had exited so furtively, but the door was closed. No chance for a discreet peek inside. *"There are only two other new mommies on the whole floor,"* the nurse last night had said. Maybe if I came back at lunch, I'd run into her.

Curiosity. It was a terrible burden sometimes.

I stopped into the nursery to find the night-shift and day-shift nurses exchanging information mixed with a little gossip and other pleasantries. They each had a baby in their arms and were talking animatedly back and forth. I paused in the doorway and waved.

"My sister—the twins' mother—is in with the doctor right now, but she'd like to have the babies brought in to her."

"We'll get them in to her," the frizzy-haired nurse from the night shift assured me. "The little sweethearts have been good as gold, but they'll be wanting to be fed soon. Would you like to . . . ?"

I held up my hands, not to accept the baby being offered, but to gently fend it off. "Oh, thanks very much, but I'm on my way into work." After my gung-ho auntie act of the night before, she probably wondered why I was so disinterested now. But I knew, if I got my hands on a baby, any baby, I'd never make it in on time, if at all. Self-preservation, you see. "I'll be back at noon, though. I'll hold them then."

Waving good-bye, I backed out of the door before I could change my mind and headed for the elevators. I punched the button and waited. Then, as an afterthought, I really did change my mind—I backed away and took the stairs instead. Down was a lot easier than going up, and I didn't want to take any chances, seeing as how Ol' Murphy the trickster had been having his way with me yesterday. The stairs seemed a much safer bet.

That is, they did until I missed the last step on the second-to-the-last landing.

Chapter 9

I had just been thinking about the conversation I'd over-heard in the service elevator, wondering if somehow the pair had been closeted away on the little-used stairs right next to it; the two shafts were close enough together, it certainly seemed possible to me—voices tend to carry in spaces like this. And then all of a sudden I felt the unmistakable sensa-tion of air meeting my right foot rather than a firm step. I grabbed for the handrail with both hands rather than one . . . but it was too late. My weight came down unchecked as my beautiful, sexy, strappy Mary Jane twisted beneath me.

I sat down. Hard.

"Ow, ow, ow, *ow*!"

Tears sprang to my eyes, hot and sharp, stinging at the corners as the shock of the moment became pain. Raw, throb-bing, agonizing pain. Totally moan worthy.

"Oh. Crap."

Sprained. It was sprained. I knew it was, darn it. Which meant either I was going to have to try to hobble-hop down the rest of the stairs—a risky venture, considering I was not always the most graceful person anyway, despite years of after-school classes at Madame Sascha's School of Dance—or I was going to have to get some help.

Where were all the medical professionals when you needed one? Wasn't this a hospital, for heaven's sake?

Probably taking the elevators. So much for being health conscious.

Maybe I should try the ankle. Maybe it wasn't serious. Maybe I could suck it up, walk it off.

Gingerly I pulled myself up to a standing position on the landing, putting all of my weight on my left foot. So far so good, except the herky-jerky movements I was making didn't feel all that great. Okay. Now just *ease* the weight down, carefully . . .

"Ow, ow, ow, *ow*!"

Son. Of. A. Beehive!

So far, so *not* good.

It was most definitely sprained, and I was most definitely screwed.

I dug around in my purse for my always-errant cell phone. There was no way I was calling 911—because I could already hear the disbelief that I knew would come when they asked my location. But who to call? Someone nearby seemed key for maximum embarrassment-elimination purposes. Not my mom and dad, they had enough on their hands. Marcus was all the way across town, and besides, wasn't it enough that our private rendezvous had been unexpectedly vetoed by circumstances beyond our control? Liss was probably already at the store, early bird that she was.

Steff! Of course!

Sniffling, I dialed her cell, hoping she had her phone on her. I was so relieved when she picked up.

"Steff?" I quavered.

"Hey, Mags! Oh boy, am I glad you called. I . . . Wait, what's wrong? Your voice is shaking," she said, as though my only word to her had just registered on her consciousness.

"Steff, can you come get me?"

"Where are you? Maggie, what's wrong? Of course I can come. Tell me where you are."

I felt the tears sting my eyes again, tears of relief. "At the hospital."

"What are you doing at the— Never mind. Where at the hospital are you?"

"Sitting in the stairwell, across from the main elevators. I think I'm only half a flight up. I was coming down, and I missed a step and twisted my ankle."

"Ouch! You okay? Did you fall-fall, or did you twist your ankle and sit-fall?"

"The latter. Everything else is okay. It's just my ankle. And, maybe, my pride."

She laughed. "Well, they do say that pride goeth before a fall."

I groaned. "No puns! Laughing kind of hurts."

"Sorry! I couldn't resist. You said everything else was okay. And besides, laughter is the best medicine."

"Obviously you are on a roll. Maybe I should have called Marcus after all."

She gasped in mock pain. "I'm hurt!"

"Funny . . . me, too."

"All right, all right. I'm on my way. Stay put."

Yeah, like I was going anywhere. If I could have gone anywhere, I probably wouldn't have needed to call for rescue.

As soon as I hung up, I noticed the low battery light blinking at me. As I watched, the phone powered down in my hand before my very eyes. I shook my head, marveling at the timing. At least I'd been able to get my message through before it had died. My angels, watching out for me.

I sat there in the semigloom beneath the flickering security light, trying not to think about my ankle or the dirty steps beneath me. But it was only minutes later that I heard the door open down below, followed by a familiar voice.

"Maggie? You in here?"

It was Dr. Dan Tucker, Steff's paramour and monopolizer of her every spare moment. Not that I should complain—Marcus had done a fair bit of monopolizing my thoughts and schedule of late, and I'd been very happy about that. I was happy for Steff, too. It was good for her to be a little off balance over a guy.

"Up here!" I called out to him.

He came bounding up the stairs like an excited puppy. That was Dr. Dan in a nutshell. A medical resident with a heart of gold, and regarded as one of the most eligible bachelors at Stony Mill General Hospital, he'd fallen for my charismatic and equally heart-of-gold best friend. At six foot four, he was taller, leaner, and leggier than any of Steff's previous hunk-o'-honeys—and towered a good head over her petite voluptuousness—but he was a sweetheart and seemed completely devoted to her, and as such, he had quickly won my respect and appreciation. Early on in their one-year relationship I had almost envied his time with her, but I realized now how ridiculous that had been, a sign that I needed to find a love life of my own and stop trying to live vicariously through Steff.

Dan rounded the landing and stopped short, putting his hands on his hips and shaking his head. "Well, well," he said, "what have we here? A damsel in distress?"

"Kind of," I said, scratching the bridge of my nose in embarrassment.

"What happened?"

Briefly I explained clumsily overstepping my bounds and the cosmic slap on the wrist that had me sitting there on the concrete stair riser babying my tender ankle and waiting for rescue.

"Let me see." He squatted down in front of me. With gentle, long fingers, he lifted the pant leg of my thankfully short cropped pants and began to explore. "Hm," he said. "Hm."

"Is that all you have to say: '*hm*'?"

"Hm."

I stopped talking and braced myself as he took my heel and my foot in his hands and very slowly, very carefully turned. In a flash, a lightning bolt of pain shot up my leg. "Ow, ow, ow, *ow*!"

"Hm. Sorry."

Involuntary tears and a running nose were officially making a mess out of whatever makeup I had managed to keep on my face through all the night's dramas and traumas. Not only had I missed out on an evening tryst with Marcus that I had been very much looking forward to and everything that it probably-mighta-shoulda-woulda entailed, but I had spent the entire night in a none-too-comfortable recliner after being stuck in an elevator and having to fend off the searching tendrils of goodness knows what kind of earthbound energies *in the dark, closed space,* not to mention overhearing something that certainly sounded to me like a sinister and questionable plot against some unidentified someone and not having a single recourse of action because the conspirators in question had left no clues as to the identities or whereabouts of themselves or their potential victim . . . and then with Mel's uncharacteristic secrecy surrounding her pregnancy, and the argument that had awakened me in the middle of what sleep I did manage to get . . . and now this . . . Well, quite frankly, it had all been a bit much.

In short, I was done.

Against my will, a single sob erupted from all those I was

holding tightly in check. With that one out, there was no help for it. It was like Mount Kilimanjaro erupting.

Dan set my foot down, a stricken expression on his face. "Oh, hey. Hey. Maggie, I'm sorry. I didn't mean to hurt you. I was just trying to assess the damage."

"It's not just you," I burbled, sniffling, involuntary sobs herky-jerking my shoulders inward. "Well, it did hurt, but it's just . . . everything . . ."

He patted my hands with his while I sniffled and sobbed into some semblance of composure. Then he said, "Stay here."

Unnecessarily, I might add.

He ran down the steps, taking them two at a time in a way that made me cringe for his own ankles. I heard the door close pneumatically behind him and then reopen just a minute later. Faint sounds of other activity from the corridor on the other side of the door drifted up the stairs on his heels as he raced back up to me.

"Ready?" he asked. I nodded, and he leaned in, lifting me up against him as he might a child. "Watch your ankle," he told me. "It's kind of hard to see here in the stairwell. I don't want to bump it."

He didn't have to tell me twice. I really didn't want Mount Maggie-manjaro to erupt again anytime soon. Especially not with witnesses.

You know, for a lean and lanky guy, he was deceptively strong. I put my arms around his neck to help him along and looked up at him adoringly. "Dr. Dan, you are officially my hero today. Steff is a lucky girl, you know that?"

He laughed, a rosy blush making him look all of fifteen. "Keep telling her that, would you?"

"I think I'll do that." At the bottom of the stairs he had propped the door open with a wheelchair. I eyed it with suspicion. "Oh, I don't have to ride in that thing, do I?"

His eyebrows rose. "You want me to carry you all the way to the ER?"

"The ER? Why would I have to go there? Can't you just wrap my ankle with an Ace bandage or two and be done with it?"

He set me down in the chair and squatted before me again to skillfully guide my feet, injured and all, onto the foot paddles. "Not if you want it to heal properly." He looked up at me and met my eye. "I'm fairly positive you've broken it, Maggie."

"What?" I stuttered out a nervous laugh. "No. That's impossible. I just stepped down wrong, that's all. It's just a sprain." I nodded and smiled up at him, as though doing that would seal the deal and make it so.

"Heyyyyy!" Steff put her hands on my shoulders and leaned over the back of the wheelchair, peering down at me, upside down. "I just got here. How's the patient?"

"I'm fine!" I told her.

"She's going to need X-rays," Dan countered.

"Really, it hardly even hurts," I insisted, crossing my arms. "Honestly."

"She burst into tears when I rotated it," Dan told her.

I made a face at him. "Traitor. And besides, that was . . . that was just . . ." I searched for the right word. "Stress."

"Well," Steff said, smiling back and forth between the two of us, "I think Dan is right, Maggie. What's it going to hurt? If you're right and it's not broken, it still needs tending to. The ER is the best place for that. So let's go, huh?" To Dan she said, "I'll take her. I'm off today and you're not."

He hesitated. "If you're sure . . . I do have a meeting to go to first thing."

She nodded, her sprightly auburn curls bouncing, meeting his eyes for the briefest of moments and then dancing away. "Thanks for doing that for me, Dan."

"You're welcome. Anytime."

Whoa, whoa, whoa. Was that tension I sensed bouncing back and forth between them? That was as impossible as me having a broken ankle from a teeny-tiny misstep on the stairs. But there was a slight edge of formality in their last exchange that I didn't understand. I felt guilty all of a sudden. I'd been so busy with Marcus. Had I missed something that happened between the two of them?

Looked like I had some girlfriend-to-girlfriend digging to do.

"Will I see you later?" she asked quietly.

I watched his response closely. He glanced sideways, away from her, opened his mouth, closed it, flicked his glance her way once more, then cleared his throat and said, "Well, as I said, meeting. I'll call you?"

And Steff, true to modern woman form, straightened her shoulders and made her face a mask of neutrality as she nodded. "Okay. Talk to you later."

I waited until she had wheeled me down the hall, away from Dan, before I spoke again. "Okay, you can let me go now."

Steff laughed behind me. "Don't think so."

"Honestly, it will be fine. It is most definitely a sprain."

"Doctor's orders, Maggie. You're going to the ER."

I flopped back in the chair, wincing when it made the ankle pain flare, and mutinously crossed my arms. "It is so not broken," I grumbled.

Chapter 10

It was most definitely broken, and I was most definitely screwed.

"Look on the bright side," Steff chirped in her perkiest voice while I watched glumly as the ER crew prepared to outfit me with a splendiferous fiberglass cast. "You get to rest as much as you want without feeling guilty for it. What color do you want?"

"Color?"

"For the cast. I mean you can go with the plain cast, which is white. Ish. But if I were you I'd go for the gusto. I mean, you're going to have to wear this thing for at least six weeks. Have some fun with it. Besides, the colored fiberglass won't show dirt as quickly."

A dirty cast. In the full heat of summer.

Sigh.

The ER nurse smiled and rummaged in a cart, pulling out a tray of fiberglass tapes in every color of the rainbow as well as some well beyond the rainbow. "Take your pick."

Well, if I couldn't be mobile, at least I could be vibrant. "That one."

"Neon yellow?" Steff raised her brows. "You never wear yellow."

"Sunshine yellow. It's a happy color," I said in my defense. "I think I need happy right now."

"Yellow it is."

When they were done, I admired their handiwork. Well, admired is probably too strong a word. Surveyed is probably more like it.

"All happied up?" Steff asked me, smiling.

"It'll do." We sat quietly a moment while the nurses finished filling out the paperwork. I slapped my forehead. "Oh my gosh."

"What?"

"I forgot to call Liss. She's going to be beside herself, wondering why I haven't come in. My phone died after I talked to you, and—"

"No worries, I called her for you," Steff said, a little smugly.

I gaped at her. "You did? When?"

"When I got off the phone with Danny. I figured you'd be a little too busy to think of it. I did not, however, call your mother. You're on your own with that."

And Marcus. I needed to call Marcus to check on Minnie and to let him know what had happened.

My face fell a little.

"What's the matter, honey?" Steff asked, taking my hand. "You look sad all of a sudden."

"Last night . . . with Marcus . . ."

Steff gasped, looking thrilled. "You didn't!"

"No. I didn't. And that would be the problem." I explained the events of the evening to her. "And now, with this thing? He's going to want to stay far, far away from me. Just look at it." I knocked on the cast for good measure. "I mean, leave it to me to luck into something like this.

Steff shook her head, her gaze stern. "Now you listen here, Maggie O'Neill. Don't you sell yourself short. Bad luck is bad luck is bad luck. It's coincidence. You didn't do anything wrong."

"I guess." But I wasn't convinced. Sometimes bad luck was more than coincidence. What if I had been unconsciously inviting it into my life? Not in a biblical sense, although I'm sure my mother would be more than happy to blame it all on my boss, my friends, and my forays into "the Dark Side." (Cue very scary music.) More in a cumulative, unwitting sense brought on by years of shoving my awareness of the truth about the world surrounding me into the broom closet. Deny, deny, deny . . . and close your eyes when it comes knocking. That's what I had done for far too long. Did I accidentally leave open cosmic doorways or portals that I should have been learning how to close, and now I was paying the price?

After handing me a prescription for painkillers, notations for care, and a recommendation that I obtain crutches to get around with ASAP, the nurses were done with me, so Steff wheeled me out into the hall.

"Speaking of man trouble . . ." I said as soon as I could be certain no one who might know Steff or Dr. Dan could overhear.

"Were we?"

"Well, I was. What's up with you and Dr. Danny?"

"What makes you think something's up?"

"Well, for one thing," I said dryly, "you never answer questions with more questions. Stop using my own perfected avoidance technique on me."

Steff laughed. "I'll have to work on perfecting a technique of my own, is that it?"

"Preferably. My techniques never work anyway, so I don't know why you would want to try them on for size."

She paused as we waited for the elevator. "Do you feel up to going and chatting somewhere? There's a nice bench or two outside."

"Sure. Sounds good, and I'm not going anywhere right away anyway with this thing."

The difference between the air-conditioning inside the hospital and the sultry air outside was enough to knock you over, but I kept telling myself I just had to adjust. And maybe there would be shade. I hoped. Steff pushed my chair over to a little garden area complete with benches and perennials waving in the dappled shade, then sat down on a bench beside me.

"So."

"So," she echoed, then paused, catching her lower lip between her teeth. It was a rare day that I had seen Steff up in arms over a guy, and yet she obviously was. She had always been so confident in herself when it came to men, and Danny obviously worshipped her. I couldn't help wondering what was up.

"Stephanie Marie Evans, spill it. You know you want to."

She smoothed her hands down her legs and over her trim knees. She looked cute as could be today in a gauzy sundress and bejeweled thong sandals, her curly hair pulled back away from her delicate face and drawn up in a high ponytail that dropped in a mass of ringlets made tighter by the steamy air. Danny had thought so, too—I saw the glint of appreciation in his eye. So why the angst and tension?

"Well," she hedged, "Danny's been acting so strangely lately."

Surprise made me frown. "Strangely?"

Steff nodded. "He's been avoiding me. We usually make plans for him to come over, but he's been too busy lately, and when we talk, I can tell that he's holding something back from me. He's never been like that, which is why this was such a surprise, and . . . and he's been distant. Oh, Maggie. What if he's seeing someone else?"

I reached for her hand. "First of all, let's not jump to conclusions. You have no real reason to believe that, so don't even go there. And second of all, are you nuts? Have you *seen* the way that he looks at you?"

"He's hiding something, Maggie. I know he is."

Now, all women have at times felt that their man was hiding something from them. You get to the point where you have spent enough time with them that you know the inner workings of their minds, the everyday sense of them, and when their behavior is at odds with what you know, it raises your intuitive antennae. So when Steff said that something was up with Dan, I tended to believe her. The question was, what was that something?

"Maybe he likes me but doesn't think that his family will approve," she continued. "I mean, think about it. What if he knows his family—his mother!—won't like me? That would have to weigh heavily on his mind. Maybe he just can't think of a way to tell me."

There was no way that anyone could not like Steff. Absolutely zero chance. "Has he given you any indication of that?"

"Well . . . no."

"And he's not going to!" I told her firmly. "Because it's not going to happen."

"But . . . it has to be something big, Maggie. Something important. Danny is never like this."

"Maybe he is worried about something but doesn't want you to know he's worrying," I offered, grasping for explanations.

"Other than whether his family would like me or not, what could he be worried about? He's almost done with his residency. Then all he has to do is be licensed and certified . . ."

"Does he have to take a test in order to do that?"

"Well, of course he has to take a test for that to happen."

"Well, that's it, then," I said. "It makes sense."

"It makes sense if you're anyone other than Danny. He's a brilliant doctor, Maggie. Smart, knowledgeable, and he has his fingertips on everything he needs when making a diagnosis. I swear the man has a photographic memory when it comes to medicine. When it comes to his keys? Not so much." She laughed at her own joke, and in that moment I saw her absolute devotion to him. It gave me the shivers, in a good way. "Anyway, there's no way he needs to be nervous about the test."

"But that doesn't mean he's not."

"Maybe." But she didn't sound convinced.

I watched as she sank back into an uncertainty-driven funk. It wasn't her usual style, that's for sure. "You really love him, don't you?"

She glanced up at me, mouth open and ready to deny it. But at the last minute, she squeezed her eyelids shut and pressed her lips together and just nodded.

"Aw, Steff. Honey." I reached out and touched her hand, joggling it from side to side for good measure just to try to get her to smile. "That's a *good* thing. Isn't it?"

She actually had tears glinting in the inner corners of her pretty green eyes. "Well, I thought so. I did. It's been coming on so long, you know, little by little, and keeps getting stronger. I just don't know what to do anymore. I don't know how I'm going to keep it from him." She lifted her gaze to mine, searching for wisdom, hoping for insight. Anything that could help her find her way through this. "How do you keep something so big inside?"

Her fear was rolling off of her in waves. This was new to her, uncharted waters, and she didn't even have a star to sail 'er by. I let the fear come into me, using my own energies to filter it and soothe it, in hopes that that would help give her a measure of peace and a chance at perspective. "Maybe you're not supposed to keep it from him?" I suggested. "Maybe you're not meant to hold it inside. Maybe you're not meant to be in control of it at all."

Her lower lip trembled, and she wailed, "But I don't want to not be in control!"

"I know, hon. But sometimes these things are decided for us."

She sighed, her brow troubled.

"Does he love you?" I asked her. "I mean, he does, obviously—it's written all over him. Has he ever told you?"

She shook her head. "We've come close to saying it, so close that I almost feel that we have sometimes. Without words."

"Are you going to tell him?"

"How can I, when I have this weird . . . feeling hanging over my head? What if he's just trying to come up with a way to let me down easy?"

There was obviously no reasoning with her. Poor Steff. She had it, and she had it bad. I had never seen her like this before. Not ever. Which meant one thing and one thing only.

Danny was The One.

And because he was The One, I knew that I would do anything to see my BFF happy and content, forever and always.

I patted her on the knee. "Leave this to me."

"Wait." She squinted suspiciously at me. "What are you going to do?"

I shook my head and gave her my most mysterious smile.

But I would say Not. One. Word. Mostly because I really had no idea what I was going to do yet. No worries, though—I would come up with something.

To keep her from asking any more questions that I wouldn't yet have answers to, I decided it was time to distract her with a little problem of my own. But how to approach it? I turned my face up to the sun, blinking through the tree leaves above the little bricked courtyard, searching for inspiration.

"Forgive me, Mags, but I think the popular phrase of the moment is, 'spill it,'" Steff quipped.

So I told her. I told her about the conversation I had overheard while stuck in the elevator with the power outage, and how much what I'd heard had bothered me. How much it was still bothering me, despite everything else that had been going on. "I know it was all very random. I know it could have been anything. Anyone. Believe me, I know that. But there was just something about it. I don't know. It's hard to even explain. There was just something about it that . . . I can't let it go." I made a wry face. "Marcus thinks I'm making too much of things."

"Maybe," Steff said, frowning. "Maybe."

"And the truth is, there is absolutely nothing that can be done about it. Maybe Marcus is right. I have more important things to worry about right now. It's just that, with everything that's happened in town . . ."

"It's a little worrisome?" Steff nodded sagely. "Understandable."

"So you don't think I'm just jumping to conclusions?"

"Oh, Maggie. Who can tell? The voices weren't muffled? I mean, you could hear clearly?"

I nodded. "It was kind of hollow sounding, but yes, what I heard, I heard pretty plainly."

She considered this a moment. "Then I guess we hope that it has a perfectly reasonable explanation. What else can we do but wait and see whether anything happens?"

I didn't know. I just didn't know. But I didn't like it.

Steff had errands to run, and I had taken up enough of her free time on her day off already, so I had her wheel me back up to Mel's hospital room after trying to reach Marcus using Steff's cell and failing miserably. I couldn't go back to my apartment—living in the basement was guaranteed to make life with a casted ankle, shall we say, *interesting*—so for the time being, it was better for me to be with people I loved.

In other words, it was time to face the music.

"Maggie! What on earth! I thought you had gone into work!"

My mother was the first to catch sight of me as Steff pushed the wheelchair through the door, carefully maneuvering through the doorway and around furniture.

"She had a little bit of an accident," Steff said to the room at large. "Nothing to worry about. Just a little bit of a break."

From her regal throne on the hospital bed, Mel was peering around the furniture that separated the room. Her mouth fell open as I was wheeled around the second bed, but then closed in a pout. "You broke your ankle? Jeez, Maggie. What were you thinking?"

She was looking at me as though she thought I'd done it

on purpose, to steal her thunder. "Well, I didn't exactly mean to do it, Mel. Jeez." I explained briefly how it had happened.

Mel sighed. "Leave it to you to try to be healthy and hurt yourself in the process."

Steff evidently thought this was the perfect time for her to exit, before things got even less pretty. She leaned down and gave me a kiss on the cheek. "Don't let 'em get you down," she whispered into my ear. Straightening again, she waved. "See you, Mrs. O'Neill. Mel. Cute babies, by the way."

My mother waited until she had left the room before telling Mel, "She always was a pretty girl. A little too much for her own good, I think."

"She could be so much prettier if she straightened that curly hair of hers." Mel jumped in with her two cents. "Maybe add some blond highlights. And losing a few pounds wouldn't hurt, either."

That did it. Mel was officially, certifiably crazy. Steff's hair was gorgeous and unique and didn't need to be a cookie-cutter copy of every desperate housewife out there in Stony Mill Suburbia. And her petite figure was curvalicious, yes, but only in the best way possible. We should all be so lucky. So either Mel had gone off the deep end at long last, or maybe it was just the tidal wave of postbaby hormones—one could always hope.

"Never mind that now. We have bigger fish to fry," Mom said prosaically. "I suppose we could make room in Grandpa's efficiency apartment."

"For what?" That was me, clueless as usual.

She raised her eyebrows at me. "Well, you can't exactly get around your apartment in that cast, can you? All those stairs down? One misstep and you could be lying there at the bottom in a heap for the good Lord to watch over in good faith, waiting for someone to come along and find you. And who knows how long that could take?"

I stared at her. She couldn't be serious. "Grandpa doesn't have space for a roomie."

Mel was no help at all. She was too busy smirking down at the baby in her arms and waiting for the explosion. So much for the nice moment the two of us had shared this morning. And it had been so convincing, too.

"We can always make room for family and people in need."

How about people in need of a new personality, like Mel? Did that count?

Eh, probably not.

"Excuse me, I have to go check in with work," I said, already wheeling myself toward the door. I knocked over a stack of magazines in the process, but there was no help for it. They went sliding half under the bed. "Oops, sorry, didn't mean to do that."

Thank goodness the door to the hall was propped open, or I would have been in real trouble. Managing a wheelchair wasn't as hard as it looked, but it did have its tricks. I was just grateful I only had to use it until I was able to get crutches, or have someone bring a pair to me. To Do Numero Uno on my agenda.

Well, maybe Numero Dos. First I really needed to figure out how I was going to live with this monstrosity on my leg.

Down in the family waiting room for the second time in two days, I plugged in my cell phone charger, which Steff had been so kind as to retrieve for me from my car before she left, and powered up. Several text messages popped up as soon as I turned it back on:

#1: *Hey, guess you're not up yet. Minnie woke me up with a tongue in my ear. Sexy.*

#2: *Still sleeping? Lucky u. :) Be gone most of day. Txt when u can, can't guarantee reception. Have to go help Unc Lou w/ load of*— The message cut off. Well, at least he wasn't hanging by the phone, wondering where the heck I was and why I hadn't called.

#3: *Oh my goodness, your friend Stephanie just told me the news. I'm so sorry, ducks. What can I do to help?* Liss for that one. Of course.

#4: *Maggie! Oh! Ow! Feel better!* Classic Evie. Carpenter, that is. Sweet as ever. She'd been helping out at Enchantments until recently when the *Stony Mill Gazette* (via Margo Dickerson-Craig, I strongly suspected) spilled the beans about Liss and her paranormal proclivities. Evie's mom had yanked her out of her after-school job at the store without so much as a by-your-leave. But Evie still somehow managed to be around on an almost-daily basis. Funny how that worked.

#5: *Ooooooooh, ouch! Busted! Literally! Sorry, bad pun. ROFLMAO.* And, classic Tara, who never let a chance for a demonstration of her renowned sarcastic wit pass her by. Good thing she had Evie's influence to temper her tendency to walk the fence between light and dark.

#6: *Tara got ahold of me, Maggie-sweet, we're on our way back. Don't worry, we'll figure things out.* Sigh. Marcus again, just minutes ago. I texted back to let him know that I was okay, not to risk life or limb hurrying back, and that I would call or text if or when I knew where I would be later on. When he sent me back a quickie text in reply a moment later that promised to kiss it and make it all better, I had to smile. Big time.

I phoned Liss first.

"Enchantments Antiques and Fine—"

"You have no idea how much I wish I had just gone into work this morning as usual," I interjected before she could complete the usual greeting. "No idea."

"Maggie! Darling! How's the ankle? Oh, you poor thing. It must be absolutely excruciating."

"I don't feel a thing," I told her breezily. "They gave me a shot of something that took it all away. Now, I don't know how long that's going to last, so I'm enjoying it while I can." I sighed. "I feel so guilty, being away from the store today. I know we have a million things going on."

"All of which will be going on tomorrow and the next day and the day after that and the day after that . . ."

"I get the picture. Are you telling me don't worry?"

"Precisely."

"Hm. Well, I'll try."

"The girls have promised to come in after school to help out. Including Evie." Liss laughed. "It seems our little psychic angel is far more rebellious than she has been given credit for. It is always the quiet ones, it seems. Is there anything I can do for you, darling?"

"Well . . . that just so happens to be one of the reasons I'm calling. The other being to keep myself sane while being mired in the trenches with my mother and sister."

"I heard about the babies. I really must be getting old. I didn't remember that your sister was having twins."

"Neither did I. But that's a story for another day."

Liss chuckled. "Wonderful. I do love a good story."

I had a feeling we were both going to love this one. And I would tell it, just as soon as I had all of the details myself, straight from the source. To Do Number Three.

"Okay," I said, getting back down to business. "It seems that one of the minor annoyances of having a broken ankle is having this massive, weighty lump on the end of your leg. It's called . . . a cast."

"I have actually heard of that, yes." Her humor crackled over the airwaves.

"Yes, well, it occurs to me that I live in a basement apartment. Down a dirty concrete stairwell that catches lawn debris every time it storms, and I will be on crutches."

"Hm. I think I see your predicament."

"And it's a doozy."

"It doesn't have to be, you know."

"My mother wants me to move into the garage with my grandfather," I told her. "I love my grandpa, but living anywhere near my mother after having worked so hard to get out from under her thumb does not sound like my idea of moving forward in my life."

"I knew I should have insisted that Geoffrey install an elevator at the house when we built it," Liss remarked, referring to her late husband. "Of course, he thought I was being dramatic. It would certainly solve your current dilemma."

Too bad for me. Sigh. Living at Liss's for a time would have been heaven compared to Ye Olde Homestead.

"Don't give up too soon," Liss said soothingly. "I'm sure we'll be able to find a solution if we put our heads together, and of course you're welcome to sleep on one of the sofas downstairs as a last resort. Let me do a bit of calling around and I'll ring you back."

I wanted to believe that an acceptable solution could be found, but I had a sinking feeling that tomorrow I would find myself waking up on the creaky old fold-out bed back home, listening to my mother plan her day around her church activities, Grandpa G, and Mel, while Grandpa G acted up with gusto and my father and I shrank into the fading wallpaper, hoping not to be noticed. It was either that or learn how to get really good on crutches really fast and hope that my mother's prediction of a tumble was just her usual pessimism run amok. I'd rather stay in this unpadded wheelchair in a dark corner of Mel's hospital room for the duration of her stay than to move back home for any length of time.

I wondered if anyone would notice a woman with a bright yellow lump of a cast?

Hm. Perhaps I should have gone with basic black after all.

Chapter 11

Another text message came in as I held my phone in my hand, weighing my next move. Distracted, I clicked through the screens:

Mags, I did a little digging for you. There were 2 deaths at hospital last night. Call when you get off the phone. Steff, digging? I had to call.

Locating a set of crutches was going to have to wait while I gave in to curiosity. I dialed Steff's cell phone.

"Two?" I asked, just as soon as she answered. Two, the same night Mel's twins were born. Two for two. I shook my head at the irony.

"Two," she confirmed. "Now it could be nothing, coincidence, nothing more. And it probably is just that. But in light of what you overheard, I just thought I'd do a little quick check with a friend of mine who handles the paperwork for the morgue. And our hospital's so small and all of the truly complicated things usually go to the big hospitals in the city, and two separate deaths on the same night . . . well, it just doesn't happen too often."

Two. Could it be? I wondered. Could one of them actually be related to the now infamous-in-my-mind elevator conversation? And, I hated to even think it, but I didn't know if Jordan Everett's death had been accidental or suspicious. It couldn't be related, could it? Was there a killer on the loose? I shivered.

"Do you know the situations?" I asked her. "I mean, the deaths occurred in the hospital. There was nothing about what I overheard that could guarantee that whatever it was that they intended to do would happen at the hospital itself, so they might not even be connected."

"One was in the ER. Heart failure, I think, with a possibility of it being drug related. The other was a woman on my floor who'd been sick quite a while with cancer. You're right, they don't sound incredibly suspicious. One sudden, one lingering. And with the possible drug-related one, well . . . I don't know, Maggie. I don't think they're what you're looking for, but I thought I'd mention it anyway."

After my initial excitement—not that two people had died (never that!), but that perhaps I was not merely imagining things due to the stress of the situation—I felt my optimism slip.

Steff went on. "Well, it was a thought, anyway. Maggie . . . you don't think there was any way that you could have been hearing . . . spirit voices, do you? Not real, live people?"

"I'm positive," I told her firmly. I mean, give me a little credit to understand the difference between daydreams and reality, please. "They were definitely not of the otherworldly variety." Even if they *were* hollow sounding and faraway and . . . Oy, continue on that line of thinking and I'd start to wonder myself!

"Okay. I'll keep my ears to the ground," Steff assured me. "Just in case."

"All right. You'll tell me what you find out?"

"Well . . . actually no."

I frowned into thin air. "What do you mean?"

"I've got to be careful, Maggie. In this day and age of patient confidentiality? I'm not supposed to be digging at all because I have no legal right to the information and no sanctioned need to know."

She was right about that much at least, and I knew it. "I don't want you to get into trouble over this."

"That doesn't mean I can't look into it a *little* more. Just in case. Rachel down at the morgue does owe me for the time I caught her smoking, um, shall we say 'Martian cigarettes' down there. *Not* that I would use that against her, really, but these things do come in handy sometimes." She paused delicately. "However, what that does mean is that I am absolutely not going to be telling you anything specific."

A little exasperated, I asked, "Well, could you blink once for yes, twice for no? Put a lantern in the window? Anything?" I was the one who overheard the conversation in the first place. It seemed only fair.

"If there is anything suspicious about either death, anything at all in the coroner's report, *someone* in the appropriate channels will hear about it, Maggie. I promise you that. But that's all I can promise." She cleared her throat. "And by the way? That does not include Danny, so please don't be mentioning anything about this to him."

Keeping something from Dan? That didn't sound like Steff.

"I don't like keeping secrets from him," she said, echoing my thoughts, "but he's too close to finishing his residency. I absolutely will not risk his involvement in any way."

Her lioness approach to preserving Dan's integrity was nothing short of vintage Steff, champion of the underdog, in the same way that she had always protected the nerdy kid on the playground when someone threatened to break his glasses. "Okay, not a problem," I promised. "Danny won't hear a thing from me."

"Thank you."

"Oh, by the way," I said, wanting to change the subject to something a little less touchy, "my mom is trying to make me move in with them while my ankle heals. I may need you to kill me before she can take me home. Nothing fancy or dramatic. A simple, old-fashioned draught of poison in my tea will suffice."

Steff laughed, which is exactly the reaction I was hoping for. "Self-fulfillment of a death prophecy is not allowed, Mags. That's kind of, you know, cheating."

"Ha-ha."

"Well, when Danny breaks up with me, you can always move in with me," she said, gloomy again.

"He's most definitely not going to break up with you, silly girl. And you're on the third floor. How is that supposed to help?"

She laughed, too. "I guess you're right. About that at least."

We hung up then with a promise from Steff to check in with me soon . . . just to be sure I hadn't rolled my wheelchair off the most convenient cliff face. Which wasn't even an option, since we live in flat-ass Indiana. Presumably that meant I was screwed, if Liss's secret notion didn't work out. I was afraid to cross my fingers for fear of jinxing the whole deal. Ol' Murphy had been riding my tail far too close for comfort lately. I was going to have to do something about that.

I tried to reach Marcus but instead received the canned message that *the cell phone user could not be reached at this time, please try your call again later*. Wherever he'd gone with Uncle Lou, he must be in and out of service areas. As an afterthought, I took a picture of my cast with my cell phone and sent it through as a photo text with the caption, "Ow."

Sighing, I reached over to unplug my cell phone charger from the wall. It wasn't easy. The cast weighed about five hundred pounds (my mother wasn't the only one who liked to get her hyperbole on when the situation called for it) and wouldn't cooperate. I was forced to roll halfway over in the chair, wrangle one knee up beneath me on the collapsible seat, and try to stretch that way. Admittedly, this probably wasn't the safest posture, but without anyone to do my reaching for me, and without any way of wheeling the chair closer to the wall, I did what I had to do.

Everything would have been all right if the weight on my ankle hadn't suddenly shifted sideways, throwing me completely off balance. I caught myself from falling entirely, thank goodness—ow—but couldn't figure out how to get myself back upright.

This was going to take some maneuvering.

The door to the waiting room opened. In scuffed a young woman in a fluffy pink bathrobe, her rounded tummy suggesting that she was a recent maternity patient. She saw me leaning over the arm of my wheelchair and froze.

"Oh my goodness. Are you all right?"

She hurried over, her flip-flops flapping, concern written on her brow and in her dark eyes. Or at least it looked like concern. It was kind of hard to tell from my upside-down vantage point. Heck, I was lucky I even took the time to register they were brown.

"Uh, hi," I said.

"Can I help you with that? Here, let me get you up."

She extended a hand, waiting until I took it and allowed her to pull me upright.

Her long dark hair had fallen forward into her face, a straight, thick sheaf of it. It was the kind of hair I'd always dreamed of, a wish made more poignant by the fact that it was a style my light brown waves could never in a million years emulate. Only after years of tears and drama had I at long last come to terms with that sad truth.

"Thanks," I told her, a little embarrassed. "I wasn't quite sure how I was going to get myself out of that one. I was just trying to unplug my charger. Guess this thing is going to take some getting used to." Wryly, I reached down and rapped my knuckles on my lovely new boon companion.

"Oh, did you just break it?" she asked.

I nodded. "I was here with my sister, Melanie. She just had twins."

"Oh, she's the one!" the young woman exclaimed. "I had my son right before her, I guess. And I'm right down the hall from her. I heard her little ones crying just a little while ago. She's got her hands full with two."

"Congratulations on your new baby." I smiled. "I think we sat with your in-laws in the waiting room. The Watkins?"

She nodded. "Uh-huh."

"Nice folks, Joyce and Harold," I added, but I could tell that I was losing her. Her attention was starting to veer off around the room. "Joyce seemed so happy to have her first grandchild, signed, sealed, and delivered. Very proud."

"You didn't happen to see a magazine in here, did you?" she said, completely off the original topic as she scanned table and countertops.

"Um, well, no." Actually, now that I looked around, I did notice that the bevy of magazines that had been on the tables while we were waiting for Mel to pop had since disappeared. "Gosh, there were loads of them in here last night." And then in my mind flashed a memory: a stack—well, a former stack once I was done with it—of glossy periodicals on the floor by the bed in Mel's room. "You know, it's possible I might know where to start the search."

"I am actually looking for one in particular," she offered as I started wheeling myself toward the door. "I thought maybe my mother-in-law might have walked off with it accidentally when I wasn't looking. I was really hoping to get it back."

"In the middle of an article, were you?"

"Something like that. So, you think you know where they went?"

"My sister has a whole stack in her room that I think must have come from here, because all the mags that were in here last night are gone. Follow me, I'll show you where. You can look through them to see if any are yours."

I waited as she opened the door. With my phone charger and cell phone on my lap and my injured ankle leading the charge, I maneuvered my way through the doorway and out into the corridor . . .

Straight into the path of a very familiar personage.

"Oh, excuse me, Miss—"

An equally familiar voice broke off suddenly, and I had a feeling his gaze had just connected with my face.

"Maggie."

I cleared my throat and steeled my emotions. "Hello, Tom." My gaze flicked to his left—to the woman on his arm—and then back again. I smiled, ever so pleasantly.

He still had his favorite aviator sunglasses on, so I couldn't see his eyes, but I knew they weren't meeting mine. "What are you doing here?"

I shrugged. "Mel had her baby. Babies, I should say. She had twin girls."

"Ah. Be sure to tell her congratulations for me."

"I will." But I didn't know why, really. Mel had never actually met Tom, unless it was in some capacity outside of being my boyfriend-minus-one that I wasn't aware of. Still, it was a nice sentiment, I would give him that much.

"Looks like you had a little trouble," he said, inclining his head toward my ankle.

When he said "trouble," why did it sound critical, as though I had caused it somehow by my actions? "This old thing?" I joked. "A minor spill, that's all. Just dumb luck."

I thought I heard him say, "Karma, maybe," but it was mumbled, and I couldn't be sure.

I held out my hand to the woman whose hand was curved around his inner elbow. She released his arm and took it, hesitating only slightly. "Hi there. I'm Maggie O'Neill."

I got my first good look at her. She was slender, wispy even, with short pixy hair that waved appealingly around her face and a long neck that was enviably swanlike. She was also taller than me, nearly Tom's height with the low heels she was wearing with her casual jeans and airy blouse.

"I'm Julie," she said. "Julie Fielding."

Dun-dun-dunnnnnnn . . .

I flashed back to the day, just a few weeks ago, to when Annie Miller had hesitantly, reluctantly, worriedly clued me in to the fact that she had seen Tom while out at a local Mexican restaurant in the company of an attractive woman. At the time Tom and I had still been "dating," although both of us had acknowledged that there were issues cropping up that were directly related to who we were as individuals, issues that we didn't quite know how to conquer, although time itself seemed to have decided that for us in the end. At the time I had also tried to convince myself that it had been his sister. Gazing up at the woman, I suddenly knew that this was without a doubt the person he'd been having dinner with. His ex-wife. The ex-wife he would never talk about. Not even ex, since they were only in the process of being divorced.

Were they back on now?

Did that even matter?

"Julie and I are here to visit—"

"Me." The Watkins woman stepped forward. Until that moment, I don't think Tom and Julie had even registered her presence behind me. I'd almost forgotten her there myself. "Hiya, Jules. It's good of you to come in."

Surprised, Julie stepped up and embraced her. "Frannie! Harry said it would be all right for us to just come up; I hope that's okay. We just wanted to stop in and see how you were doing." With her hands on Frannie Watkins's shoulders, she leaned back to survey her. "Should you even be up? You just had a baby, for heaven's sake."

Frannie waved her hand to dismiss the concern. "You'd be surprised how quickly they get you up and around these days. Don't worry, I'm not doing anything I'm not supposed to."

Except probably helping me back into my wheelchair, I thought guiltily.

"Frannie and I are cousins," Julie politely clued me in. "Second cousins, I guess, but family nonetheless."

"Good thing you stopped in early," Frannie told her. "Little Harry and I are being released later tonight."

"So soon?"

"No complications in pregnancy or delivery, so it's a one-day stay. Insurance dictates." Funny, I could feel her getting antsy about the impromptu visit, even though it was, as Julie Fielding said, family. "Listen, Maggie here was about to help me with something. Why don't we go do that, and I'll meet you in my room in a few minutes?"

Perhaps Julie had sensed her preoccupation as well. "Oh, that's all right. We can't really stay. Tom is taking me out to a lovely dinner tonight," she said, leaning into his arm and smiling up at him.

I froze. I couldn't help thinking that the mention of their upcoming dinner date was for *my* benefit. Why else would she have mentioned it? I hadn't even had *lunch* yet!

For one completely, ridiculously irrational moment, I was *that* girl. The girl who has left one boyfriend behind and has moved on, but the instant the previous guy showed signs of moving on, too . . .

Yeah. Zing went the strings on the harp played by my own personal little green monster.

Disgusted with myself, I intentionally summoned the image of Marcus into my mind's eye. Marcus, who made every bad day somehow better. Marcus, my friend and my soon-to-be lover, if I had anything to say about it—stupid yellow cast be damned.

I just wished I didn't know that Tom had been purposely exploring his options *before* we had officially called things off. Say what you will about my jumping ship to Marcus so quickly, but at least it hadn't been planned. It wasn't intentional.

I looked into Tom's gray eyes and found him watching me, too. I lifted my chin. Things were better this way, better for everyone.

Still . . .

"I hear the band at Finnegan's Reef is really good," I couldn't resist mentioning, intentionally referring to the place where Marcus and his bandmates were currently playing Wednesday nights and weekends. "Maybe you should take her dancing, too."

His eyes betrayed nothing, but the slight tightening of his jaw spoke volumes. Let's just say that I knew that he knew that I knew he knew . . . "Maybe I will."

"Oh, Tom, really? I love dancing. It has been ages," his clearly not-so-ex-wife gushed. Although she was doing a good job of appearing unaware of the edgy connection between Tom and me, I knew—I sensed—that she wasn't oblivious to it at all. Perhaps that was why she reached down and took his hand as I watched on. From my seated position, it was right on eye level. I couldn't have missed seeing it if I'd tried.

"Women sure do have a way of staking their claims, don't they, Margaret? Even when their claims are in the past."

There it was, Grandma's voice aloud in my ear, again. Complete with self-satisfied cackle at the end. I sighed, wishing the voice would go back to being that soundless one in my head. Although at least this time it was a quiet one. But really, consciences can be a real pain in the neck sometimes.

Especially when they made you think.

Was that what I was doing? Trying to stake a claim? Of course I wasn't. Things between Tom and me had never been quite right. We had both sensed that, and seemingly we had both come to that conclusion around the same time. If Tom wanted to get back together with his ex-but-not-ex-wife, who was I to complain? I should be happy that he was moving on with things. After all, that's what I was doing.

Still, I was relieved when the two of them decided to go, leaving me to head back to Mel's room with Frannie Watkins at long last. She had been just as anxious as me to get on with things; something told me she wasn't as close to her cousin as all that. Either that or she had other things on her mind.

"There you are! I was looking everywhere for you."

We had barely made our way around the corner when Frannie's husband came out of her room as we passed by, their baby in his arms. Frannie jumped guiltily.

"Hi, honey." Her accompanying wave was a little weak.

"Hi. I just got here, and Little Harry was waking up in his bassinet. I didn't see you, so . . ."

"I just left him for a minute, Harry, I promise," she rushed to explain in an agitated voice. "He was perfectly safe."

The lapse forgiven, Harry glanced my way and smiled. "Hello there."

More babies. Sigh. I smiled a greeting back at him and nodded toward the baby. "Could I?"

He angled his arm so that I could see the tiny eyes peeking out from the folds of a soft blanket.

"Look at those eyes," I cooed. "Have you ever seen a baby with such big, dark eyes? They couldn't be changing already, could they? No, it's much too soon. And look at those lashes!"

The proud papa patted his son lightly on his padded rump. "You think that's dark? Look at what he got from his mommy." Gently, carefully, he peeled back the fuzzy blanket and with a big calloused palm slipped the knitted cap from the baby's head. Out sprang a head full of dark, curling waves. "A full head of hair! Just what every man needs, let me tell ya," he said with a glimmer of humor, with no need to run his hand over his own receding buzz cut to demonstrate why.

With a soft cry, his wife padded forward, her hands reaching for their baby. "He'll catch his death," she insisted, tugging the cap back down to the baby's downy eyebrows. She stroked her fingertips in a sweet, soft caress along his cheek, a flicker of emotion feathering over her brow as she gazed down at him.

Turning away suddenly, she cleared her throat. "I was just on my way to find a magazine to flip through, and this lady said her sister had some in her room."

"Oh. Okay. I'll just take Junior and wait for you here, then." He looked down at the pale blue bundle in his arms and his expression softened. "Come on, Junior. Let's go see if your diaper needs changing."

"Wow, your hubby changes diapers," I commented up at

Frannie as we continued on to Mel's room. "That's a keeper for sure."

She nodded. "He's been wanting to start a family for a long time. This is a dream come true for him."

She sounded so . . . I don't know . . . vague? Distracted? In fact, come to think of it, she had seemed that way since she walked into the waiting room. Something wasn't right in Frannie Watkins's world today, I would guarantee it.

It hit me then. *There are only two other mommies on the entire floor*, the night nurse had said, and then later that night I had seen a man with dark hair coming out of a room. Sneaking out of a room, in the middle of the night, following what certainly sounded like an argument of some kind. What was his name? I had forgotten in all the events of the day. Frannie herself had mentioned she was right down the hall from Mel just a little while ago. But it hadn't clicked with me until just now.

The room that Harry Watkins had emerged from was the exact same room.

Chapter 12

No wonder Frannie Watkins was out of sorts today. I didn't know who the man had been or what the connection between Frannie and her after-hours visitor was, but it couldn't be an easy one.

Curious.

A moment later I could have smacked myself. Good heavens, I was turning into as much of a "Nosy Parker" as my sister and mother. Shoot me now! Whatever connections existed between them, it was their business. It certainly wasn't mine.

"Now you're learning, missy."

Yeah, thanks for the vote of confidence, Grandma C. Now, butt out, wouldja?

"Here we are, room twelve twenty-three," I said, pushing against the mostly closed door.

"I was wondering when you were going to come back, Mags," came Mel's voice from the far bed. "You keep disappearing."

I steeled myself, put a neutral smile on my face, then led the charge back into the trenches.

Or should I say, the viper's pit? Because who should be sitting on the chair and love seat opposite Mel but my long-time nemesis, Margo Dickerson-Craig (emphasis on the hyphen, please—she'd be the first person to tell you it was important) and her partner-in-gossip, Jane Churchill, each with a twin cradled in her arms.

Ol' Murphy was obviously in top form. How many times did this make in the last couple of days that he'd reared his ugly head? I was starting to lose count.

The three women had formed a sort of coffee klatch after Mel and Greg had moved into the upscale subdivision of Buckingham West. Before I even found out about the alliance of the terrible trio, they had cemented together via their thirst for scandal, their taste for the illicit, and their hunger for one-upmanship. It was a friendship that would live in infamy.

"Well, look who it is," Margo smirked.

One person with a personality, coming right up, I thought to myself, smirking right back. But I took the high road. My new nieces were in the room. They didn't need to be exposed to such negativity. They were already surrounded by it . . . poor things.

"You just missed Mom. She just left. Where *did* you disappear to?" Mel asked.

I shrugged. "Never mind that now. Come on in, Fran—"

"Frannie Watkins!"

The sudden screech of recognition bounced off the walls and my eardrums. With it Mel had sat up straighter on the bed; she sank back now instantly, grimacing, her hand held protectively to her abdomen. "Ow, ow, ow, ow, *ow*."

There was a lot of that going around today.

Frannie stopped in her tracks and stared. "Melanie? I had no idea it was you down the hall. They said the girl in here had had twins——" Her searching gaze found the two empty glass bassinets, then the two babes in the arms of the two wenches, I mean, women. "Wow, you did. I had no idea you were having two. Never in a million years . . . you were so tiny."

Were we back to discussing Mel's petite uterus? Oy.

"I would have stopped in earlier, had I known it was you," she continued. "Honestly, I thought you were pregnant with just one. Gosh, I feel bad now. I'll be going home this evening."

"You two know each other, I take it?" I asked, trying to keep my sense of humor.

"From Baby Bellies," Mel confirmed. "My fitness class. I was going until Dr. Jonas ordered me on bed rest."

"Twin girls?"

Mel nodded. "Sophie June and Isabella Rose. You?"

"A little boy. Harry the third. That was pretty important to my husband. Not Harold, though. I put my foot down about that. I thought two Harolds in a row were enough." She laughed a little self-consciously. "Speaking of the baby, I'd better be getting back. H3 is going to be wanting to eat. That's what I've decided for a nickname for him, you see. H1 will be grandpa, H2 his dad, and he'll be H3. How else are you supposed to keep them apart? Besides, Harry is waiting for me. My Harry. My husband, I mean." She groaned and shook her head. "See what I mean? It's self-defense."

Mel laughed politely.

Frannie glanced at me. "Well . . . I don't mean to be rude . . . But if you have those magazines handy?"

"Magazines?" Mel asked, looking at me now, too.

"Mom must have picked up one that had been left in the waiting room by the Watkinses when she brought in the stack for you to flip through earlier," I explained. Embarrassed because I wasn't going to be much help in my somewhat incapacitated state, I was forced to point to the stack of magazines on the floor. "I would help, but . . ."

"That's okay." Frannie crouched down in her bathrobe and slippers and began to flip through the stack swiftly. "Oh, thank goodness!" Finding what she wanted, she straightened the stack.

I caught sight of the magazine as she rose carefully to her feet. It looked like a men's sporting magazine, like one my grandfather would have enjoyed. She caught me looking and blushed.

"I scratched down some personal thoughts in it while I was in labor," she quickly explained, waving it slightly in my direction. I thought I saw something fall from it, but it happened so fast and when I looked around her feet, there was nothing there. Oh well. It was probably just one of those annoying inserts anyway. "It's my husband's magazine, really, but I wanted to capture what I had recorded there before it ends up getting lost in his bathroom reading stash." She turned to leave, pausing at the door. "Congratulations, Mel, on the babies."

"You too, Frannie."

It hadn't even occurred to me that Margo and Jane had been uncharacteristically silent throughout the bulk of this exchange between the two new moms. But now that Frannie had gone, Jane got up quietly behind her, passed the baby she'd been holding over to Mel, then tiptoed stealthily over to the door to watch Frannie retreating down the hall with her prize. She closed the door just as quietly on its pneumatic hinges, then turned back to face the rest of us.

"What's up, Jane?" Mel asked, her face betraying a bright curiosity. The baby had awakened in midshuffle and was now making snuffly noises. On mommy autopilot in the way only very experienced mothers can be, Mel reached for the recently prepared bottle and plopped it in her mouth. "There you go, Isabella."

Jane's face displayed an avid excitement known to gossip-mongers everywhere. "I know her, too. She and her husband are clients of the firm." Jane "worked" at her husband's law firm on a part-time basis. Mel had told me once that Jane did it gratis, solely for the benefit of having easy access to private information she might not otherwise be privy to. In other words, Prime Scoopage. "Greg might even have been the partner to handle their case last year," she told Mel, "if I remember correctly."

"Case?" Mel echoed.

My intuition kicked in. I had a sudden feeling as to where this was heading.

"Their *divorce* case."

Yup, that's what I thought. Greg was a divorce lawyer, a partner at the firm of Turnbow, Whitehouse, Churchill, and Craven, along with Jane's husband, Phil. Young, smart, and very savvy, Greg had risen quickly through the ranks of the midsized law firm and made partner by virtue of his seemingly effortless ability to see his clients through one of the most emotionally difficult times of their lives without losing their shirts in the process.

The Watkins family had struck me as being very simple, down-to-earth people. Not the kind who would be overly worried about preserving all in a divorce case, because fairness and equity were a way of life to them. Not Greg's usual type of client, surely.

"Divorce!" Mel exclaimed. Her eyes lit up at the scoop. "But how—"

"Obviously they didn't go through with it," Jane said. "Harry Jr. backed down soon enough when Frannie found out she was pregnant. By all accounts, his desperation to have a child played into the dissatisfaction with the marriage, so when that was taken out of the equation . . ." She let her voice trail off meaningfully and shrugged, leaving everyone to come up with their own conclusions.

Not so much of a scoop after all. I could see Mel's interest waning.

And so could Jane. But her information wasn't quite spent after all. She stood at the end of Mel's bed, her hands clasped ever so piously before her. "Perhaps," she suggested, "he wouldn't have been quite so hasty if the private investigator's report had been forwarded to him."

Two pairs of eyebrows rose in response to Jane's revelation: one set Mel's, the other's, Margo's. I was trying to remain neutral, rather than play into their need for scandal . . . but I will admit, I was paying attention. The only difference between me and Mel? Her interest in gossip and intrigue was purely for the titillation factor. Mine was to further my understanding of human nature. At least that's what I told myself. The need to understand was strong within me; it always had been. Why people did the crazy, mixed-up, sometimes completely nonsensical things that they did. Inquiring minds (mine) want to know.

"He hired a private investigator?" Margo asked. The twin in her arms was beginning to snuffle and shift around, too.

"No," Jane said. "We hired the private investigator. It is standard operating procedure in divorce cases at the firm for, shall we say, families of extended means. Since the Watkinses own all the gas stations in town, they have a significant amount of cash, property, and investments in their portfolio that needed to be protected."

So the down-to-earth Watkins family was rolling in it . . . who knew? They certainly didn't flaunt it. Unlike some people I knew. Case in point? I rolled my gaze dispassionately toward Margo, who had a brand-new Vera Bradley satchel purse at her feet, an expensively maintained mani-pedi, shoes and clothes that probably cost as much as a week's pay for me, and who sported a fresh blow-out for her (*cough*, bleached, *cough*) blond hair.

"So, Jane," Mel prodded, "what did the investigator find?"

Jane sat down again, stretching out her moment in the spotlight for as long as possible. "Well, I don't know if I should say. It is privileged information, you understand."

"You know us, Jane. It absolutely goes no farther than this room," Margo told her solemnly.

I tried very hard not to roll my eyes. Trust me, it was a supreme effort.

Mel shot me a look. "*Right*, Maggie?" she demanded.

But I couldn't help it when my eyebrows stretched upward in disbelief. "You're worried about *me*?"

She forced me to agree to those terms before she would allow Jane to continue.

"What they found," Jane said in a voice that quivered with the excitement of the moment, "was that she had been having an affair."

Mel sucked in her breath in delight. "And the husband didn't know?"

"Not a clue. Evidently that wasn't a contributing factor to their divorcing."

Mel and Margo exchanged a glance, as though they were sharing thoughts telepathically. And maybe they were. There was almost an electric back-and-forth telegraphing of energy hanging in the air.

"Why *were* they getting a divorce?" Margo asked.

Jane hesitated—not because she was having second thoughts, but for effect. "Because he wanted a family and they were having trouble and he thought she was taking measures to avoid getting pregnant."

The entire conversation was making me feel slimy by default . . . but there was a hint of something important lurking there.

"When was this, Jane?" Mel asked her.

"Hm. No more than a year ago, certainly."

There was a moment of silence as four women, yes, including me, began counting backward. Because if a standard pregnancy lasted for forty weeks, that was ten months of the "no more than a year" right there.

"He called it off because they'd reconciled," Jane said simply.

They'd reconciled . . . and all of a sudden, poof, baby. What fortuitous timing.

Or was it baby, then reconciliation?

"And someone at the firm made the unilateral decision to just file the private investigator's report in his file for future reference. Just in case it ever came back to that, the report would be there." She laughed. "The whole situation was so notable because of how it suddenly came to light, and because of how it just as quickly was tucked away into the closet again. It always bothered me, that the husband never had a chance to make that decision for himself . . . but that's family law for you."

Mel's brow furrowed. "Well, I wouldn't want anyone making that decision for me," she said decisively.

Margo and Jane said nothing. Nothing at all. Not even a single murmur of agreement.

And all of a sudden I was hit by a strong, heavy feeling that completely distracted me from the gossip about poor Frannie and Harry Watkins. Completely unrelated . . . but not, somehow.

And that made no sense whatsoever.

Sometimes intuition can be frustrating. Visions, symbols, feelings—the "sign" language of Spirit—all are often given via a type of metaphysical shorthand. It would be much easier if one's spirit guide could just make it standard operating procedure to appear before them and either speak in complete sentences, or hand them a scroll or even a computer printout or something. Instead, a message from beyond might come in any form and often must be interpreted according to the belief system and experiences of the recipient. Which made it a very tenuous process at best. Still, for every message that went undeciphered, the ones that made a real difference could not be discounted. I was grateful for every last one of them.

Of course that didn't help me to understand how Mel's situation could be in the least bit tied to Frannie Watkins. The two were shirttail acquaintances at best.

"I wonder who she was having an affair with," Margo mused.

The rest of us seemed to be wondering the same thing.

"Oh my God!"

Melanie had slapped her hand to her forehead, jarring baby Isabella awake. The baby began drawing again at the almost empty bottle, forestalling any squalling that might have been about to erupt.

"What?" Jane asked, breathless.

"I had completely forgotten this," Melanie said. "You remember I told you all I had met Frannie at Baby Bellies? Back before I had been relegated to bed rest?"

Margo and Jane nodded encouragement. I pretended not to be listening too closely, but I totally was.

Isabella had actually finished her small bottle. Mel turned the baby up onto her shoulder and began to gently pat and rub her back. "Well," she began importantly, her eyes flashing, "a guy came early to pick her up one night. While the rest of us were in the middle of our mom-ified lunges and hippo squats, I could see her in the coatroom with him, thanks to the mirrors on the wall. They were arguing. He grabbed her arm, she pushed him away." She paused then, a mischievous glint in her eye. "Cute guy, too. Dark and dangerous. Motorcycle hottie in a black leather jacket. Not my type, but Maggie here would like him well enough."

Out of the corner of my eye, I could see Margo surveying me with a sudden renewed interest. "Really? But I thought Maggie was seeing, oh, what's his name? That bland sheriff's deputy?"

Bland? I was insulted, on Tom's behalf.

"Tom Fielding," Melanie supplied, ever so helpfully, as she patted her daughter's back. "But that's over."

That would be Special Task Force Investigator Tom Fielding to you. And why was she helping Margo out with my business, anyway?

"Well, that didn't take long," Margo said.

A little unkindly, I thought.

All the things I would like to say to her but shouldn't started boiling in my brain. I stared at her. I fumed.

Perhaps sensing my supreme annoyance, Mel handed Isabella off to me—I accepted, gratefully, happy for the distraction—and then motioned to Margo to bring Sophie to her.

"So. Maggie." Margo straightened in her chair and smoothed her now wrinkled linen capris, the light in her eyes making her resemble a viper on the make. "Who are we seeing now?"

"Marcus Quinn," Mel supplied, laughing when I gave her the Evil Eye. "Quite the hunk-o'-honey. Tall, dark, very good-looking. A little bit of the bad boy, I think, though. The last time I saw him, he was wearing his hair tied back at his neck and a pair of black leather pants." She nodded at their horrified faces. "Seriously."

And who should choose that very moment to knock on Mel's closed door? Your favorite bad boy and mine, although I sometimes had a hard time thinking of him that way these days: Marcus, of course.

He popped his head in, a hand covering his eyes just in case. "Okay for me to come in?"

I can barely express how happy I was to see him just then. All the events of the day came crashing in on me at once, and they expanded outward in one great big bang worth of emotion. "Marcus!" I squeaked. I didn't even care that Mel and her cronies were watching on in amusement. I was holding Isabella, so I couldn't roll my wheelchair over to greet him properly. I had to wait until he found his way over to me.

"Brought you something," he told me.

I giggled. He was holding his hands behind his back, but . . . "Er, I am so not noticing the length of crutches stretching south of the border there."

"What?!" He spread his legs just a bit and glanced downward between his knees. "Oh, that's cheating, Maggie May-I." His blue eyes sparkled with good humor into mine as he leaned down to kiss me. "Just had to be sure it was the crutches," he teased with a wink. Then he glanced down at the baby in my arms. "Cute baby."

"Speak of the devil," Mel interrupted conversationally. "We were just talking about you."

"Were we?" Marcus glanced back and forth between me and Mel and the others. "All good things, I hope."

Jane's gaze was still parked in a southerly direction. "I'll say." The last ended on a swiftly indrawn breath as Margo's elbow connected with her ribs. "I mean, it's a pleasure to meet you."

For once I was glad he wasn't wearing the black leather pants which were so vintage Marcus. After all, they were what had originally caught my eye. Well, that and the hair that waved just so around his nape. And the playful glint in his eyes. And then there was that first kiss that neither of us saw coming, and . . . well, yeah. With Margo's track record and Jane's obvious appreciation? I felt both my pride and my protective nature kick in simultaneously. *That's right, girls, he's all mine.*

A smile slid into place on Marcus's face, as though he had been reading my thoughts. And for all I knew, he had been. Drat him.

"Uncle Lou and I just got back. Did you get my text?"

"Oh!" I had forgotten to plug my cell phone back in, and it was nowhere near charged enough even to blip a new message warning. "No, sorry. Dead cell phone battery."

"No probs. Aunt Molly had a pair of crutches out in the garage from the time she sprained her knee last winter, so I brought them along just in case you didn't have any yet." He glanced around the room. "Um, do you?"

"No, I haven't had a chance to get out yet," I told him with an appreciative smile. "Actually I haven't even had a chance to figure out how I would be getting home. I can't exactly drive Christine with this monstrosity, now, can I?" I tried lifting my ankle, but honestly? I was starting to get a bit tired, and I had an idea that the shot for pain they had given me when they casted it was starting to wear off, because the whole thing was beginning to throb.

"The yellow looks good on you."

"Aw, thanks. I think."

"And I brought my truck."

"Thank you times two. Now if you have a solution to the housing issue I am facing, I'll be yours forever."

He winked at me, and I had a feeling any reticence had everything to do with our keen listeners. "I'll get back to you on that."

Now that he was here, I was enjoying a resurgence of hope that he would rescue me. Did I mention hospitals were not on my list of favorite places? Between the sticky, plaquelike energy, the weird night, the broken ankle, and now Mel's so-called friends, I knew I was approaching the top of an empathic volcano that was reaching maximum pressure capacity. I could feel it building within me, and if I didn't find a way to release it soon, the energy migraine I felt encroaching on the fringes of my consciousness would be a best-case scenario. I needed to get away from this place, from these people, before things got any worse.

Despite my weariness, I sat up a little straighter, a little prouder as I faced them. "Ladies. As you might have guessed, this is my boyfriend, Marcus Quinn."

"Marcus was the one who came out to my house a couple of months ago when we had that . . . problem. You remember, Margo," Mel reminded her. And then she looked at her askance. "Of course, you did leave awfully fast."

I groaned, though I did my best to school my expression into neutrality so as to betray nothing to the others. The incident Mel had referred to so casually was one of the most frightening, most otherworldly experiences of my life to date. And of Mel's, I should hardly need to remind her. It was not something to be taken lightly.

Mel had been ordered to bed for the bulk of the summer due to complications with her pregnancy, and like any dutiful sister, I'd had no choice but to honor my mother's request that I help out. Certainly Greg wouldn't have been able to handle Jenna and Courtney, a houseful of cleaning duties and responsibilities, and a more-than-full-time career as a hotshot family attorney, so Mom and I had done our best to fill in. But I'd never expected to find that the strange paranormal occurrences in Stony Mill had wormed their way into one of the newest and most highbrow subdivisions in town, and after discovering that it wasn't solely relegated to the psychic abilities of my two young nieces and their protective spirit guides—whom Mel and my mother liked to refer to as their "imaginary friends"—but in fact was a dark entity of unknown origin and significant power that reached far beyond the realm of my limited experience, I knew then that I had little choice but to call for reinforcements. In other words, Liss and Marcus, and their magickal Bag O'Tricks. The two of them had come out to Mel's house without question, without protest, without a thought as to previously scheduled plans or inconveniences. Together they had pooled their considerable energies and talents in order to send the dark spirit packing, back to the nebulous existence he had come from, and they had worked to ensure that whatever portal he had used would not be utilized by others of his ilk. All simply because it was I who had asked them for help. Because they knew they were needed.

And how had Mel chosen to repay them for their generosity of spirit? By exposing them as witches and purveyors of paranormal pastimes. And as you might guess, around these parts where Sunday morning church service attendance almost—*almost*—beats out attendance at the bars and strip clubs on Friday nights, no witch is a good witch, no spirit is a good spirit, and anyone who partakes of such deeply disturbing offenses must therefore be no good by default. Popularly held beliefs and traditions are hard to fight . . . especially when the town newspaper gets in on the act. Before you could say "String them up, stake them down," word had spread around our small, provincial town. Liss had been turned away from City Hall for a permit she had been trying to obtain, and business at Enchantments was down. Way down. And as much as Liss would have liked to blame it on the blistering summer weather, we both knew the truth of it.

Mel knew nothing of this. Mel was as oblivious to any sense of wrongdoing in the matter as she was to the nature of the spirit she had allowed into her house through ill-advised and uninformed use of a Ouija board with the very same friends who were sitting with her in this hospital room today. To Mel, the spirit had been taken care of. Vanquished from her home and banished from her responsibility, and along with it went her fear.

It was never good to get so used to the spirit world that you let your guard down. An open channel was the meta-physical equivalent of leaving a master key hanging from the brass door knocker on your front door, along with a sign that says, "Come on in, help yourself."

A light had gone off for Margo at Mel's reminder. "Oh, I remember Marcus. I do indeed," Margo said, gazing at Marcus and me with renewed interest.

I could see the brain waves blitzing madly behind her eyes. I braced myself, waiting for what I knew would be coming next.

Chapter 13

"So. You're the wizard in town. Mel told us about what you did."

Marcus laughed. The sound was gentle and relaxed, but his energy was on guard, his shields on intercept-and-deflect mode. "Someone has been reading the Harry Potter books, I take it?"

"Harry P—" Margo sucked in her breath. "I would *never*!"

"Too bad," he told her. "Fun, fascinating, and fabulous— that can be pretty hard to find in literature these days; I highly recommend them. But just so that you know, I don't call myself a wizard."

"No? Well, what do you call yourself, then?" she demanded, rather imperiously, I thought. "A warlock?"

With a smile smooth enough to charm a cobra—and maybe that was his point?—he raised a conciliatory dark brow in her direction. "How about . . . dangerous to know?"

"Oh . . . oh, my . . ."

His tactic worked. In an instant, Margo went from confrontational to profoundly, blissfully mum. I could have kissed him.

"I think I read in an article last Halloween that they're just called male witches now, Margo," Jane offered up helpfully, unaware of her friend's discomfort.

Marcus nodded pleasantly. "That's right. Since we're discussing semantics, the word 'warlock' in the olden days referred to an oath breaker. And since I value my integrity and honor, that label isn't one I choose to own."

"Oh," Jane said, a little confused. "Well, that makes perfect sense, then."

"Here, Maggie-sweet. Let's get you up out of that chair and try these crutches on for size, eh?" Marcus said. "Who'd like a turn with the baby?"

Mel reached out and pulled the two bassinets toward the edge of the bed. "Would you mind setting her in her crib?" she asked him. "I'm getting a little tired, I think."

Marcus leaned over and wrapped his hands around the tiny, blanketed form nestled snugly in my arms, lifting her against him like an old pro. "Aw, come here, little one," he crooned in a way that made my heart beat a little faster. His eyes, oh so blue, lifted to mine, and all of a sudden I was finding it difficult to swallow, or even breathe. Then he straightened, the baby cradled against him, and as I watched he jostled and rocked her gently.

I don't know what it is about the sight of a tiny baby in a man's big hands, but it was an image guaranteed to jar loose the mechanisms of even the most tightly wound biological clock. I could feel mine stuttering doggedly to life, and I had to take a deep breath and try to lock it down in the farthest dark closet in the corners of my mind.

Now. Was. So. Not. The. Time.

"Which one do I have?" he asked Melanie.

Mel the Madonna smiled beatifically up at him. "That would be Isabella. And this," she said, gazing down at her daughter in a way that made me forgive her instantly for being a gossipy wench, "is Sophie."

"Isabella, pretty Isabella," he crooned over her. Checking the name card on the bassinet to be sure he got her in the right one, he set her gently down and stroked her pink cheek. "You are going to be a heartbreaker someday."

Oy. So, *so* not the time.

Turning back to me, he said, "We can do this two ways, Angel."

Marcus's favorite movie was an oldie but a goodie called *Romancing the Stone*, and he liked to quote it whenever possible. He also liked to tell me that I resembled a young Kathleen Turner, and that was the first thing that had attracted his attention. I'd take that as a compliment any day—Kathleen Turner back in the day was H-O-T *hot*, and if Marcus wanted to see me through those particular rose-colored glasses, I was more than happy to let him.

"Quick like the tongue of a snake?" I quoted back, playing the game.

"Or slower'n the molasses in January."

"Hm. I pick slow," I told him. "At least it's cold in January. This cast is starting to get itchy already."

He laughed and extended a helping hand to get me to my feet. Balancing on one foot while he fiddled with the height of the hand rests on the crutches wasn't as easy as it looked. By the time he was finished with one, I was ready to sit back down again.

"Oh no you don't," he said, catching my backward glance at the wheelchair. "Let's get you some practice on your new set of stilts."

I didn't relish practicing within full view of either Margo

or Jane, so as soon as I got the swing of things, I headed for
the hall with Marcus in pursuit.

"Whoa, whoa, whoa there, Turbo," he said. "Not so
fast."

I slowed down, then stopped altogether in the corridor.
"Sorry about that. I just couldn't do this in front of them."

"They are a bit . . . intense, aren't they?"

"That's a nice way of putting it. I can't believe I just spent
the last hour or so with them. That's a full sixty minutes of
my life that I can never have back."

Marcus got back to business. "Let's see you do this," he
said, indicating the crutches.

"Didn't I just . . . do . . . this?"

"Humor me."

Putting on my this-is-silly-but-whatever-you-say face, I
swing-hopped my way down the corridor, pirouetted on one
foot and two stilts (elegant, let me tell you), then swing-
hopped my way back and flashed him a saucy look. "How's
that?"

A slow, lopsided smile curved his mouth. "Did anyone
ever tell you that you look really pretty when you're trying
to be cheeky?"

I wrinkled my nose at him, but I liked it, I liked it.

"See?"

"What do you think?" I asked, sticking out my cast,
which went from my pink-painted toenails to just below the
knee.

"I don't think I've ever seen anything so cute. Except
maybe your sister's babies. Whose idea was the yellow?"

I grinned. "Mine. Why be dull?"

"Oh, Maggie-sweet, you are anything but dull," he
drawled in a low growl, his eyes flashing at me. And then
he slipped in close a moment and, putting his arms around
me, kissed my temple. "Did it hurt?"

I sighed, melting into him. "A little," I admitted. "But nowhere near as bad as I would have expected a broken ankle to feel. It is starting to throb a little now, though."

"We should get you off your feet."

"Aw, so soon? I just got back on them."

"No sense rushing things. The novelty will wear off the crutches pretty fast when they start rubbing your skin raw."

A broken ankle, an ugly cast, chafing, and possibly having to move in with my mother for the duration? This was getting better and better.

That reminded me. "I am so screwed. My mom wants me to stay with them because she doesn't think I can handle the stairs down to my apartment on stilts. I mean, crutches."

"I hate to say it, but she has a good point. Those stairs are on the steep side. Have you ever used crutches before? Apart from just now?"

"Sure," I said confidently, as if it was no big thing.

He looked at me askance. "When?"

And then I blushed. "Well, at church once. Someone had left theirs behind, and we kids took turns racing up and down the hall with them while we were supposed to be having catechism class but the teacher was running late."

"How old were you?"

I blushed even harder. "Eleven."

"Ah-ha."

Hm. He had a point. "So you think I should do what my mom suggests and move in with my grandfather."

"I didn't say that." He kissed my temple again. "I could take care of you."

I blinked. I think time stopped for a moment. The words were so quiet, the gesture so unassuming, I thought for a moment I'd imagined it. Then: "But . . . well . . . your house has quite a few stairs going up the front steps, too, Marcus . . ." It was the first thing that popped into my head.

He reached down and in an instant lifted me into his arms
as he might a small child. Emitting a squeak of surprise, I
dropped the crutches with a clatter and threw my arms
around his neck.

"Any questions?" he asked.

No, I didn't think any were necessary, really.

"But you have other things to do," I said, trying to come
up with a way that he could ease out of the offer gracefully if
he needed to.

He shifted me in his arms with a bounce that made me
gasp and hold on tighter. "It could be fun."

Yeah, I could see that, too.

Oh, where was the voice of my conscience when I needed
it most?

My mother would have a cow, I tried to reason.

He lived even farther away from Enchantments than my
mom and dad did.

I would never hear the end of it with Mel.

Or Tara and Evie.

Um . . .

"So, what do you think?" he prompted.

I was saved from having to answer right away when the
door to our left opened and I realized we had been standing
outside of Frannie Watkins's hospital room.

"Oh, hello," Harry Watkins said with some surprise as he
found us practically on his wife's doorstep. He looked down
and saw my crutches sprawled there at Marcus's feet. "You
didn't fall, did you? Here, let me help you with that."

I blushed again as Marcus set me down carefully and with
his hands at my waist allowed me to find my balance on one
foot as Harry retrieved my fallen crutches for me. I was doing
a lot of blushing of late, it would seem. I peeked over at
Marcus and felt my cheeks warm. Something told me it was

going to become a habit if I moved in with Marcus for a few weeks.

My heart beat a little faster at the prospect.

"We're just getting ready to take Little Harry home." A beaming smile brightened Harry Watkins's round face. He puffed out his chest with pride. I looked up into his pale blue eyes and knew that I would like him instantly. He was a big man, as big as his father, with the same bulwark chest and massive arms. Country stock, salt of the earth. Uncomplicated and straightforward. People like the Watkinses, like Grandpa G and my dad and my mother were once a staple of Stony Mill. Once we were a town of simple people, simple pleasures. Only recently had it struck me how much things had changed.

Frannie Watkins came to the door of her room, fully garbed in a maternity dress that now hung on her medium-sized but no longer pregnant frame, her sleek dark hair clipped back in a low pony. The poor thing, she did look tired. Dark circles shadowed her eyes, stark against her pale ivory skin. She held her son in her arms, cradled there in a light blanket, an outdoor sun hat covering his head down to his eyebrows. "Are we almost ready? I have the bag packed, and . . . Oh, hello there, Maggie. I see you're up and about." She smiled wanly.

"Are you feeling all right?" I asked her. "You're looking a little tired."

"Oh, you know." She waved a hand to dismiss concern. "A lot happens in the first twenty-four hours after giving birth. All I need is a good lie down in my own bed. I need to get home."

"I brought the van around!" Harold Watkins Sr. had just come sailing around the corner, and hard on his heels, too-tling along in her mom jeans, white tennis shoes, and slouch socks, was Joyce. "We'll load 'em on up and get the three of you home. We'll just follow along in my truck."

Joyce sent a friendly smile my way. "Goodness, you had an accident since the other day. Poor thing." She patted her son on the arm. "I'll just go and get a nurse, dear."

"Aw, thanks, Mom."

She was back in a jiffy, nurse and wheelchair in tow, and by that time the men had already loaded themselves up with bags, books, gift bags, flowers, congratulatory balloon arrangements, diaper bag, and more. It boggled my mind, the amount of "stuff" that having a baby generated.

"We can take it from here," Joyce told the nurse. "No sense in you having to go all the way down with us."

"Well . . ." the nurse hedged, "it *is* Hospital policy."

"We won't tell if you won't. I'm sure you have plenty of other things you would rather be doing instead.

Setting the baby paraphernalia back down, Harry Jr. spread the seat out and readied the footpads. Braced as I was on my crutches, I looked longingly at the chair; I could use a good rest right about now. But instead I held onto Marcus's arm and hop-skipped out of the way with one crutch as Frannie allowed herself to be catered to one last time before going home. She had to juggle a little bit with her purse as she settled her son into a safe position. At the last minute, with her attention elsewhere, the big bag toppled over the arm of the chair, spilling to the floor.

"Oh!" Immediately Frannie handed the baby over to her mother-in-law and was reaching down for her things.

"I'll get it, Fran," Harold Sr. said.

"No . . . No. I've got it."

Harry knelt down, too, as she started scooping and scraping items together.

"So that's where this went! I thought I was going to have to buy another one." Harry held in his hands the magazine that Fran had retrieved from Mel's room. Frannie opened her mouth and then snapped it closed again as he began to flip through it. "I don't think I got to read even a single article while Frannie was in labor, and there were a few in here I had my eye on."

Was I the only one who saw the tension on her face as she watched, riveted, as the pages fluttered by beneath his fingers? It eased when he folded the magazine in half lengthwise with a sigh and tucked it away in one of the bags.

The rest of the flotsam Frannie plunged back into her bag without thought or concern for the mess or organization. With everything under control, she zipped the top closed and stuffed it securely under her arm, then sat back with a sigh of relief and waited, her hands on the arm rests of the wheelchair.

"Here, I'll just hold the baby, hm?" Maybe I wasn't the only one who noticed Frannie's edginess, I decided as Joyce angled a concerned glance toward her daughter-in-law. But her gaze softened as she looked down into the face of her new grandson. "Look at this little hat," she cooed. "Isn't that the most adorable thing."

The words "adorable," "precious," and "cute" come up an awful lot in the company of new moms and grandmas. And even aunties; I had to admit, I'd dropped a few of them myself in the last twenty-four hours.

Joyce leaned down to him, peeling back his hat to kiss his brow. But she came back up with a gasp. "Oh my word!"

Harold's head came up at the alarm in her tone. "What is it, Joyce?"

"Mom?"

She pulled the hat the rest of the way off, staring, then looked up, eyes stricken. "Harry! Wh—what happened to his *curls*?"

All of our gazes were drawn like a magnet to the baby's

head, where dark hair had been clipped none-too-neatly close to the skull, the remnants making choppy crisscross patterns over the baby's scalp.

Confusion flickered through Harry Jr.'s pale eyes as he turned to his wife. "Frannie?"

Frannie frowned, annoyance flashing in her eyes. "He had a bad case of cradle cap. The nurses suggested it would be best. Easiest. We used blunted cuticle scissors. It was perfectly safe."

"But . . . his curls," Joyce said mournfully. She looked ready to cry. Harold came up and tried to comfort her as best he could with his hands full, but there was no consoling her. "His beautiful curls."

"They'll grow back, Mom," Harry Jr. tried to reassure her. She nodded, sniffling.

No one consoled Frannie for having to carry out the task in the first place.

Hospital policy dictated that the baby be held in his mother's arms in the wheelchair going out. Reluctantly Joyce relinquished the baby over to Frannie. She accepted him woodenly. It was almost as though the burst of energy she'd expended to reclaim her things had completely done her in. She appeared . . . spent. Though Harry Jr. looked as though he might like to have carried his infant son himself, manly duty won out. He loaded himself back up with bags and baby belongings. Joyce took the helm of the wheelchair.

"Well, folks," Harold Sr. said to us, "looks like we're ready to head on out. You two take care. Especially you, young lady," he said to me with a friendly, paternal twinkle. "That looks like it might hurt."

The four of them shuffled off slowly, and then veered off down the main corridor. I turned back to Marcus.

"Ready for some more practicing?" he asked me.

"Well, if it's a choice between that or returning to face the firing squad in Mel's room, then I guess I can." I tossed a saucy look up at him. "Although, I must confess. I'd rather practice kissing, with you."

He laughed. "I don't think you need any practice at that." But then he backed up along the hall and crooked his finger for me to come hither. "Come on, then, Hopalong. I'll wait right here for you."

Incentive. A very important part of the art of negotiation.

"Although I have to admit," I continued, "I am kind of hungry, too. I just realized, I haven't eaten much today."

"Want to go?"

I nodded. "And how. Just let me say 'see you later' to Mel for now."

Margo and Jane were still there, so I made my farewells short, sweet, and to the point of being insipid. Did I mention they were brief?

As I turned to leave the Terrible Trio behind, I saw that Marcus had paused at the end of the second, vacant bed to bend at the waist. A flash of pale blue caught my eye as he straightened with something in his hand.

"Uh-oh."

"What is it?" I asked, clumping along toward him.

I glanced down over his arm. It was the bassinet card for the Watkins baby. "That must have been what I saw fall to the floor," I exclaimed as realization struck. "When Frannie was in looking for a magazine. At the time I thought it was probably just one of those annoying inserts and didn't think too much about it, but . . . I guess maybe I should have. Do you think you can catch them?"

"I can try. Stay here."

My long and lean boyfriend went flying through the corridors as discreetly as possible. I decided that making my way toward the elevators would be preferable to acting the part of gimpy statue in the hall, but he was back before I had a chance to get very far. He shook his head. "No dice. They're gone."

"I'll hold it for her," I said, coming to an immediate decision, "and I'll call later to let her know that I have it, safe and sound. Things like this mean an awful lot to a mom."

"You speak from experience, do you?" he said, teasing.

"Okay, to a *woman*, then. Mementos, you know? Things to help you remember." I leaned against him, grateful when he put his arm around me. "I'm getting too old for all this. I'm seriously pooped."

"Stay there," he said again, leaving me just long enough to grab my wayward wheelchair from earlier. "Your chariot, madam."

He made me ride in a wheelchair the rest of the way down to the lobby, and thankfully the elevator trip was uneventful. I could have predicted that, though. Odd occurrences like last night's elevator events didn't happen unless I was alone. And in the dark. It was the way of the Murph.

Getting me into his old, beat-up truck took a little doing—the bench seat was higher than my hip, even with me standing balanced on the curb, so I had to back up to it and Marcus had to grip my hips (grinning away, natch) and lift me carefully into the seat.

"This could be an interesting few weeks," he teased.

Oy. He was not kidding.

Blushing furiously, but not without a little reveling in my own personal power, I sat modestly on the passenger side waiting while he put my crutches in the back and got in beside me. "So, where to?" he asked me.

"How about Annie's again? We never did have more than coffee last night."

It didn't take much in the way of convincing before we were heading downtown. The moment Marcus turned onto the main route, my stomach began to rumble in anticipation, and I knew it was a good choice. Just the thought of one of Annie's double fudge caramel cheesecake brownies was enough to make me feel faint.

"Hey . . . isn't that the girls?" Marcus asked, bringing me out of my drool-induced reverie.

He pulled up to the side of the road faster than I could even focus, and reached across me to roll down my window with the manual knob. "Shouldn't you two be in school?"

Tara sidled over to my door. She was wearing a pair of black capri leggings, an above-the-knee tunic-cami combo, and her beloved lug-soled ankle boots. Black, gray, black. Add in her choppy, chunky ink-black hair, and the overall look was quite Dark Tinkerbell. "School got out twenty-five minutes ago, cuz. Duh."

Marcus glanced at his watch. "Oh. Sorry."

"You stand corrected." She gripped the window frame and leaned her head in. "Holy cow, you did break it! Thought maybe you just really needed a day off work. Kidding!" she said with a wicked little grin. "What in the name of the Great Goddess is that thing on your foot, though?" If that crinkle on her nose wasn't the look of utter repugnance, then I didn't know what to call it.

I laughed. "It's called . . . wait for it . . . a *cast*."

"It's yellow."

"I noticed." I could be wrong about this, but something told me that Tara would have gone for basic black. And no doubt she would have rocked it.

Evie came forward then, too, waving at me. "Oh, it must

have been awful," she said, her china-blue eyes wincing. "Every time I think about it, I can almost feel it snap myself. You poor, poor thing!"

"We're on our way down to Annie's for a late—okay, a very late—lunch," I told them.

"Oh good," Tara said, reaching in for the door lever and pulling the door open with its usual squeak. She tossed her messenger bag casually into the truck bed. "You can give us a ride."

Now, Marcus's truck is by and large considered a two-seater. One bench seat in the front with a small storage ledge behind it. That didn't deter Tara, though. She was either thin enough or moldable enough to squeeze through the narrow opening behind my seat, perching like a quasigargoyle on the ledge behind Marcus. Being somewhat more endowed in the boobage area, Evie had things a little bit harder, but wherever Tara went, Evie was sure to follow; eventually she managed to wedge her way in. I grinned over my shoulder at the two of them, thinking that it was a good thing Marcus wasn't the type of guy who stored a lot of stuff in his truck.

Marcus laughed, looking at them in his rearview. "You look like two sausages back there."

"Yeah, yeah. Could we get a move on, please?"

"Oh, I don't know," Marcus said, even as he was looking over his shoulder to check for traffic, "it's kind of fun having you stuck back there."

"Yeah, well, my mouth still works fine, and I'm a little cranky about a test I totally failed at school, so watch it, cuz."

I rather enjoyed Tara's banter. Some might find it rude and mouthy, and it was, but once you got to know her, you realized that she didn't really mean much of it, and when she did mean it, there was likely good reason for it.

"You're going to the store, too, Evie?" I asked.

"Oh yeah."

"What about your mom?"

She shrugged prettily, or as prettily as she could with her knees drawn up to her chin and Tara's knees wedged sideways into her. "She always tells me how important it is to be community oriented, to help out. It's not like I can just leave Liss to struggle, right?"

She had a point. I'm not sure her mom would see it that way, but . . .

"We found out a little more about Jordan today," Tara told us as we skirted the crosstown after-school and -work traffic on the meandering path that was the state route through Stony Mill proper. "Guess what he died from."

It didn't seem right to play guessing games on the cause of death for someone so young, so I just waited for her to go on, because I knew she would.

And did. "Evidently they think he died as a result of heart failure from an enlarged heart. Preliminarily."

Not another murder at least. What a relief it was to hear that. The poor kid.

"Some of the guys have been whispering about steroids and other drugs," she continued, "causing the heart trouble."

"Steroids?" Marcus said. "In our guys?"

"Surely not," I put in. I mean, that was something that only happened at a higher level, right? Professional level, or at least college with an eye toward turning pro? I asked that question of Marcus.

"I dunno, Maggie. The world has been changing faster and faster lately. There are stories everywhere like this. Sports is just one avenue that has gotten really messed up at all levels."

"But steroids are illegal," I persisted. "And he's a kid."

Behind us, Tara uttered a bark of a laugh. "You're joking,

right, Mags? Drugs are out there, ready and available to anyone who has it in their minds to try them. And yeah, there
are a couple jocks who think they have to do 'roids—or
worse—to get their game on." She made a wry face in the
mirror. "Idiots."

"It's dumb," Evie weighed in with her soft, quiet percep-
tions, "and I think they even know that on some level.
But something or someone convinces them they have to
try it. And if they even think they see the kind of improve-
ments they're looking for, it's instant justification to keep
doing it."

Marcus nodded at the girls' perspectives. But . . . "Okay,
call me behind the times, call me crazy. But, if there are los-
ers on our street corners selling drugs to our kids, shouldn't
the cops"—Hello, Special Task Force Investigator Fielding!—
"be, I don't know, doing something about it?" Especially now
that we had a boy dead because of it?

"What are they gonna do? Arrest every high schooler at a
party who's passing along weed?" Tara made a rueful face.
"There are pushers, no doubt about it, but they get the kids
to do a lot of their business for them."

"It's out there, Maggie," Evie echoed the notion. "Defs."

Yet another way that Stony Mill had been changing, perhaps a little behind the rest of the world, but still keeping
up with the Joneses? Somehow that always turned out to be
a bad thing.

Miraculously Marcus found an empty spot in front of
Annie-Thing Good and took it before anyone else could
swipe it from us. He'd opted to let the girls walk from Annie's over to Enchantments, since it was only a few blocks
and since they were wedged so tightly into the narrow space
behind us that I was afraid we'd need pry bars to get them
out. Amazingly enough, as soon as he got out and leaned his
seat forward, they unfolded their limbs from their pretzel-

like poses and slipped out with nary a pinched nerve or aching back between the two.

"We gotta get going," Evie said, coming around to give me a bouncy hug. "Liss is expecting us. Hurry up and feel better!" And then she blushed. "I mean, don't hurry on our account. It's not like you can rush these things. I mean—"

"She means, hurry up and get your ass back to the store . . . cuz we'll miss you if you're gone too long," Tara explained gruffly as she elbowed Evie aside for the briefest, stiffest hug possible. And yet, it melted my heart, because I knew what displays of "weakness," even among friends, cost our tough little elf.

"Right!" Evie agreed.

I watched fondly as the two of them set off, the sprightly pixie and the lighter-than-air sylph, chattering away with Evie's long blond ponytail twitching back and forth as they walked, keeping time.

"Kids," Marcus said with a smile, appearing by my open door.

"I was just trying to remember what it was like to be that age," I mused. "Sometimes it seems like only yesterday . . ."

"And sometimes it feels like a million years ago," he finished for me.

"Exactly." I turned in my seat toward the open door and let my legs, including the Casted Wonder, dangle in readiness. I looked up at Annie's big picture windows, the golden light, the happy bustle, the chattering groups of people, friends, neighbors, classmates. How could death, ugly death, happen in places like Stony Mill? Suddenly I felt the weariness of the day descending on me.

"You've changed your mind."

It wasn't a question. He was reading me again, as he always did so well. I took a deep breath, my shoulders lifting with the effort. "I guess I'm more tired than I thought. I was up half the night with the babies while Mel slept off the anesthesia. And then! Then there was the argument down the hall that woke me up out of a sound sleep once I finally did get a chance to close my eyes." I didn't tell him it was Frannie. I don't know why. Maybe because I was all gossiped out about Frannie, thanks to the Terrible Trio. It had left a bad taste in my mouth, and after all, I wasn't sure it was anyone's business but hers and Harry's, in the end.

"Listen," he said, his voice a soft and gentle caress, "why don't you stay here? I'll go in and get us takeout, and you can rest."

I wasn't going to argue.

Annie came out to see me, despite the seemingly ever-present crowd waiting for her luscious tasties. She wore a scarf to tie back her frizzy strawberry hair, pulling it away from her face that was as usual shining from within. Her hands were dusty with flour, which she was wiping off with her much abused apron. Today I couldn't see the T-shirt, but I was sure it was a good one—they always were.

"Honey! I heard what happened, and I just had to come out here and see if there's anything I can do for you." She reached through and gave me a floury, cinnamon-sugar hug. She smelled like cookies and fritters and apples and choco-late. It was ten times better than any perfume.

I shook my head. "Nope. Not really. It's just one of those things, I guess."

"The trials and tribulations of life," Annie agreed, her mouth making a wry moue. "But what does this mean about the upcoming N.I.G.H.T.S. investigations we've got planned? We're fast coming up on that time of year, you know . . ."

"*That time of year*" meaning autumn, when the veil grows

thinner and the line between this reality and the next becomes . . . blurred.

"Well, you know I'll be there," I told her. I was getting used to the whole paranormal thing at last. Accepting it, and accepting myself. And in acceptance, there was curiosity. I would admit to that. Not comfort, but a need to understand. "I'm not going to let this thing hold me back. Just give me a day or two and I'll be fine."

I hoped.

" 'Kay. Well, duty calls. I'd better get back in there before they start rioting and looting the place. It's been real busy of late."

"The price of being a witch in the kitchen," I teased her.

She laughed and raised her hand in a wave. "Call you soon."

Marcus came back out as Annie went back in. They did a little two-step in the doorway that made me laugh in spite of the now throbbing ache in my ankle.

He got in the truck, filling the small space with the scent of apples. He reached behind the seat to deposit a large paper sack.

"Yummy," I said enthusiastically. "I don't know what it is, but my mouth is watering already."

"Just a little surprise. You'll see." He started the truck again but sat there with his palms flat on his thighs.

"Something wrong?"

"We need a destination." He smiled over at me. "Have you decided?"

Should I, or shouldn't I? Hm, hm, hm. In the end, it seemed the only acceptable—in many ways, *more* than acceptable—option.

I nodded. "Your place."

If he was surprised by my decision, he didn't show it. "No to Grandpa G?"

"No to my mother."

"Have you thought about what you're going to tell her?"

I shrugged, trying for nonchalance. "I'll cross that bridge when I come to it. She has more important things to focus on right now. Whether she realizes it or not, she doesn't need me there, mucking up the works."

"Well, you can muck up whatever you want to at my house," he said with a grin.

I laughed. "I'll keep that in mind."

"Minnie will be glad to see you," he remarked as he put his truck in gear and started to back out of the diagonal parking space in front of the café. "Maybe with you there she'll stop molesting my poor old Garfield."

"Your what?"

"My Garfield. You know, big, orange, fat cat, snarky sense of humor?"

"Well, of course I remember. But I didn't know you had one."

"Well, now you do."

I laughed. I couldn't help it. "And, er, *how* has Minnie been molesting it?"

"The little minx searches him out no matter where in the house I put him, gets on top of him, and . . . well . . . goes to town, kneading the heck out of him for hours and purring like a motorboat the whole time." He arched a brow at me. "It's really quite shocking."

"I'll bet. She doesn't do anything like that at home."

"Maybe all the testosterone at my house brings it out in her," he suggested.

"Right." I nodded sagely. "Garfield is rather a manly beast."

"I am going to pretend you didn't just insult my own beastliness."

We arrived at his house in a jiffy. He parked at the curb,

climbed out of the truck, and opened the gate before coming back to get me. I had expected him to set me down and get my crutches out, but he wasn't kidding with his Tarzan chest-pumping display in the hospital hallway. He made me put my arms around his neck (*hmm, gosh, I don't know . . .*) and swung me up into his arms so effortlessly that he made my head spin. And then he kissed me for good measure. Between the spinning equilibrium and the lengthy kiss, by the end of it I was seeing stars. In a good way.

He kicked the truck door closed with his foot (*swoon!*) before carrying me up the front steps and across the deep porch to the front door, where he did not set me down but instead fumbled with the key and the latch until he had it to where he could push the door inward to admit us. Not only did he carry me across the threshold (*um, double swoon!*), but he carried me all the way inside and down the hall to his bedroom, where he finally laid me to rest . . .

On top of a blanket of fresh rose petals.

My eyes opened wide and I turned my head this way and that to take in the spectacle that was Marcus's normally masculine bedroom.

The dresser tops and tables were each lined with a string of red jar candles, all burning brightly and casting their cinnamon scent into the air. The fragrance blended nicely with the rose petals, which were various depths of pinks and reds, scattered on the bed and in a circle on the floor around it. In the center of the dresser, reflected in the mirror, was a vase filled with more of the lovelies, not modern hybrid tea roses popular at street vendors and grocery stores nationwide, but huge, cabbage-y, old-style English roses. The kind that bring with them visions of Beatrix Potter, cottage gardens, and tea from an old china teapot at a charming, wrought-iron table beneath a protective oak.

I covered my mouth with my hand as I stared, trying not to cry.

"It was Liss's idea," Marcus explained, obviously pleased with my reaction. "She called me when I was on the way back with Uncle Lou. She felt so bad for you, and she just wanted you to have this. It was my idea to ask her for extra petals for the room, though," he said with just a hint of shy pride. "And the candles, too."

His idea. Swoon Part Three, for the win. "It's beautiful."

"So are you." Any more swooning and we would be heading into overtime. "Are you ready to eat yet? We have Annie's Asiago French onion soup and gourmet grilled cheese on ciabatta. And one of her double deep-dish apple pies."

That must have been the source of the stomach-tempting apple scent in the truck. "Starved. But . . . I *think* I might need my pain prescription filled even more. In all the excitement between the girls and Annie's, I forgot about it."

"Why didn't you say so? I'll go do that. Did you want some pie before I go?"

I smiled up at him. "I'll wait until you get back."

As I dug the prescription out of my purse and filled out the name and address info, he brought out a soft T-shirt nightgown and fuzzy robe.

I looked at him askance. "I *hope* those aren't leftovers from an old girlfriend."

He laughed at me. "Nope. Liss brought these over, too."

"Oh. Well, okay, then."

Marcus leaned in for a soft, lingering kiss. "Don't go anywhere," he said. "I'll be right back."

Chapter 14

I wish I could say that I sat up waiting for his return. That would have been the nice girlfriend thing to do. That's actually what I meant to do. I waited until he was gone to struggle out of my clothes and into the nightie and robe, and then collapsed again into a heap on the bed. I didn't want to peel back the coverlet—that would have disturbed the rose petals, and they were too pretty to do that. So instead I hopped over to snag a knit blanket from the chair in the corner, then hopped back to the bed, wrapping myself up like a cocoon against the air-conditioning, which was set altogether too low. Minnie apparently agreed with me. She wandered in at last, probably in search of her stuffed orange loverboy, but seemed excited to see me all the same. After a goodly amount of earlobe licking and hair chewing, she settled down into a furry black ball and purred herself to sleep in the crook of my arms.

*　　*　　*

I dreamed.

Or I thought I did. I roused slightly in the dark of the night with an urgent thought written on the fabric of my mind.

Jordan Everett.

And Steff.

But I couldn't remember why, and in the end, it didn't matter. I went back to sleep as suddenly as I'd come to.

The next thing I knew, it was morning and I had awakened to a bright light coming through the windows. The candles had been blown out at some point during the night, and the bottom half of the knit blanket had slipped upward from my feet and was now pooled around my bare knees. It had formed a perfect hammock for Minnie, who had stretched out on her back between my legs, all four feet up in the air and her white underbelly displayed shamelessly for all the world to see. The rose petal bit stuck to her nose completed the picture. She looked unbearably cute.

So did Marcus. He had draped his long body crossways on the big leather wingback chair I'd taken the blanket from, his arms crossed over his body in a way that made his biceps bulge most intriguingly and his head resting against the wing and looking none too comfortable. He still wore the jeans and T-shirt he'd been wearing at the hospital yesterday, but had removed the leather cord from his hair. It hung down across the sharper angles of his cheekbones and clung to his five o'clock shadow, just asking to be brushed aside.

No rose petals on him, though.

His eyelids fluttered, blinked open. "Hey," he said. "You're awake."

I smiled. "You, too."

"Am I?" He laughed and stretched his arms over his head.

"Erg, I'm getting too old for this. I think every muscle I own is complaining right now."

I patted the bed beside me.

"You sure?" he asked. "I don't want to hurt you."

I nodded, patting the bed again. Right now, just seeing him across the room was hurting me. I needed him closer. *Muuuuch* closer.

"Just a sec."

He went into the bathroom for a minute—well, a few— and came back carrying a glass of water and my prescription, setting it on the table next to me. "You might need this."

"Right now I just need you."

The grin he flashed at me could only be described as lecherous as his gaze swept the full length of my body on the bed, sending sizzles to bits of me that most often go undescribed. He leaned a knee onto the bed and eased himself down with his hands until he lay beside me, facing me.

"Hi," I said softly, riveted by his eyes.

"Hi back," he returned, just as softly. He touched my cheek with his fingertips, just grazing my lips until they parted with my shallow breathing.

And then he swooped in to capture them, drawing me up close to his body. All thought left me in a rush. I could feel his heart thudding against the flat of my palm. My other hand was currently flung around his neck, holding on for dear life. His? Let's just say they were playing Lewis and Clark, searching for hidden pathways to a known but elusive land of treasure and booty.

I mean, bounty.

All of that stopped abruptly when he yelped and sat upright.

A motion which knocked my propped leg abruptly off balance.

Fiery needles of pain shot up from my ankle as the heavy cast bounced off the mattress.

"Ow, ow, ow, ow, *ow*!"

Instantly contrite, Marcus sat back on his knees on the bed and gently lifted my casted ankle onto a pillow. "Oh jeez, I'm sorry, Maggie! I was afraid of something like that happening."

"Ow. What was that all about?"

"It was Minnie," he said, swearing. "She decided to use my back as a scratching post. Or maybe she was getting back at me for locking Garfield away in the closet, I don't know. Are you okay?"

"I'll live," I said, gritting my teeth against the pinpricks, which were actually more like toothpicks. Or maybe ice picks.

"Here," he said, pressing the glass of water and the bottle of pain medicine into my hands. "You'll probably want this now."

"Thanks." I read the label, extricated one from beneath the wad of cotton, and popped it into my mouth, attempting out of habit to dry swallow it. It didn't work. Instead, it got stuck on the back of my tongue, halfway down, and it tasted *bad*. Gagging, I took a gulp of water, and then another.

"Bleah," I said when I could speak again. "Oh my gosh, that's awful. Bleah. Ack."

"Here," Marcus said, pressing the glass up to my lips again. "Drink more."

"What on earth do they put in these things?" I complained. The flavor was so awful that it filled my entire mouth, clinging to all moist surfaces (aka flippin' E-V-E-R-Y-W-H-E-R-E). I smacked my lips a few times, but it just wasn't going away. "Yuck. I don't know what's worse: the pain or the taste."

"Here, lie back down again. That's right," he said sooth-ingly as I reclined back in his arms and he cradled me against his chest. He stroked my hair, my arms, over and over. "Just relax. Breathe. Let the pain go."

It was better, and I knew it wasn't because of the pill. Nowhere near enough time had passed that it could be taking effect that swiftly. It was the Marcus effect. As my muscles released the pain that had made them contract in protest, I grew brave and turned my face toward his neck and shoulder. Nuzzling. Breathing in his scent. Blowing his hair against his neck.

"Maggie?"

"Hmm?"

"You know, you're going to have to stop that."

I answered by pressing my lips to the spot just below his jawline where his pulse drummed visibly against his skin. But when I parted my lips and touched the tip of my tongue there, he swallowed once, hard, his Adam's apple bobbing convulsively, then with a growl he lifted my chin and raised my mouth to his, pressing me back into the pillows in a way that said *Excuse me, but I think I'll have some of this*, and yet somehow managing to keep his body angled away from my legs.

I don't know how long we remained like that, locked to-gether at the mouth, hands reaching, bodies humming. But pretty soon, something else was humming. And then the humming turned into buzzing. And then the buzzing into out-and-out bleeping.

Groaning, frustrated, Marcus reached behind himself and slammed his palm down on the Snooze button on the alarm clock. "Now, where were we?" He scooped me back into his arms for another deep, exploring kiss.

When his cell phone began tweedling away on the dresser

top across the room, we both knew we were done for. Marcus
lay back against the pillows a moment, scrubbed his palms
up and down his cheeks a few times, all the while muttering
under his breath.

I started to laugh. I couldn't help it. "I don't think any
spells are going to bring it back at this point, you know."

"I wasn't spelling. I would have, if I thought it would
work in this situation."

"More cinnamon, maybe," I teased. "Or maybe more
roses. At least they smell nice. Did you put garnets under the
mattress? Patchouli in the candle flames?"

Still frustrated, he brushed aside my teasing. "Didn't Liss
tell you? They're just mood setters without the real
magick."

"Oh? And which part is the real magick?"

He wouldn't say. He just sat on the foot of the bed, deep
breathing and working hard at releasing all the pent-up
energy.

Men. They really are from Mars, sometimes.

Getting to his feet, he snatched up his phone from the
dresser. "Yeah. Hang on. I'll call you right back."

"What time is it?" I asked, shifting myself around against
the pillows so that I could see the alarm clock. *Oh. Holy.
Jesus.* "Is this thing right?"

"Yeah. Why?"

Why? "It's eight thirty."

"Right."

"The store opens at nine thirty."

"Yeah. And?"

"It's Saturday!"

"I repeat: And?"

I scooted on my rear end over to the edge of the bed and
retied the belt of the robe around my waist. The crutches

were all the way over by the door. How on earth had they gotten there? Marcus must have moved them. Probably to ensure that I didn't attempt the bathroom without his help. "Saturday's our busiest day at the store," I told him, fretting. "Liss needs help. My help. Can you hand me my crutches, please?"

"That depends. What do you think you're going to do with them?"

I blinked at him. "Well, I think I'm going to go to the bathroom and wash up. You know. Get ready to go?"

"Well, hang tight. You haven't eaten in, what, two days?"

I thought back. "Friday night, Friday morning, Thursday evening. Um, yes, that's about right."

"And you just broke your ankle yesterday."

"Right again. The crutches?"

"Maggie, you're not going to make it in by nine thirty."

"Well, I might be a little behind, but I've got an hour if we hurry."

Instead of handing me the crutches, he went back over to the dresser and picked up his phone, quickly punching in a number. Patently ignoring me, mind you. "Hi, Liss. It's me. Sorry about that, I needed a minute. Yes, she's up. Yes, she's being a handful. No, that's okay. I'll take care of it. We'll see you in a bit. Gotcha. Bye."

I raised my brows. "And what was that all about?"

"That," he said bluntly, "was all about you taking care of yourself and not hurrying into the store just to get there before the front door is unlocked. That was about you taking the time to eat some breakfast, allow your pain meds to kick in, and be sure you're not going to topple over on those crutches out of sheer exhaustion."

I just stared at him. "You really are cranky, aren't you?"

Shaking his head and muttering under his breath again, Marcus stalked out of the room. I heard him clanging pots and pans together in the kitchen a moment later.

Mars. Definitely. Or maybe even a little farther out. Like Pluto.

Breakfast wasn't such a bad idea, I decided as I finished off the last bite of a cheese and tomato omelet, cooked to perfection by my genius-in-the-kitchen boyfriend.

"Yummy," I told him, flashing him what I hoped was my prettiest smile. "Thank you. You are good at that."

Minor ego strokes and honest gratitude. Very important to the male of the species.

"You're welcome." His mood was softening. Time and a hearty breakfast can assuage all overextended libidos. At least for a time. And then: "That's not the only thing I'm good at, you know."

I smiled. Softening, but not completely over it. Not yet.

But over it enough to help me in the bathroom. A shower was out of the question—I didn't have the time nor the expertise with the yellow lump encasing my ankle at present to manage it—but Marcus helped me with towels as I cleaned up as well as I could. My hair I twisted up into one of my uber-handy clips, letting the mass of waves poof out from the top in a springy high pony. The only makeup in my purse was a small tube of moisturizer, an eye pencil, and a combo lip-and-cheek pencil in a pretty poppy shade, but I made do with what I had, and actually? I didn't think I looked half bad. Spartan, sure, but fresh and clean.

After that, it was back into my wrinkly clothes from yesterday. Or was it the day before? It couldn't be helped. Maybe I could beg Steff to run down to my apartment to pack a bag for me and bring it to the store.

"Very pretty," Marcus said as I swing-hopped my way out of the bathroom at last.

I preened for him and blew him a kiss as he headed for the bathroom himself.

"Oh no. None of that for you now. You missed your chance for today."

"Darn," I said. "Well, I guess later today is out of the question then, hm?"

"Well, let's not be too hasty . . ."

My purse was on the bed. I made my way carefully there and sat down to grab my cell phone from the riot of stuff in its depths. As usual, the silly thing hid from me, so I ended up pulling things out until I found it. One of those things was the pale blue identification card that Frannie Watkins had dropped. "I almost forgot about this. I'll give her a call."

"Goo' i'ea," Marcus said around a mouthful of toothpaste.

I pulled my cell phone out at last . . . only to find it dead as a doornail. I had completely forgotten about charging it last night. Luckily I still had my charger in my purse with me, so I pulled it out and reached over behind the nightstand to plug it in. I powered up my phone.

1 New Voice Mail Message

The voice on the message was unmistakably my mother's. Nothing new in that. Eight out of ten voice mail messages did stem from my mother. But what was new was the tone of her voice. For the second time in three days, she sounded . . . worried.

"Maggie, this is Mom. I don't know how to tell you this, but we are in trouble again. Greg did not go home to the girls last night. Margo Craig called me this morning to let me know and to ask me where he might be. She was not happy to have been taken advantage of so callously, but she has agreed to keep the girls with her today while we try to locate him. I have a call into the office, but he's not there, either. I just don't know what to do. Call me when you get this message."

Whoa. Whoa, whoa, whoa. This was big. This was weird. This was totally and completely unexpected.

What. On. Earth?

I glanced over at Marcus, who was now standing in the doorway to the bathroom with his toothbrush parked in his foamy mouth frowning at me. He'd heard every word. I bit my lip. What to do? I knew I should have talked to Mel yesterday. Something had been wrong, something she was ignoring. I just didn't know what it was, and with Margo and Jane there, there was no way that I could have broached the subject. But I should have, somehow. I should have made her talk to me.

I couldn't help wondering what she was going through right now, alone at the hospital with two new babies, away from her girls, and with a husband who had gone missing.

And then there was Steff and the sudden distance between her and Dr. Dan.

And Frannie Watkins and the mystery man she had been arguing with that night, and the strange haunted look in her eyes before she'd left the hospital.

And Jordan Everett. Yet another Stony Miller taken too young.

And the whole elevator intrigue . . . which still troubled me, even though it seemed unlikely that the two deaths that had actually taken place that night in the hospital were connected to what I'd overheard. But did that mean there was still danger out there for someone? Somewhere?

Was the whole world in the process of going crazy? Was that it? Would I wake up tomorrow to find my mom and dad separating, or Grandpa G suddenly sporting hoop skirts and singing show tunes from his hoverchair?

Never mind about that last one. Grandpa G had a wacky sense of humor—I wouldn't put it past him.

The bassinet card stared up at me from the comforter, which still had wilted and crumpled rose petals all over it. What a sad end to a beautiful thought and effort. Sigh. I picked up the card. *Harrison Michael Watkins*, it read. *Male. Weight: Eight pounds, six ounces.* Ouch. *Height: Twenty inches. Head circumference: Thirteen inches.* Double ouch. *Blood Type: O Negative.* And there beside it all was the most adorable baby footprint in ink, with its five pearl-perfect toes.

"Marcus?"

From the now-closed bathroom door drifted, "Hm?"

"Do you have a phone book handy?"

"Bed stand. In the drawer."

Sliding my way up the bed, I reached into the drawer and pulled out the phone book. I flipped through it toward the end of the alphabet. "Watkins, Watkins. Here we go. Abraham Watkins. Clarence. Eleanor. Fritz and Frieda." That one made me smile. "George and Wanda. Ah. Harold and Joyce Watkins, and Harry Jr. and Frannie Watkins. Bingo."

Harry Jr. and Frannie Watkins, 111369 Mount Holyoke Rd, Stony Mill, 555-4242.

I dialed the number and waited while it rang. Once. Twice. Three times. Four.

Five.

Hm.

When it reached the tenth ring, I figured I'd better give it up and try back later. Obviously no one was home, or else they just weren't answering.

Marcus hurried up his clean routine, rushing through a quickie shower and shaving off the dark beard that had made him look very dangerous and pirate-y. He emerged five minutes later, bare chested with a damp towel slung low on his hips, and quickly rummaged through his closet to come up with some fresh jeans, a clean shirt, and his favorite chunky boots. I had done a double-take the minute he walked out of the bathroom and now found myself watching his every move through the room, instantly distracted from the day's early morning dramas.

I made myself turn away, before he caught me looking and we allowed ourselves to be . . . sidetracked. No time for that.

Still, I did peek. A little.

Especially when he stood before the dresser mirror combing his hair and fastening it low at the nape. There was something about the shape of a man's body standing in that position, the width of the shoulders, the play of muscles, the way the towel clung to his hips, and how certain movements made the biceps pop out in a way that made my mouth go dry.

All right, I'll admit it. I watched. The whole time.

"Ready?"

We headed toward the front door. As he opened it, Marcus scratched Minnie behind her ears and shooed her off toward the bedroom since I had a feeling we were going to need to make a stop or two and it was too warm to haul her around in the carrier. I used the crutches to follow him out onto the porch. I was game to at least attempt the steps, but there was no handrail, and as soon as he saw me looking in that direction Marcus took my crutches from me and swept me up into his arms again.

I wasn't complaining. A modern girl I might be, but there was something very primal and attractive about a man who could exhibit Tarzan-like strength but still harbor a softness and tenderness for his woman, too. Besides, it allowed me to be up close and personal with my guy and gave me the excuse to just gaze at his face in completely smitten admiration without looking like a total loon.

Sigh!

Outside, the sun was already slanting across the porch floorboards like crazy, and the heat was rising. But the sky was blue, without a hint of the usual steamy haze we "enjoy" this time of year, and the trees waved at us with the onset of a cheery breeze. It was going to be a beautiful day.

Marcus carefully placed me on his truck seat and went back inside to get my bag. I took my cell phone from my pocket and immediately plugged the car charger into the truck's cigarette lighter, powering back up. My phone already had a light charge, but it hadn't been plugged in long enough and needed a much longer time on the charger, so for now this would have to do.

Off in the distance, a police siren wailed, disturbing the day's perfection. Or was that an ambulance I heard? Or a fire truck? I could never tell the difference. Still, I cast out positive energies toward whoever might be needing them in whatever situation they found themselves in on this almost painfully beautiful Saturday.

I tried my mom's cell first, but it rang busy. So did Mel's. Of course. They were probably on the phone with each other. Knowing them, it could be a while. With that in mind, I tried the store next.

"Hey!" I said as Liss sang her usual cheerful greeting into the phone.

"There you are, ducks. How are you feeling today? Will you be spending the day resting, I hope?"

"Well . . . I had intended to come in this morning."

"Absolutely not. You need to rest with your foot up, Maggie, to keep the swelling down if you want it to heal properly."

They had mentioned something about swelling, but I had kind of been distracted yesterday. Maybe that was why my foot felt a little like an overinflated inner tube.

"Well . . . I'm in the truck now, actually." Before she could scold me for not taking proper care of myself or allowing someone else to care for me, I said, "But only for a short jaunt."

Briefly I explained that yes, I had wanted to go into the store today, but the phone call from my mom had thrown a monkey wrench into the works. "I really need to get ahold of them and find out what is going on."

"Good. Go back to bed and do that. I'll be fine here. Tara and Evie had a band conflict today, but never fear, I have it all under control. In fact, I am basking in the peaceful glow."

"Liss . . . I am worried about Melanie. If it's true, what Mom said . . . well . . . she is going to need my support."

"That's all we can ever give our loved ones, my dear. Loving support as they find their way through the eddying floes and mucky tide pools of life. Melanie will be fine. She's strong, like you. Whatever happens, she will come to know herself a little better, and that is never a bad thing, now, is it?"

That was Liss for you, as thought provoking as ever. Every day I thanked my lucky stars that I could call her my friend. Life in Stony Mill wouldn't be easy these days without her.

Marcus put my bag on the seat beside me and got in behind the wheel. "Liss won't let me come in," I told him. "In fact, she ordered me back to bed."

Marcus laughed. "Surely she knows you better than that." I wrinkled my nose at him. "Where to, then?" he asked, turning the key in the ignition.

"I'm not sure. Can we get some coffee? I still haven't gotten through to my mom or my sister."

"Yup." He put the truck into gear and pulled away from the curb as I tried my mom again. Still busy. No sense in trying Mel, then. I dialed up Steff next instead.

As soon as she picked up, I blurted, "Steff! You're never going to guess what's happened now!" at the exact same time that Steff wailed, "Oh, Maggie! I'm so glad you called!" All thanks to the wonders of Caller ID. My nerve endings went on high alert, my news for the moment postponed. "What's wrong, honey? You sound upset."

"It's Dan. We had a terrible fight last night."

"I thought you weren't going to see him last night," I said. "Wasn't he busy?"

She sniffled on the other end. "I wasn't supposed to see him. Well, I had wanted to, but he was busy. Or something. But he called me after all and asked me out to dinner. And when I asked him a couple of nonchalant questions about the boy who died the other night in the ER, he flipped out on me!"

Oooooh, that was probably my fault. Guilt, guilt, guilt. "That doesn't sound like Dan." Dan, the voice of logic and reason? Dan, whose caring and compassionate nature drove his foray into the field of medicine and whose gentle bedside manner rivaled Steff's own?

Jordan Everett . . .

The thought came out of nowhere. Now my subconscious was getting in on the action. I frowned. What was it about Jordan Everett that was so important?

"He did, though. He told me in no uncertain terms that the boy's death was none of my concern and to make sure I kept it that way so that I didn't find my head on the hospital chopping block. He was so adamant about it, Maggie. It's so unlike him. Honestly, I think I took more offense at his high-handed attitude about the whole thing than to him being concerned about me asking questions in the first place.

It didn't feel like concern to me. It felt like . . . him laying down the law, and it got my back up, and I was stupid about it, and . . ."

She started crying, and I felt like a complete heel for asking for her help to begin with. What if my curiosity had gotten her into trouble? What if it had gotten her fired? That would be bad enough. But if it had forced a wedge between her and the love of her life? I don't think I could live with myself.

"Listen, Steff. Don't worry. Danny loves you. I know that. You know that. I think Danny knows that. I saw the way he was looking at you. All couples have their disagreements. Sometimes they're silly"—I glanced over at Marcus, remembering how momentarily grumpy he had gotten over the repeated interruptions to our attempts to get up close and personal—"and sometimes there are bigger issues at hand. You either get over them or work past them . . . or the problems overwhelm the relationship." For some reason that brought instantly to mind the hidden, behind-the-scenes vibes I'd gotten from the situation between Mel and Greg. "I don't think that's happening here with you and Danny, okay?"

"Okay."

"Just breathe."

"I am."

"And don't worry."

"I'm trying." She sniffled again, and I heard the liberal use of a tissue brushing against the mouthpiece of her phone. I smiled, shaking my head. She really, really had it bad. I'd never seen her so head over heels for a guy in my life. Maybe that was why she felt so lost now when faced with the potential of a relationship gone sour before its time . . . or maybe it was just *this particular* relationship.

My money was on the latter.

Marcus had stopped the truck in front of the Java Hut and was gesturing broadly to let me know he would be right back. I waved him on.

"What were you going to tell me?" Steff asked just then, reminding me.

"Well, first of all, I was going to *ask* you whether you'd throw some of my clothes in a bag and bring them to Marcus's house."

"Of course. You know that."

"Thank you, love you, owe you. And secondly: it's Mel."

"Is something wrong? Something with the babies?"

"No, no, nothing like that. It's—" I laughed, but in truth it was a mirthless sound because the problem was affecting so many people in my life. "It seems as though the time has come for relationship issues, and I don't mean just yours. Maybe it's something in the water."

"Ha-ha."

I told her about the voice message from my mom. "I wouldn't be so worried about it if it wasn't for the timing," I said. "Mel is in the hospital. She just had twins. Even if they were having problems, how often does a man just up and leave his wife, the mother of his children, when she is at such a vulnerable state in her life? What would it take for that to happen? How much has gone wrong in order to lead up to that level of dissatisfaction?"

"And you're certain that something didn't happen to him? That he is . . . missing . . . on his own accord?"

"Honestly? Yeah. I think there's something going on. I don't think there's anything mysterious or sinister about it . . . except as it relates to his marriage to Mel."

"But what if you're wrong? Maggie . . . what if Greg's disappearance is directly related to your overheard elevator conversation?"

It might have been a viable option, if . . . "The voices

I overheard were referring to a woman, Steff. So Greg wouldn't fit."

"Oh. I see. I guess I didn't realize that."

"That's probably because I just realized it myself," I told her, sighing. Strange, how memory worked. Or didn't, as the case may be.

"Well, then, hm. Has anyone called the police about him being missing?"

"I don't know. If they have, no one has told me. But I'm pretty sure as an adult he would have to be missing for twenty-four hours before the police will even fill out a report."

Jordan Ever—

I sighed. All right. All right, already!

"Steff? Can I ask you a question? The kid who died in the ER—" *Boy* . . . "Was that by any chance Jordan Everett?"

The pause on the other end of the line told me Steff's jaw had just dropped open. "How did you . . . I didn't tell you that. I wouldn't have—"

"No, it wasn't you. Don't worry, you didn't divulge. But it was, wasn't it?"

"In the interest of keeping the peace with my Danny, I can neither confirm nor deny . . . but does the word 'es-yay' answer that for you?"

So it was him. Which meant that his death was completely out of the picture for certain, too. Because even if I had misheard the men as saying "she" for "he," he had died *before* I even left for the hospital. Tara had mentioned it at Annie's Thursday night when we stopped for coffee.

"Thanks, Steff. For everything. Listen, I have to go. I need to talk to Melanie about Greg. I just know there is something she isn't telling that might shed some light on her situation with him."

"All right. I'll talk to you later."

"And Steff?"

"Yeah?"

"Hang in there."

"I will."

I folded my phone and sat for a moment with it in my hands, thinking. Next to me, Marcus cleared his throat, bringing me out of my reverie. "Trouble?"

I looked up, a little disconcerted to realize Marcus had gone into the Hut and had returned with two jumbo coffees without me realizing he was back. I reached for the cup he held out to me, grateful for it. "When is there not?"

"Steff?"

"And Mel. And . . ." I reached in my bag and withdrew the baby bassinet card. "You know, I tried calling the Watkinses' place earlier, but I couldn't get an answer. Since Liss insists that I shouldn't come in and we're already out and about, maybe we should knock another thing off the To Do list and try to deliver this to Frannie and Harry Jr. before Frannie realizes it has gone missing."

Marcus shrugged. "Sure. Where do they live?"

I gave him the address, hoping he knew where it was, because I had no idea where Mount Holyoke Road was. Luckily Marcus had the gift for road names and directions that I was sadly lacking. He headed over in the direction of the Buckingham West subdivision, turning off two subdivisions ahead into one named Sherwood Forest. Of course.

Sherwood Forest was far larger than Buckingham West, which was fairly sizable to begin with, with homes built in what appeared to be the mid-eighties. The houses were starting to show a little bit of age here and there, but all of them appeared to be nicely maintained and updated, so the subdivision itself was not at risk of fading into real estate oblivion anytime soon. The property owners had money, good middle-class money. Nothing too flashy, nothing too modern, but always present.

We wended our way around a dizzying number of curving, winding, twisting, turning streets seemingly typical of all midwestern subdivisions. Thank goodness Marcus knew what he was doing, because I would have been lost in there forever. At last we turned onto Mount Holyoke, which again twisted, turned, curved, wound, and wended, until the house numbers began to approach the sequence of digits we were searching for.

Ahead of us, the road seemed to be blocked by a number of vehicles and people. If the house number we were searching for didn't come up soon, it looked as though we might need to find an alternate way around the hubbub.

"Uh-oh," Marcus said.

He had his sunglasses on; I was shade free and had been squinting against a glare on the windshield. "What is it?" I asked him.

"Trouble."

Chapter 15

Marcus pulled over to the side of the road, parking against the curb in the nearest available space. People were milling about all around, standing in their yards and staring up the road with their hands shading their eyes against the sun's brightness.

He reached across me and rolled down my window. "Excuse me," he called to a young woman with a baby in a front carrier strapped around her waist, who was currently standing on the sidewalk, taking it all in.

The woman drew nearer, relaxing a bit when she spotted me in the passenger seat. "Can I help?"

"We were just wondering what was going on up ahead. We have something to deliver to a house up the road, and it doesn't look like we'll be getting through anytime soon."

"Oh, so you haven't heard?" Excitement gleamed in her eyes; she fairly vibrated with it. Whatever it was had snapped her out of the same-old same-old of her life as a stay-at-home mom, and she was enjoying it from that aspect at least.

"Someone found a body this morning at one of the houses up there. An intruder, so they say. Right here. Can you imagine?"

"Thank you," I told her. She wandered back over and stood in the grass, swapping information with an older woman who had just come out of her house to take a gander.

My God. Another unexpected death, so soon after Jordan's. What was happening in this town?

"Well?" Marcus queried. "What do you think we should do?"

I tried to look proper and respectable and not the type of girl who would allow her curiosity and—yes, fine, all right already—a little bad luck to get her into trouble. Given the elevator conversation and my recent history with death and destruction in Stony Mill proper, was there really any question about whether I wanted to know what was going on? Felt the need to know what was going on? I folded my hands primly in my lap, even as I arched a brow at him and said, "Well, obviously I think we should go see if we can find out what happened."

"I think *we've* forgotten something." He directed a glance toward my cast, in all its sunshiny glory.

"*We* haven't forgotten anything. *We* have crutches."

"You can't possibly be considering going down there on crutches, Hopalong."

"Oh, but I can," I said with confidence. And I opened the truck door to prove it.

Shaking his head (I preferred to think in admiration, rather than with long-suffering duress), he switched off the truck and hurriedly came around to my side before I could slip down from the tall bench seat. I was eager to show him that I had attained a stately level of elegance and grace already on the underarm stilts, but Marcus was just as eager to stay by my side, helping me along like a granny with a walker on wheels.

"You could just stay here in the truck while I run down and see what I can find," he suggested.

"It's eighty-eight degrees outside. Already."

"There's a breeze."

"It feels like ninety-eight in the truck."

"You could keep the A/C blowing."

I made a wry pout. "You're just afraid I'll fall."

"Or get tired. You did just break your ankle, Maggie."

"But I'm not an invalid. Besides," I told him with a wink, "I suspect I'll get farther playing the sympathy card than you'll get playing the tall-dark-and-handsome card."

"Well . . . you might have a point there. Although I think winking and pouting like that might win you a few, too."

"Hm. Thanks. I'll keep that in mind."

"Pretty is as pretty does, Margaret Mary-Catherine O'Neill. It only keeps them with you so long. And your hem is unraveling."

Grandma Cora's voice crackled in my ear again . . . only this time it was once too often.

I stopped short. "I've about had enough of that, Grandma C. In my head is one thing, in my ear is quite another," I said before I realized I had in fact uttered the words out loud. And then I frowned. "Wait . . . What?"

Did the voice just say my hem was unraveling? I glanced down at my foot. My nonplastered foot. And what did I see? A thread dangling down toward my foot from where the hem on my pants had begun to work loose.

Marcus had stopped and was looking at me strangely. "Maggie? Are you . . . okay?"

"Shh!" I said, harking an ear and listening intently. But it was no use. I couldn't force the voice. It happened when it wanted to, and only when it wanted to. And that was just like Grandma Cora, too. She was a strong woman with strong opinions and equally strong convictions, and if she set her mind to something, it was unlikely she would be swayed. Grandma Cora was not one to be forced to do anything.

"Maggie. Hey." Marcus stuck his face in mine, waiting patiently until I acknowledged him. "What's going on?"

I hated to admit it to him. I mean, it just didn't sound like a good thing to say. "I've been hearing voices. Well, a voice. One in particular, I mean. And it sounds like my Grandma Cora."

"And Grandma Cora has . . . passed."

I nodded. "Years ago. I've always heard her as the voice of my conscience. Even when she was alive, I would hear her voice in my head, telling me to 'be a good Catholic girl, Margaret,' or 'Say your prayers, Margaret,' or 'Margaret Mary-Catherine O'Neill, listen to your mother, because you don't know when God will take her from you and you will wish you had her still to tell you what's what.'" A sheepish glance was all I could manage. "Grandma was big on sayings. And she was big on being a good Catholic."

"But you're not just hearing her as the voice of your conscience anymore, are you?" Marcus guessed.

I shook my head. "I'm hearing her in my ear. Just like I'm hearing you. I guess that officially makes me the newest resident of Crazytown."

"Not necessarily. Have you ever heard of clairaudience?"

I shrugged. "Sure. But you have to be a psychic to have it. And I'm not one."

He smiled. "Maybe. Maybe not. You did say that your abilities have been a little wonky lately and sometimes seem stronger, or even seem to be expanding sometimes."

"Yes, but . . . a psychic has visions. Third-eye stuff. And they're precognitive."

"And you have dreams."

I opened my mouth to protest again, but all of a sudden I couldn't. Because what he had said sparked a thought, one I wasn't quite ready or able to put a finger on.

Instead, I ducked my head away and said, "Let's go see if we can't make it up to the Watkinses' house on foot." The house number we were parked in front of was 111357. It couldn't be far. From the looks of it, it was situated right in the thick of things.

Marcus shrugged. "We can talk about it later."

And he would make sure we would, too. That was just the way he rolled.

We made our way slowly up the road, keeping to the sidewalk rather than the road, where the goings-on resembled a block party more than an emergency scene. The closer we got to the house number we were searching for, the closer we came to the police cruisers and milling police officers blocking the thoroughfare, until it became obvious that they were stopped right in front of the Watkins residence.

"Uh-oh."

"Yeah. Trouble."

I stopped long enough to take the card out of my purse. Whatever the trouble was, it seemed that it was big enough to be a thorn in the side of anyone and everyone involved. And I was most definitely not. Involved, I mean.

One of the police officers lifted his head as we approached. He squinted at me. "Hey, Maggie. Looking for Tom? He's over there, up by the house. Why don't you wait for him at the curb, though, huh? We've got a lot going on just now."

"Ahem," Marcus said into my ear. "Evidently someone didn't get the memo."

"Yeah. Handy, that. I mean . . ." I couldn't tell if Marcus was annoyed or not. I glanced up at him. Oh, good. Humor still intact. I should have known it would be. "We have per-mission to go closer. Do you think we should?"

He considered this. "I don't know any other way to hand the Watkinses' property over to them, do you?"

"Uh-uh. We'll just stay out of the way and . . . skulk a bit. In plain sight."

"Sounds like a plan." We stayed at the fringes of the Watkinses' lawn, pausing where a full hedge that separated the yard from the neighbors touched upon the bordering sidewalk. Marcus leaned in just long enough to whisper, "Just remember the sympathy card, should we need it."

"Good idea," I whispered back. "What about that cuteness factor?"

"Being cute won't get you out of the kind of trouble this can bring on, sweetness. But playing dumb might help. I know, it goes against your preferred style, but now's not the time to get picky."

Hm.

We wandered up the sidewalk. Well, Marcus wandered, I hop-skipped-swung. I felt my stomach muscles get tighter and tighter in my abdomen, the sensation creeping up toward my chest. Something bad had happened here. Something very bad.

"I feel it, too," Marcus muttered. He swiped his hand back over his hair. "It's still here. Still happening. It's not over yet."

That would be why it felt unsettled and urgent. Oh boy. "Can you tell what it was?"

"Someone's died. A man. His energy is still here. Like an imprint."

Unsettled and urgent.

I could feel the spirit energy, too, swirling and buzzing around my head and shoulders like a swarm of angry bees. I shook my head, willing it away. *Not here. Not now.*

Was this the death we—all right, *I*—had been afraid would happen? No, it couldn't be. That wouldn't make sense. The conversation in the elevator had suggested that whatever was intended to happen would be planned. Whatever happened here had to have been incidental.

I gazed up at the house. Number 111369—no question about it, this was the Watkins house. The front door was open, the storm door propped wide so that it couldn't close. There was a white cardboard box on the porch, long and narrow with a cellophane view pane. The doughnuts that it had held had spilled out; some of them had been trampled. The rocking chairs on the front porch had been pushed down, out of the way, the space they usually possessed now claimed by tool chests full of what appeared to be evidence-gathering equipment administered by a fully outfitted crime scene technician in a plastic suit, booties, and medical gloves. One of the potted geraniums on the front step had been knocked over, spilling its dark red flowers to the ground like so much blood. There were two vehicles parked in the driveway, one a sedate and aging sedan like my mother drove, the other a high-profile, high-dollar pickup truck. The car's passenger-side door stood open, as though someone had left it in a hurry and forgotten to shut it. Farther up the road I could see a few officers checking over a motorcycle that was parked in front of a neighboring house. More police officers were milling about on the Watkinses' lawn, both front and back, and going back and forth from the house to a windowless conversion van that was license plated to the Indiana State Police.

Tom must have called out the big guns for this one. Either him or Chief Boggs.

Chief Boggs was the head of our small town's illustrious police department. He was an interesting character—emphasis on "character"—who most often resembled a junkyard bulldog, complete with burly chest, and who was known for his unholy addiction to Annie Miller's apple fritters. People in Stony Mill loved him; he was personable, good-natured, didn't talk down to them, and made time whenever possible to be visible to the business owners in town. To that end, he was a savvy man. He was not, however, a smart man. Probably the smartest thing that he had ever done was to appoint Tom Fielding as Special Task Force Investigator to act as a liaison between the SMPD and the county sheriff's department, especially since the sheriff himself was a by-the-book stickler with little humor and even less patience for the more voluble police chief . . . or anyone else, for that matter, if the rumors commonly held were true.

I clutched the card in my hand, wondering what the right thing to do was.

Marcus approached the next-door neighbors, who were shamelessly watching the proceedings from their side of the well-clipped hedge, to ask what had happened. He came back just a few minutes later. Cupping my elbow, he murmured into my ear, "The Watkinses' home was broken into sometime last night, and the intruder was shot on the premises. Some guy named Nunzio. There is some confusion as to why it took so long for them to report the incident."

A break-in, a shooting. Good grief, what could possibly happen next? How utterly terrifying. Frannie Watkins must be beside herself.

No wonder no one had answered the phone when I called this morning.

"The police are questioning everyone right now. The neighbors have already given a statement. They didn't see anything, they didn't hear anything. Their dog slept through the night without a peep."

Something about this was leaving me with a very bad feeling. Frowning, I surveyed the neighbor's house, and then the Watkinses' home, respectively. The houses in general were

large on the plots of land that held them, claiming as much
square footage, and hence open floor space, for the buck as
possible. As with all the other homes in this subdivision,
the space between houses was actually quite narrow. There
was no way that a gunshot could have gone unheard, even in
the middle of the night. Or should that be, *especially* in the
middle of the night? Sleeping neighbors or not, when the
rest of the world is quiet, sounds tend to echo and reverber-
ate. Someone should have heard it. Everyone should have
heard it.

"What do you want to do?" Marcus asked quietly.

"Tune in," I replied without thinking. "Is there a place we
can sit?"

Tuning in was a way of centering yourself within your
own personal space, digging down deep to regather all wayward strands, feeling yourself utterly, and then allowing your
Guides or the quiet of the world around you to give the answers you seek. For me it worked best to just let come what
may. Marcus was a clearer channel; it might be possible for
him to call to the energies and see what . . . or who . . .
would respond.

At least, that's what we were hoping.

He helped me across the strip of grass along the edge of
the road and held my hands to carefully lower me to the
concrete curb, where I attempted to keep my cast out of
danger. We sat there together, quietly, as the chaos moved
around us as though it were an actual entity, with an energy
and thus a body and a being of its own. So many people, so
many thoughts, so many concerns, so many distractions.

We sat together, holding hands, but that was the extent
of the outward display. There was no chanting, no swaying,
no ritual involved. There was just us, being fully present in
the moment, deeply aware of our surroundings to the minut-
est fiber of our being.

To anyone else we would look like a normal, everyday couple doing a normal, everyday thing.

To Marcus and me, this was normal. An everyday but very important part of who we are . . . and for me, it was so nice to be able to share that side of myself with someone who understood.

I breathed deeply, letting the dappled shade and sunshine from the tree over our heads wash over me.

Next to me, Marcus quivered and jolted suddenly. His soft-focused eyes fluttered. I sat up, paying attention.

"Yeah, the energy's still here," he said. "More like an imprint, really," he repeated, feeling his way through the details he was getting. Male, for sure. I am almost positive it's our guy. I'm getting . . . dark. Young. Kind of . . . macho, strutting, in-your-face."

"And he was shot."

"Sudden passing. With an exclamation point. *Unh!* Like that."

"Why did he break in?"

"He . . ." Marcus frowned. "I'm not getting it. It feels all confused. I don't know."

Baby . . .

That one came to me, punctuating my thoughts unbidden. "Was it about the . . . about the baby?" I asked shyly, still working to not feel silly and inept about my intuition.

Marcus cocked his head as though listening. "And blood."

Anthony Nunzio . . . The name was reverberating through my thoughts, like a foam rubber ball bouncing softly off the invisible walls. Where did I know it from?

From the house emerged a squadron of uniformed personnel—police, medical, and who knows what else— preceding and flanking a stretcher being carried aloft by two

EMTs. Marcus and I both craned our necks to watch the procession, not even bothering to disguise our inquisitive stares. The white sheet covering the lumpy figure was more to protect the sensibilities of curious onlookers than the dignity of the victim-slash-intruder himself . . . but ended up accomplishing neither when a stray gust of a breeze swished in out of nowhere, lifting the sheet aside and flipping a corner of it back. A collective gasp rose all around us, and for a moment, time stood still. From where we sat, I caught sight of a dark and contorted face that seemed oddly familiar . . . just like his name.

But familiar from where?

A sudden voice behind us intruded, distracting me utterly from my struggling memory. "Well. Look who it is. Welcome to the Freak Show."

I turned around, but I didn't need to in order to know who was standing there. The unfriendly epithet said it all. "Tom."

"Maggie." He didn't acknowledge Marcus at all. Marcus returned the nonfavor. "I don't suppose I ought to ask what you're doing here. I would like to know how you knew . . . but I don't suppose I ought to ask about that, either."

I shrugged. "Just lucky, I guess."

"Uh-huh. I can see that. Some might call it jinxed. Or cursed. Yeah, some might call it that."

I shrugged and inclined my head toward the Watkins place. "Pretty shocking, huh?"

"Murder always is. I gotta go." He turned on his heel.

"Wait."

"Yeah?" he asked without looking around.

"Who was it?"

"No one. Just a regular guy, a hospital maintenance worker who liked to go to bars and hang out and ride his motorcycle. No priors, except years ago when he was a teenager, he had some trouble with drugs. He didn't have any on him, but maybe he was still using. The autopsy will show that." He did turn to look at me then, a hint of antagonism there for me. "And that's all I'm going to say about that. You want anything else, you'll have to use your"—he made the oogly-spooky motion with his hands—"powers."

"But you said it was murder. How can that be? He broke in. Wouldn't it be self-defense?"

He didn't answer. He just stalked off toward the state police vehicle, the stark navy of his uniform making him seem thinner, taller, and somehow more reserved than he actually was.

Marcus's jaw was set in stone.

"He doesn't mean anything by it," I assured him. "He's still angry with me, but he's moving on. I'm sure of it." My cell phone buzzed in my pocket. I fished it out. "Uh-oh. It's Melanie."

At least I was in semishade. Who knew how long this conversation was going to take? Marcus was already indulgently shaking his head and getting up to go talk to the neighbors again.

"Hi, Mel. How are you holding up?"

"You heard? Of course you did. Mom told you, didn't she." It wasn't a question; it didn't need to be. We both were painfully aware of the way Mom operated. Mel had learned from the best. "Oh, Maggie. What am I going to do? I just really don't know what I'm going to do."

She started to talk about Greg and how she had known he wasn't really focused on the family, but she really thought she could make up the difference, that even though he was working all those hours, she really thought if she kept things going with the house and the girls and managed the gardener and the cleaning service and the errands and making sure he and the girls were dressed properly, that she could keep him happy.

"How could he do this, Maggie? How could he just . . . leave, without a word?"

"Mel. Honey. Have you spoken with him?"

"He's not answering his cell. He called in to the office and let them know he'd be out a few days. His phone calls are all being vetted by staff. His partners say they don't know where he is. I know they're lying, but I don't understand why. What should I do?"

I snapped into action. My opinion of Greg had never been great—he was always a little too familiar when he had drunk too much at family parties—but I never thought he'd stoop to this. "This is what you're going to do. You are going to pick yourself up, dust yourself off, and you are going to take care of your little girls. You are not going to worry about what Greg is doing, or what Greg is thinking, or what Greg is feeling . . . because Greg is a grown man, Mel, and he needs to behave like one. You are going to worry about yourself, and you are going to worry about recovering from surgery, and you are going to worry about how to keep your girls from hearing about what's going on between you and Greg for the time being. You are going to worry about preserving their happy little world."

She sniffled. "I know you're right."

"Melanie, why did Greg not know you were going to have a C-section?" We might as well cover all the unguarded bases at once, while she was off balance and vulnerable. Fewer opportunities to keep up with the deception that way. "He didn't know about the twins, either. Or if he did, then he's a very, very good actor."

"Really, do we have to go into this—"

"I think we do. And trust me, I've got a lot of other things going on right now myself," I said, looking around me.

"All right. Fine. He didn't know about the twins."

"You know, that's not the kind of thing you keep from your husband, Melanie."

"You so sound like Mom right now."

"And don't try to change the subject."

"I just . . ." Mel started to say one thing, but then changed her mind and opted, I gathered, for the truth. "He wasn't happy about the pregnancy from the beginning. I think he thought I'd planned it. But I didn't, I swear it. It just happened. And you know Greg never bothered himself to go to the prenatal appointments. So when the ultrasound showed two babies . . . well . . ."

"You decided you'd let it be a surprise."

"Exactly!"

"Oh, Melanie."

"I was hoping it would be a *good* surprise!" she defended herself.

"Well, yeah. But . . ." I was trying to see this from Greg's side, for the sake of fairness and equality. But then . . . "You know what? Who cares if he wasn't happy with the pregnancy. Sometimes you get dealt a few unexpected cards in life. That doesn't mean you don't have to play the hands you're dealt."

"Exactly!" she said again.

"I'm not condoning you not telling him, mind you," I told her, "but I have your back, sis. I'm here if you need me. You know that." Even if she was a selfish, ridiculous, scandal-mongering, manipulative princess sometimes.

"Thanks, Maggie. I mean it." She sniffled. I think I got to her self-involved little heart. "I think he's been seeing someone, you know. I don't know who . . . but I'm ninety percent certain of it."

I wish I could reassure her, tell her that she was being silly, that it was the worry and the unknown talking her into it, but something about it rang true. "Don't worry about that right now. Got me?"

"Okay."

"You get some rest. We'll deal with the Greg situation later."

We. Because we were family, and that's what families do. Even when they don't always get along.

I sat there a moment with my phone in my lap and dug my hands into the grass, letting the energy tension from Melanie drain from me, returning it back to Mother Earth. It was the easiest and quickest way I had ever found of releasing external energies and emotions. I felt better in no time.

Funny, how conversations carried sometimes, even amid all the chaos and activity in the area. Was it the wind that did it? A stray, unseen breeze? Because all of a sudden I could hear bits and pieces of what two officers were talking about up on the front porch.

Scraps, really, but clearly audible.

". . . the address . . . his pocket . . ."

". . . said they don't know him . . ."

". . . call put through to his number from theirs . . ."

". . . have been expected?"

Before I could even think about what all of this might mean, my attention was drawn toward a small motorcycle putt-putting slowly up the road toward all the activity. Hm, on second glance, not a motorcycle. More like a moped but sleek, bullet-shaped, and silvery, like molten metal. It drove up in front of me and parked. A tall slim figure slid off and started unfastening the helmet's chin strap.

"Ooh. Nice Vespa," Marcus murmured, appearing at my shoulder.

The helmet came off, and slender fingers purposely tousled the dark brown pixie cut of Julie Fielding, who, I noticed, was not wearing cute heels and an airy blouse today, but was instead garbed in a fitted denim jacket to ward off road rash in the event of a spill, black skinny jeans, and ballet flats. Despite having just removed a helmet that would have turned my hair into something that resembled a second-grader's papier-mâché art project, she somehow managed to look cute, cool, and casual-but-not. Still, she did at least acknowledge the heat of the day by slipping off her jacket and tossing it carelessly over the handlebars.

Marcus had already turned away, evidently distracted by something behind us, when she saw me there on the curb. "Oh, hi. Not another spill, I hope?"

I couldn't tell if her concern was genuine or if there was an element of snark there. I decided to ignore it if it existed at all, and shook my head. "Just resting."

"Oh, good. Have you seen my husband?" She pulled a pair of Jackie O shades from the V-neck of her fitted T-shirt and put them on to survey the surroundings. I felt a whisper of near envy trickle through my veins. Somehow she managed to look Euro chic in an outfit that would have made me look dumpy and sad.

"He was up at the house a few minutes ago. You might check there. Oh! Except I don't think they want people wandering around. You might want to check with one of the officers and see if they can reach him for you."

She smiled. "Thanks, but I think I'll take my chances." And as my gaze followed, she slipped something out of her back pocket and slowly and purposely clipped it to her belt.

It was a state police badge.

I should have known. Not only was she impossibly well put together, but she was a cop, too. Tom had never mentioned that.

It made sense. But as a part of an opposing police organization. The Staties and the local boys didn't always see eye to eye, from what Tom had once told me. That, too, made sense.

She flagged down the sheriff's deputy closest to us. "Hey, Johnson! Tell Chief Boggs I'm here, would you?"

"You got it."

She headed off across the lawn with an easy stride.

"Soooo," Marcus drawled in my ear. "The wife is back in the picture, eh?"

I didn't need to look at him to know that he was grinning broadly. Happily, even. "Uh-huh."

"Good," came his blunt response. "Maybe now he'll call his goons off."

"What do you mean?"

He shrugged. "I'm pretty sure that's who's been watching my house, that's all. Or maybe it's the man himself, just trying to keep track of *your* comings and goings."

"Tom?" I blinked, trying to deny it. "Oh, Tom wouldn't . . . I mean, I don't think . . ."

Hm. He was kind of the suspicious type.

Oh, hell.

Julie Fielding stepped purposely over the dropped box of doughnuts, turning and glancing down as she paused, obviously taking note of the detail. It occurred to me then— who brought the doughnuts in the first place? Someone who didn't know about the intruder lying dead on the floor, obviously. The way I figured it, the chain of events must have looked something like this: Intruder breaks in. Intruder meets untimely death by armed home owner. Attach to that scenario the bit of info that the neighbor had given us about there being an unexplained delay in the phone call to report the incident, and that pretty much covered it. So who had brought the doughnuts and dropped them in shock or

dismay or horror or all of the above? I wondered if it had
something to do with the owner of the sedan whose passenger door even now remained wide open.

". . . confession . . ."

My head came up as the word floated across the lawn.
There was a confession? What sort of confession? A confession suggested Tom was right, that the intruder's death was
intentional. *Who?*

I exchanged a glance with Marcus.

The answer came sooner than I expected, when a few
minutes later Harold Sr. walked out of the house with his
grizzled, bearlike head held high and a grim expression on
his face. Though he was flanked by an officer on each side
from just behind him, he walked with dignity and without
handcuffs to keep him contained. Instead, he was allowed to
enter the back of the police cruiser of his own volition. One
of the officers gave him a manly pat of encouragement on his
shoulder.

On the porch, a stoic Harry Jr. came out, his arms surrounding his mother Joyce, who was quietly weeping as they
watched the proceedings. As the door of the cruiser closed
behind her husband, Joyce turned and buried her face against
her son's denim button-down work shirt.

"Wow," I said to Marcus, suddenly deeply and intensely
sad. Tears stung the corners of my eyes. Poor Joyce. She
seemed like such a nice, pleasant lady, and had been so happy
to be a grandmother. Her whole life must seem like it was
falling apart right now. The whole family was at risk of it.
"Just . . . wow."

Marcus grimaced, but seemed beyond words. It was beyond unexpected. It was outrageous. I tried to make sense of
it. Why would Harold Sr., a sedate, respected member of the
community, have shot an intruder in his son's home who
wasn't an intruder because somehow he was expected? Did

that mean that the victim had been invited to the house? And if so, by whom? According to the snippet of conversation that had drifted to me on the breezes, the Nunzio guy had their phone number in his pocket. Why? And why had Harold Sr. been at his son's house in the middle of the night in the first place? Anyone? Anyone?

Perhaps the victim and Harry Jr. had been friends and he'd called him over to discuss some matter, and somehow it had all gone horribly wrong. Oh, but didn't one of the officers say that they (and by "they" I was assuming he'd meant Harry and Frannie) had said they didn't know the man?

Dark . . .

The word Marcus had channeled suddenly brought to mind the darkness at the hospital. It had been pitch-black in the elevator that night, and then there had been the spirit activity, too. Nebulous. Unfocused. Random. Maybe the spirit activity had been a message from the other side whose purpose was solely to be sure that I. Was Paying. Attention. Now.

That notion started to make more and more sense to me the longer I considered it.

In a rational world of science and logic, a "normal" person would shrug off the timing of the hung-up elevator and the subsequent power outage that had affected only the elevator itself. Equipment malfunction, they might say. Just one of those things. Nothing to make a fuss over. But Stony Mill no longer seemed to exist within the framework of the rational world I had been led all along to believe was the norm. If the last nine months had shown me anything, it was that. So when spirit energy cropped up and tapped me on the shoulder, was I more inclined than most to sit up and take notice? You bet your sweet ass I was. The trick was in deciphering what the message was supposed to mean.

I wasn't always the best at that. But I was willing to try.

Could the conversation I had overheard that night be related to this, since the OD that the woman from the morgue had told Steff about was a no-go? *Could* Harold Sr.'s voice have been one of the two I had heard? He was at the hospital that night. Maybe that's what the spirit message was about. Could it possibly be that he had been planning Nunzio's death all along? And if so, why?

Oh, but wait. Again, it didn't fit. Not at all. Because like I'd told Steff, the voices I'd overheard had been talking about a woman. "She" wouldn't know what hit her.

And that's when a chill shivered through me. What if this Nunzio guy had been the other unseen someone? What if *Frannie* had been the intended victim all along? But if that was true, what was the connection? There would have to be a connection.

Why on earth would Harold Sr. want to kill Frannie?

I shook my head. Now I really was jumping to conclusions. First and foremost being the idea that the conversation I'd overheard belonged to the situation unfolding before us. But if not, that meant there was still another unidentifiable, unsuspecting female out there in the greater Stony Mill area, and somehow that possibility was even worse.

She won't know what hit her . . .

I shuddered, remembering.

Maybe it really had been an accident. A girl could only hope.

Anthony Nunzio . . .

The name whispered through my head tantalizingly, full of promise. There was something about it. Just a regular, everyday kind of guy, Tom had said. Works—ahem, *worked*—for the hospital. Maybe that was it. Maybe that's why it was familiar.

Stupid painkillers. My mind was mush.

Frannie came out of the house and stood there with the baby in her arms, standing separate from Harry Jr. and his mother. Harry barely registered her emergence, so focused was he on the image of his father raising a meaty, work-worn hand to him against the glass of the rear window in farewell. There was something so disturbingly poignant in that single gesture. My heart wrenched painfully.

Frannie's dark hair, so neatly brushed and contained when she'd left the hospital yesterday evening, was now draped in tangles around her shoulders, and her pale skin was marred by purple smudges beneath her eyes. That was understandable, considering all that she'd just been through. With her eyes locked on the man—her father-in-law, for heaven's sake—in the backseat of the cruiser as well, she lifted the baby to her chest and stood with her lips pressed to his downy soft head, her arms holding him tightly to her. Protecting him. For all her seeming indifference at the hospital, for all her vague disquietude, today she seemed almost uber-focused, very much the lioness guarding her cub.

That, too, was absolutely, wholly, and completely understandable.

In the doorway behind her hovered Julie Fielding. She reached forward and put a gentle hand on her cousin's shoulder. "Maybe we should go back inside, Frannie, huh?" she suggested quietly.

But Frannie felt my gaze on her and raised her chin in my direction. I waved, then let my hand drop, feeling foolish. To my surprise, she wandered over in our direction.

"What are you doing here?" she asked, obviously bemused.

"Uh, hi, Frannie." I took a deep breath, knowing how odd it must seem to find us there in the midst of all . . . this. I held up the bassinet card. "We were just hoping to return this to you. I knew it would be important to you. We . . . we honestly didn't mean to show up in the middle of all this, though. It just worked out that way. I did call, but . . ." I let my voice trail off.

She stretched out a hand and snatched the card from me, clutching it against the baby's swaddled back. "Where did you get this?"

"It must have fallen somehow, or . . . well, I'm not sure, actually," I told her, realizing just how true that was. It had been on the floor in Mel's room. I was just guessing that the card is what I had seen falling from the magazine. "Marcus found it. We knew you would be missing it."

"What is it, Frannie?"

Harry Jr.'s voice came drifting over to us. Frannie started, tucking the card away before turning toward her approaching husband. "Nothing, Harry."

Harry had come to see what was up. "Oh. Hello," he said, recognizing us.

"We didn't mean to interrupt," I told him. "Especially in light of . . . everything."

He nodded, his brow furrowing slightly. "If you don't mind my asking . . . why are you here?"

I cleared my throat. "We just came to return something to your wife. Something you all dropped yesterday. We didn't intend . . ." I shrugged, helplessly.

The tension relaxed just a bit. "Well, that was kind of you. What was it, Frannie?"

Her dark eyes darted to mine. "Nothing important, Harry. Just a . . . something that the hospital had given us before we left. That's all."

"Oh." His brow furrowed a bit in obvious confusion and distracted consternation. "Well, isn't that nice. Thanks, folks, for coming all the way out here like that. It was . . . Well," he said again, obviously at a loss for words. He cleared his throat and took the baby from Frannie's arms. "I don't mean to be rude, but . . . well, I'm sure you can see we're in the middle of something at the moment."

An understatement, surely. "Of course," I said.

"Take care of that leg, now," he told me, masterfully turning Frannie around with a big hand on her shoulder and retreating to the house where his family would be momentarily safe from the prying eyes of the neighborhood watch.

I watched them go, wondering at the change that fatherhood had wrought in Harry Jr. When I had first seen him, I thought him rather pale and bland. Nice, but somewhat uninspiring. Today, he seemed almost . . . a man. Taking charge with the best of them.

"Did you see that?" Marcus asked, bending close to my ear.

"Hm?" I hummed, distracted by my own musings.

"Did you see that?"

"What?" I turned my head this way and that, trying to figure out what he meant. Julie Fielding was still standing by the open door, watching me as I watched the Watkinses retreat, a probing look on her pretty face.

"She crumpled it."

Julie? She had a clipboard in her hands, but as it was made of metal it was most definitely not crumple-able. She caught my eye and raised her brows. I turned away from her curious stare and lifted my mouth to Marcus's ear. "What are you talking about?" I whispered.

He laughed indulgently. "Where are your thoughts running off to? *Frannie.* She crumpled the card you gave her."

"She . . . The bassinet card?" I frowned. "How odd. Why would she do that? After all the trouble we went to to get it back to her?"

"Maybe she's not the sentimental type," Marcus said as he helped me back across the lawn to more level ground.

"Maybe."

With our only excuse for being there behind us, there was nothing left to do but leave the investigation to the pros and make our exits.

"Just a moment."

Before we could go anywhere, I saw Julie Fielding following us. Marcus stopped, politely waiting for her to catch up.

She held up her clipboard. "If I could just have your names, addresses, phone numbers . . . I would really appreciate it. Just a formality, you understand," she said when I opened my mouth to protest that we had just wandered on scene a short time before. "See? Chief's guys are making the rounds with everyone in the neighborhood."

So they were. And that is how I found myself an official part of an honest-to-goodness homicide investigation.

"Thank you," she said matter-of-factly when we had both complied. There was a breath of a pause, and then with her gaze never lifting from the clipboard, she murmured, "Marcus Quinn. You probably don't remember me, do you?"

Marcus smiled; only someone who knew him as well as I did would notice that it didn't reach his eyes. "I remember. How are you, Julie?"

"Fine. Really. I am." Another breath of a pause. "How is Ray?"

"Surviving," Marcus said, the nonsmile in a tight holding pattern.

She nodded, looking for a moment as though she might say more, but in the end, she didn't. She just flicked the button on her pen and tucked it up tight in her palm before turning back toward the house and its still-open front door.

"Back to work she goes, I guess," I whispered to Marcus. "Whatever that is. Interrogating and investigating, I guess."

"More like counseling and interrogating," Marcus whispered back. "You know, psychologist-style. She up and moved down to Indy to work with the state police when her husband found out about her and Ray—our bass player. Tore Ray up pretty good. I imagine Fielding didn't like it much, either."

No, I don't imagine that he did. Somehow that made me feel even worse for our problematic almost-but-not-quite relationship. But better to cut our mutual losses than to draw it out when the magic just wasn't there.

"Wonder what she's doing back here?" Marcus mused, turning just enough that he could surreptitiously watch her disappear inside the house once more. My gaze snagged on Tom, across the way. In my mind, the answer was pretty obvious.

Well, whatever had brought her back, it was perfect timing for Frannie and her family. In the days to come, they were going to need a bit of handholding from someone who knew them well.

We were quiet all the way back to the truck, our mood somber and reflective. Marcus helped me in. I was so lost in my thoughts that I didn't even realize where he was taking me until he turned down the hill off Main onto River Street.

"Liss made me swear I wouldn't come in today!" I exclaimed.

He shrugged with a silly smirk. "She didn't make me promise I wouldn't bring you in. Besides," he said, "I thought you could use some energy recoup time, after the events of today. And yesterday. And the day before that."

I laughed. "Maybe I can, at that. And a cup of iced fresh-brewed Roobikoos tea might be nice, too."

He parked in an empty customer space in front of the

store, hurrying around the beat-up old truck to help me down to the curb. "We won't be here long enough to worry about taking up a spot reserved for customers," he assured me even though I'd not said a word.

The displays in the front windows were the same—I'd only been gone a day and a half—so why did I feel so much like the prodigal daughter returning home at last?

It wasn't often that I entered the store through the front door. The brass bells tinkled sweetly overhead as I clumsily crossed the threshold with a clatter and a bump. Instantly my nose was assailed by the familiar scents of cinnamon and tea, coffee beans and vanilla, all underscored by notes of paper and linen and a million bulk spices and herbs all blending into one sweet symphony. Yes . . . this had become home to me, in so many ways.

"Maggie O'Neill! What on earth . . . didn't I tell you not to come in today?" Liss rushed forward to place an arm solicitously and securely around my waist as I thumped across the old, creaky wooden floorboards, as though she expected I might collapse forward at any moment.

I stopped a moment to get a better look at her—ah, the Edwardian clothing styles were her choice for today: wasp waist, peplum jacket, and a narrow skirt that dropped to her ankles. Definitely not a crutches-friendly outfit. Well, I'd be lucky if I could walk in that skirt even without crutches. They didn't call it a hobble skirt for nothing.

"What is it, dear?"

I shook my head and leaned my cheek against hers. "Just that it's good to be here," I said with a relieved sigh and then kissed her on said cheek for good measure. "It's been a heckuva day."

Liss aimed a measuring stare at Marcus. "Didn't I tell you to keep her home today?" she fussed as I made my way over to the ribs-high counter, which made a fine brace to help me turn myself around and back into a stool.

"Have *you* ever tried to make Maggie do something she doesn't want to do?" he countered.

"Well, I can't say I've ever had to." Smiling with her eyes, Liss glanced over at me, and I shrugged as if to say, *I don't know what he's talking about.* "Hm. I do see what you mean, I think."

Marcus waved Liss off the moment she headed for the counter. "You sit down. I'll do it."

"You folks got room for one more?"

I turned on my seat to see a big, sweet face peeking around the corner from the back room. Genevieve Valmont was a member of the N.I.G.H.T.S., a former nun of a certain age who had given up living a life for the church out of the blue one day; no one knew the full story as to why. Now she lived a life of simple pleasures running a bait store on the lakes north of town. She might be big and burly, but the rough exterior hid a heart the size of all five Great Lakes put together.

"Gen popped in yesterday morning right after I heard the news about your ankle," Liss explained, "and since the girls started back to school on Monday, she volunteered her services here at the store until we get you up and running."

"Running. Ha. That might take a while," Marcus teased. He ducked when I threw a to-go packet of organic honey at his head.

Gen came forward and gave me a big bear hug. "One of the benefits of being retired," she said, brushing aside my words of gratitude. "But don't get any ideas about me staying or anything." She pulled with discomfort at her sedate sweater and black slacks. "I'm not exactly used to dressing up anymore, ya know." Leaning conspiratorially toward me, she whispered, "I much prefer my overalls. The epitome of comfort. But I suppose they don't do much to help sell high-end stuff like what Enchantments has to offer, huh?"

I gave her a reassuring pat. "I like them just fine."

"So, what brings you in today," Liss asked as Marcus slid a steaming cup of lemongrass tea in front of her, "in defiance of direct orders?"

"Well," Marcus said, clearing his throat, "*I* did it, actually. Don't blame Maggie. She was off in her own world until we got here."

I took a sip of my iced Roobikoos (he remembered!) and wrinkled my nose at him from over the rim of my cup. "I was, a little. So much has happened." And from there I had to share the whole sordid tale, from beginning to end. Babies, weirdness, a broken ankle, a missing husband, a murder, a confession, and all. Marcus helped me fill in the details as he knew them. Between the two of us, it didn't take long.

"Well, now. That was *some* trip to the hospital," Gen said when we were done. "New babies are always exciting, but . . . wow. When you do it up, you really do it up. And two more deaths in this town . . . Lord have mercy. What on earth are we to make of all this? That's what I'd like to know." She shook her head. "I know Harold Watkins. Not well, but . . . I always thought he was a good man. Salt of the earth. Makes me wonder what could have happened to get him riled up enough to . . . kill someone."

Marcus nodded in agreement. "He is a good man; at least, I've always thought so. I know my Uncle Lou thinks so, too. But they say we all have it in us. To kill, I mean. For the right reasons, of course."

What would those reasons be, I wondered? I tried to think of anything that could induce me to take another person's life. None of the usual motives, certainly. Not power, not greed, not ambition. I didn't roll that way. But to protect someone I loved with all my heart, whose very existence was in danger? Depending on the circumstances, yes, I liked to think that I would find the courage within myself to rise to the occasion if said occasion dictated the need. As with most areas of life, there were no blacks and whites, no absolutes. Each situation had to be judged on its own merits, or lack thereof.

But I wasn't kidding myself. I knew not everyone thought the same way. Not even another "good guy." The question was, what would induce Harold Watkins to kill? And how was Nunzio related to all this?

I couldn't help but think it *must* have something to do with Frannie.

"I can't get it all out of my head," I confessed to all. "I keep running through my time there at the hospital. From beginning to end. I feel like I'm forgetting something. Missing something. Something big. Something that *might* be important." Marcus reached out and linked fingers with my own.

"Like what, darling?" Liss asked. "Something that you saw? Something you heard?"

"I don't know." Frustrated, I rubbed my forehead hard with the heel of my free hand. "Maybe it's silly. Maybe I've gotten so used to having been in the wrong place at the right time, maybe I just expect that to come into play this time, too. Whether it's divine guidance or intuition, or just plain dumb luck doesn't really matter in the end, does it?"

Marcus took my hand. "You can't feel responsible for not having the answers, you know. You can't be in sync with everything. No psychic is a hundred percent. And sometimes, what you do tune into is accidentally misinterpreted. A miscue."

"Not everything, no." Not that it mattered, because I

wasn't even a true psychic. Not really. Not like Evie. Not even like Liss. Just enough that I knew that something I couldn't quite put my finger on from the last few days was important, and that whatever it was, it wasn't forthcoming.

"You're trying too hard," Liss observed. "Intuition simply cannot be forced. Have you never noticed that the connections are easiest when you occupy your thoughts with something mindless and menial, allowing your intuition to work its magick behind the scenes?"

I frowned, not immediately understanding. "Something menial."

"Some task that doesn't take a lot of brain capacity. One that allows your body to work on autopilot," Liss elaborated. "Oh, you can sit in front of your black scrying mirrors and crystal balls, certainly, but it's so much easier to simply get busy and let your mind empty itself. And that's when your Guides start dropping the real whiz-bang-doodles at your feet."

Hm. I'm not sure I've ever been the actual recipient of a whiz-bang-doodle in any way, shape, or form . . . but I would take her word for it.

Gen offered, "I've always enjoyed sitting on the end of the dock, fishing for whatever wants to come up and take a nibble."

"I've always been partial to scrubbing the floor," Marcus said. And when we girls looked at each other and giggled in spite of ourselves? "What? It's very methodical and soothing."

I didn't know about Liss or Gen, but the last time *I* had come across Marcus scrubbing the floor, he was on his hands and knees wearing his black leather pants. The ones that had very early on emblazoned themselves in my mind's eye because of their habit of stretching ever so impressively across some very attractive parts of his anatomy. Still grinning, I patted his hand. "You do have very clean floors."

"Thanks." He looked at me askance through blue eyes sparkling with good humor. "I think."

"Never mind that, ducks," Liss told me. "You go home and take a long, hot bath tonight, and see where that gets you. You'll be surprised what comes around."

Skeptical to the end, I glanced pointedly down at my ankle, which was once again complaining about dangling in midair. "I don't know if you've noticed . . ."

Not to mention the pain meds that made my head spin just the littlest bit mixed with hot bath water sounded like a killer combination.

"So? I'm sure Marcus can come up with something to keep your cast dry."

The absolutely scandalous level of interest Marcus suddenly displayed at the prospect of helping me with the intricacies of my bath made my heart skip a beat.

And with that suggestion planted securely in his mind, Marcus seemed all the more eager to get me home. To . . . *rest*. Yeah, that's it. Rest.

"Oh, wait a moment! I nearly forgot." Liss disappeared behind the velvet curtain that led to the back office, returning a moment later with a small box. "For Melanie, dear. Just a little something witchy that no new mummy should be without."

I took the box from her. "Something witchy, huh? Um, nothing that Mel will see as . . . scary, right?"

Her laughter tinkled through the air, pure and perfect lightness of being. "Do I look like the type of person who would gift a woman whose body is being ravaged by invading hordes of hormones with something designed to set those very invading beasties on fire with fear?"

"Hm, good point. You're far too civilized for that." I hefted the box in my hands. "Dare I shake it?"

"It's a pretty little mobile crafted out of the most beautiful crystal beads. Very good energy. Protective and very soothing. I would have purchased two, you know, had I known in advance of the impending arrival of twins. I'm usually spot-on as far as expectant mums go, so that rather surprised me, I must say."

Join the crowd. "Protective and soothing sounds perfect. Especially with Greg gone missing."

"Poor Melanie," Liss tsked. "I take it she was caught unawares by her husband's discontent?"

"She was in denial."

"The more open she is to change, the easier the next months will be for her. Resist the energetic tides, and she will find herself powered along by forces much stronger than she could ever be. She needs to use this time to go inward, to grow strong and bolster her sense of self. How she deals with this will determine the next grand design in her life."

I gazed with surprise at Gen, who didn't usually offer much in the way of metaphysical insight. Thanks to a lifetime of hiding her ability, Gen was far more circumspect than that. Seeing the dead . . . that couldn't have been a popular motif among her peers. Certainly at St. Catherine's we had been taught that the dead should stay dead, no ifs, ands, or buts about it. "Thanks, Gen. I'll tell her."

"Melanie will be fine, dear," Liss said reassuringly. "She's a strong girl."

That I could agree with. Melanie had always come out on top. Granted, her life up until now had been one shining gold moment after another, but it didn't matter. She had always possessed an innate sense of trumping right over anyone who might stand against her. Despite her moment of vulnerability at the hospital, something told me the outcome of this current hiccup in her life would be no different.

Greg would be smart to watch his back.

Marcus took me home (where there was a full bag of clothes waiting for me on the porch—thank you, Steff!), and after seeing me safely ensconced on the edge of the bed, he went into the adjoining master bath to run a tub full of hot water. I could tell that Liss's suggestion had really seized hold of his imagination, because he seemed to have little else in the forefront of his mind. Lifting my cast up onto the bed with a sigh, I settled back on my elbows to watch him as he adjusted the knobs, set out fresh, fluffy white towels, and—be still my heart—lit a couple of candles.

"Wow," I told him as he came back into the bedroom, drying his hands on a towel, "you really go all out."

"For you, yes." He put his hands on his hips and leered down at my prone figure. "Although, if you're going to display yourself so invitingly, I might have to rethink the whole bath idea. Or at least postpone it."

There is nothing like coming into one's own power as a woman, of knowing just what effect every movement has on her man. Feigning a yawn, I stretched my spine and rolled my shoulders, all the while watching him through lowered lashes.

But then there is nothing like a man who knows his own power over a woman, either. Not in an aggressive way, but in a way that leaves no doubt as to what is going on in his mind. Especially when he leans in ever so slowly like a jungle cat, leveraging his body over yours. Taking you with his energy without touching a single part of you.

"Especially," he whispered, allowing himself a brief nibble at the base of my throat, "when you do something like that."

I was breathing much faster when he just as slowly peeled his energy and his body away, leaving me to wonder who was the victor in that all-too-brief tussle of the sexes. He extended a hand and pulled me to a sitting position.

"Bath first."

Well, at least *that* left the evening open-ended. I got to my feet and reached for my buttons . . . and froze, suddenly shy as I realized he was intently watching my every movement.

It wasn't that he hadn't seen bits and pieces of me in all my, erm, glory, but I had never actually purposely . . . undressed . . . in front of him. This was new territory.

So much for claiming my feminine power.

If he'd noticed my hesitation, he didn't say anything. Instead, he got up and headed for the door, calling back, "You go ahead while I get you a fresh cup of tea. Your robe's on the end of the bed."

Robe. Yes. I slipped out of my clothes in a heartbeat and reached for it, grateful for its deep folds. Marcus was back before I had even had a chance to sit back down. He set the mug of steaming tea (chamomile by the scent wafting upward on the vapors) on the vanity, then stepped aside to let me through into the bathroom.

It hit me then. There was no way around it. I would not be able to lower myself into the tub without assistance. Not without risking life and limb. Both lower extremities, and my neck, to boot.

While my mind worked a mile a minute figuring all of this out, Marcus it seemed had already made the same calculations on his own. I felt his fingers tug at the knotted belt of my robe. Almost at the same moment, he leaned in and gently kissed me, effectively stifling my embarrassment.

Had I been embarrassed? Really? At that precise moment I couldn't imagine why.

His hands grasped mine as he backed away and slowly, irrevocably, he lowered me into the bathwater, maintaining eye contact with me the whole time as he took care to keep my casted ankle from slipping over the edge. The temperature of the water was perfect, hot enough to make me tense up as my skin became accustomed to it, but not hot enough to make me yelp and try every possible movement to prevent scalding the whole of my backside. I forgot my moment of modesty as a boatload of bubbles and a wave of water closed around my body. Leaning my head against the angled back of the tube, I closed my eyes with a blissful sigh.

"Oh, wow. This feels . . . fabulous. What a good idea."

"I'll say."

I slitted my eyes open to peep at him. He was standing at the end of the tub, a folded towel held forgotten in his hands and a light of naked interest glittering in his eyes that sent an arrow of longing straight through me. When he realized I was watching him back, he cleared his throat and carefully, solicitously lifted my ankle in order to place the towel as a cushion beneath it. Then he rose again, stuffed his hands in his pockets, and said, "I'll just . . . give you your privacy and wait out here."

My privacy? I blinked, confused, as he shuffled back to his bedroom, his shoulders hunched.

He's trying to be a gentleman, Margaret Mary-Catherine O'Neill. And you, might I say, have no shame.

Hm. Grandma C? Now is not the time, okay? Stuff it.

He left the bedroom door open at least. If I leaned forward just so, I could see his denim-covered legs lounging on the bed. Much too far away.

A nice, relaxing bath. Yeah.

I did relax, though, much to my surprise. I must have

been more tired than I thought because my eyes drifted closed and my mind began to waft around on the dream currents of never-neverland almost instantly. I wasn't sleeping so much as floating.

And then, just as Liss had predicted, a lightbulb went off.

Tony Nunzio, dial 212 . . . Tony Nunzio, 212 . . .

Tony . . . Anthony . . .

My eyes flew open and I stared at the bright lights above the vanity in dismay.

Anthony Nunzio.

That's where I'd heard the name before.

Frannie's special midnight caller.

It was him. Frannie's mystery man and the intruder in her home were one and the same.

Why had it taken me so long to remember that?

I blame the painkillers. I'm usually much quicker on the draw.

What had he said to her that night? The words were faint in my memory. Was it really less than forty-eight hours ago? Somehow the last two days seemed to fill a lifetime.

Regardless, the incident at the hospital proved one thing a lie: the Watkinses had told the police that they didn't know their intruder.

At least one of them did. And I was willing to bet, maybe even more than one.

It was the knowing again, that deep sense of truth that came sailing out of the nebulous nothingness, just as Liss had promised it would if I but silenced my thoughts. That certainty that said You. Are. On. The. Right. Track.

But which one? Who besides Frannie knew about Tony Nunzio? Who besides Frannie would care?

Who would care that Frannie and Tony . . .

That they what? That they had shared some sort of association between them? It certainly seemed likely. Even probable. Showing up, after hours, when her husband and family were likely to be away. Skulking about in stairwells and shadows, waiting for the most opportune time to approach her.

To approach her *for what purpose,* though? What was it he'd said?

I relaxed back into the warm water and closed my eyes, willing myself to drift. It had worked once just now; there was a good chance it could happen for me again.

At first all I saw was the darkness penetrated by distinct red swirls where the vanity lights were burned into my field of vision. I let my focus go softer, shift inward, until my breathing began to slow, naturally, into a deep and rhythmic continuous wave. Ebb and flow. Flow and ebb.

A blank screen appeared in my mind's eye, white and shimmering in the fluid darkness. Bemused, I stared at it, watching it bob in and out of sight—out, the harder I focused on it, and in, the more that I let come what may. I breathed deeply through the excitement that had cropped up at the first sign of this new turn in my abilities and worked hard to just be still, of mind and of body.

"Get away from him . . ."

The memory floated through my mind, crisper and clearer than it had been that night at the hospital when sleep deprivation and confusion had ruled the moment. I resisted the temptation to latch onto it and clutch it in my hands, turning it over and over in my mind to try to wring out the rest. *Patience,* I reminded myself. *Let it come.*

"Get away from me."

"Gotta get out of town for a while . . ."

"I heard about the kid . . ."

"They'll want to know where he got it . . ."

All of a sudden Jordan Everett popped into my head again. Jordan whose death was a result of heart failure attributed, most likely, to either steroids or other drugs, verdict still being out as to which. Oh my God. It made sense. Tom had said Nunzio had had run-ins relating to drugs in his past. What if he never stopped? What if he just got smarter about it? Or just lucky enough not to get caught? *Until Jordan died.* Had Nunzio been supplying drugs to kids in town? Kids like Jordan? Maybe that's why he told Frannie he was leaving.

But he would be back.

"Stay away and leave us alone!"

There was something in Frannie's voice that had caught my ear, a low and throbbing urgency that was out of place in the drowsy-lambs-and-dancing-butterflies dreamworld that was the norm for New Mommyland. It was obvious she was afraid of him for some reason known only to her, even though he didn't seem to be threatening her in the brief exchange I had overheard. But there are many ways to threaten, to influence. To manipulate. Maybe she was afraid for other reasons. Not necessarily for her own welfare, but . . .

The baby.

Marcus had channeled that when we were sitting on the Watkinses' curb, trying to connect with the otherworldly energy we still felt there. *Baby.*

More memories were tumbling in, end over end, merging into some sort of primordial soup in my head. Conversations, gossip, odds and ends and snippets.

"Oh . . ."

Jane Churchill had mentioned that the divorce file Greg's law firm had prepared contained evidence that Frannie had been having an affair. Mel herself had seen Frannie arguing with a strange guy in the coatroom at the mommy-to-be exercise class she attended. A cute guy, a dark and dangerous motorcycle type.

I'd seen Anthony Nunzio only twice, and only in passing . . . but the description matched what I'd seen.

Was Tony Nunzio Frannie's former lover?

"Get away from him!"

Baby.

Whose baby? Harry Jr.'s? Or Tony Nunzio's? And what did all of this have to do with Nunzio being interrupted at the Watkinses' home in the middle of the night, and shot dead?

"Marcus!" I called out.

"You rang?"

His deep voice came from the doorway, much sooner than I'd expected it to. My eyes flared widely. He was standing there, one shoulder leaning against the door frame, his thumbs hooked in his belt loops.

"Uh, hi," I said, because I couldn't think of anything more pithy to say, because I suddenly couldn't help wondering whether he'd been standing there the whole time I was meditating.

His attention did not waver in the slightest. "Hey."

I became suddenly, acutely aware of just how much skin I knew I must be displaying beneath the bubbles, which were disappearing fast. But I caught myself. I didn't have time for self-consciousness now. "I just remembered something!" I told him excitedly. "Several somethings, actually."

His gaze remained enigmatic, but my breasts were tingling beneath the warm water, and I had a feeling it had nothing to do with the fizzing properties of the bubbles. "Did you, now?"

Focus, Maggie-girl . . .

I cleared my throat. "Remember when I told you about what happened at the hospital the night Mel had the babies?"

"The elevator thing?"

"No, I mean the argument I overheard down the hall. What I don't think I mentioned at the time is that it was coming from Frannie's room."

"Yeah?"

He might as well have said, *"Hmm?"* I resisted the urge to wave my hand in front of his eyes (*Men!*) and instead explained, slowly, "I saw the man she was arguing with," as I waited for him to catch up. "It was Nunzio, Marcus. The intruder who was shot in the Watkinses' home. They are one and the same."

When I saw his eyebrows rise, I knew I had snared his attention. Or at least he'd managed to stop ogling my . . . "You sure about that?"

I nodded. "Positive. I saw him clearly at the hospital. Not so much this afternoon, but it was still him. I'm sure of it. It just took me a while to place the face."

"I thought they said they didn't know him."

"That's what they told the police, yes. But obviously Frannie knew him. Marcus . . . I think . . ." I couldn't finish the thought . . . but then, I didn't have to.

Heaving a sigh, Marcus leaned his head back against the door frame. "All right, let's do this. There's more to this than a straightforward confession from Harold can account for, isn't there?"

I nodded. "I think so. I have no real proof, just . . . hunches and things heard first- and secondhand." I paused, trying to get all of my thoughts and impressions to gel together. "I also found out through one of Mel's friends that Frannie had been having an affair. I think . . . I have good reason to think it was with Nunzio." Briefly I explained my thinking behind my supposition: the gist of the argument, and the coatroom scene that Mel had witnessed at Baby Bellies.

Marcus stared at me. "If that's true . . ."

"I think Frannie had a secret, and I think it went deeper than having a lover."

Baby . . .

The word burst out of my mouth, unbidden, as soon as it entered my thoughts. Yes, the baby. So many more things were occurring to me now, blip after blip of memory. Joyce's explanation to my mother that putting pressure on a young married couple has the potential to end in heartache for everyone involved, and how Harry Jr. and Frannie had been on the verge of splitting when they miraculously reconciled, with an equally miraculous pregnancy cropping up shortly thereafter to seal the deal. The urgency in her voice when she told Nunzio to get away from him. To get away from the baby. Her strangeness about the baby's dark curls. Even then, her explanation of cradle cap did not ring true, and we all knew it. Even her strange behavior with the bassinet card.

"The baby isn't Harry's," Marcus breathed. Reading my mind again? "Holy shit."

I had begun to shiver violently; the water had begun to cool without me paying attention, but it was psychic tremor, too, a reaction to the energy flowing in and through me. Marcus was on top of things, though. He grabbed a bath sheet and helped me gently to my feet—well, *foot*—wrapping me efficiently and securely in the big fluffy towel with nary a peek. Well, none that I noticed, anyway. When I was dry, he switched out the towel for a robe, swept me up in his arms, and carried me to the bedroom.

It would have been romantic if my mind wasn't already in uber-focus on things like:

Blood . . .

That was another tidbit Marcus had channeled. I didn't know why it floated into my consciousness just now. Of course there was blood—the man had been shot.

"You know, I keep going back to the conversation I over-heard in the elevator, trying to make it fit; I can't help it, it keeps coming back to me. Is it at all possible . . . do you think . . . *could* it have involved the Watkinses? Because . . . what if Frannie was the intended victim, and not Nunzio?"

He considered this a moment in all seriousness. "That would mean that Nunzio was a part of some plan . . ." he said slowly.

"And somehow ended up the victim," I finished for him. "It would fit, wouldn't it? '*She* won't know what hit her,' they said. What if Nunzio was hired help, so to speak? And what if, when he visited Frannie in the hospital after hours and they argued, what if he was trying to somehow warn her?"

"Hired help. You mean, hired thug?"

I shrugged. "He did seem to be trying to convince her of something. He was going to be lying low for a while, he said. Getting out of town. Something about the Everett boy—the boy who died. Well, he didn't name him outright. But it fits."

"Drugs? Dealing? Including to the Everett boy?"

"Tom did say Nunzio had a history with drugs."

Marcus shook his head. "I don't get it. Why would Harold Sr. hire Nunzio? To do what? Kill Frannie? Scare her? And why would Nunzio try to warn her? A surge of conscience?"

"If it was a surge of conscience, maybe that would explain why he went to the Watkinses' home to begin with. Another attempt to convince her?" I suggested.

"Hm. Maybe hurting or scaring Frannie aren't the only possible explanations for what Nunzio might have been hired for," Marcus suggested pensively. "Assuming he was hired at all." He sat down on the edge of the bed next to me.

"What do you mean?"

"What if his job was simply to lure Frannie away from Harry?"

Intrigued by this new thought, I said, "Go on . . ."

"Say you are Harold Sr. Say your only son is married to a girl you don't think is right for him, for whatever reason, or that you think might hurt him. Say you've got money to burn, enough to hire a known local reprobate to, you know, sweep her off her feet?"

"Okay. So Nunzio and Frannie have an affair that is financed by Harold Sr. Then what?"

"Say Frannie and Harry Jr. separate for other reasons, and Harry files for divorce."

I was trying to see ahead along his line of thinking. "Only Frannie finds herself expecting. And that is what Harry Jr. always wanted—remember, Joyce herself said that. So did Jane—she said one of the reasons he'd filed for divorce in the first place is that Harry Jr. thought she had been taking measures to keep from having children." The Alanis Morissette song "Ironic" came to mind. "So . . . Frannie tells Harry, and they work things out. Only Nunzio finds out and surprises her—"

"Because he wants the kid, too?"

We looked at each other, surprised at how quickly we had speculated through a scenario that rang with potential.

"Maybe that's why he tried to see her at the hospital," I mused. "To warn her about her father-in-law and to let her know that he had to go away for a while, but that he wanted to be involved in his son's life."

"Which could present a problem for Harold Sr. Especially if he didn't want his son to know about his . . . arrangements on his behalf."

Which could potentially equal a motive for getting rid of him. Maybe Harry Sr.'s confession wasn't as far off the mark as it had originally seemed.

"But . . . why at Harry Jr.'s house?" I persisted. "That is probably the biggest sticking point for me. If it really was his intention to get rid of Nunzio permanently, why wouldn't he choose a neutral location? An out-of-the-way back road or some other isolated spot, rather than a crowded subdivision and with family present to boot? Something that wouldn't implicate himself or his family?"

"I don't know. Maybe something went wrong. Something that forced his hand?" Marcus suggested.

But what? What could that be?

"What if Nunzio wanted to meet with Harry Jr. and tell him the whole story?" he continued along the same line of thought.

"That would suggest altruism on Nunzio's part, which might be a problem. Besides, a phone call was made to him from the Watkinses' residence, remember?" I reminded him. "Someone there asked him to come."

"Not necessarily altruism. It could just as easily have been intended as blackmail. And maybe Harry Jr. was returning an earlier call, accepting a request to meet?"

"Hm. And then maybe Harry Jr. confided in Harold Sr. about the meeting—"

"Hence the need for Harold Sr. to eliminate Nunzio?"

That still seemed iffy to me at best. Again, Nunzio was killed at Harry Jr.'s house, while his wife and new baby were home. I had a hard time believing that a devoted new dad would risk something going terribly wrong while his wife and newborn son were in residence, no matter how pissed off or threatened he felt. Obviously we had to be missing something.

I shook my head. "It just doesn't make sense. Harry Sr. could have just paid him off if he wanted to be rid of him so badly, couldn't he?"

"Maybe he wanted too much for his silence. Or maybe the

paternal instinct was too strong. Or maybe Nunzio found his conscience after the fact."

Maybe. Too many maybes.

"Or maybe it wasn't Harold Sr. at all," he continued. At my sharp look, Marcus shrugged. "All this time we've been talking through the reasons Harold Sr. could have done what he said he did as though it's set in stone, simply because he is the one who confessed. And yet we both have entertained thoughts that it just didn't ring true, haven't we?"

I nodded, folding and refolding the edge of my robe.

"So maybe we should pause and rewind a sec, huh? What if it wasn't Harold?"

"Who, then?" I asked. "Harry Jr.?"

"Why not? He was alone with his wife and new son. Who would have had a better opportunity?"

He had a point, actually. I sat a moment, ruminating on this. "Why?"

"The most obvious reason would seem to be: He found out about his wife's affair."

Or he found out about the baby. Or both. But how? "Jane said the PI report was buried in the divorce file."

"Mm-hm. So deeply buried that no one else knew about it, huh? So deeply that no one has ever talked about it, right?"

I bit my lip. Jane had certainly talked about it easily enough. "I guess that's true. Someone at the firm could have leaked it." We seemed to have two viable suspects, then. One was in police custody at his own hands. The other, safely at home with his wife and baby. "But even if that's true, why would Harold Watkins have confessed?"

The answer was simply complex and complexly simple: "Love," Marcus said with a confident shrug, leaping to his feet to pace back and forth in the space between the bed and the door.

Love. It was a many splendored thing, it was a battlefield, and it made the world go 'round. It will even go on and on. And the love of a parent had to go down as one of the strongest bonds possible, even in the messed-up world we lived in.

"To protect his son?" I couldn't help flashing back to the poignant image of Harold Sr. sitting in the backseat of the police cruiser, stoically holding up his hand to the window as a last good-bye to his wife and son.

"His *only* son," Marcus added. "His only son who desperately wanted a family, a two-car garage and summer barbecues, and a dog sleeping on the front porch. The whole picket-fence life."

Would a man like Harold Sr. be willing to give up his own life with Joyce in order to give his son the life he'd badly wanted?

The image of him gravely leaving his family behind said yes.

"He's sick, you know," Marcus was saying.

"What?" My eyes darted to his. "I didn't know that."

He nodded. "Joyce was practically force-feeding him his heart medicine that night, while you were stuck in the elevator. Maybe *that* would be incentive enough, do you think? To see his son happy? His grandchild taken care of?"

That was the problem. I could see it. I could more than see it. I was totally feeling it.

But before I could give into the feeling, I heard my cell phone ring in the other room.

"I'll get it. You stay put."

From the living room, I heard the inevitable shuffle through the flotsam of my bag as the phone tweetered on, then Marcus answering.

"Hell— Oh, hello, Mrs. O'Neill. Yes, Maggie's here. I'll put her on, just a moment," he said as he walked back into the bedroom, having already been on his way.

He handed me the phone. "Hi, Mom—"

"Maggie? Thank God. Oh, I don't know what I'm going to do, this is so unlike her and—"

"Calm down, Mom. This is so unlike who?"

"Whom, dear. It's Melanie."

Melanie again? "What's wrong?"

"She's left the hospital. Oh, I just don't know what's gotten into her! She couldn't check herself out without a release from her OB/GYN, so she just up and disappeared on the nursing staff. I found her—she isn't so beside herself that she's no longer answering her cell phone—but she is dead set that she has too many pressing details to take care of to stay at the hospital another night. Little Isabella and Sophie are safe and sound in the nursery, thank goodness—she couldn't sneak two low-birth-weight babies off the floor without raising an alarm. But that should tell you something as to her emotional state. And that's not the whole of it . . ."

I'll admit it—I drifted. My mother has a tendency to ramble when she is upset or uptight, and now was one of those moments. Of course, maybe in this one instance she had a right to. It did seem to be a *teensy* bit erratic on Mel's part to leave without her doctor's permission. Usually she'd be all for milking the pampering of an extended hospital stay. I guess the whole abandonment prospect was more than enough to drive any hormonal new mommy over the edge.

"Are you going over to her house?" I interrupted.

"I can't! The girls from Bridge Club are due here at any moment, and I have a quiche in the oven, and—"

"Tell her we'll go."

Marcus's voice cut into my mom's monologue, and I gaped up at him in surprise. *You sure?* I mouthed. He nodded.

"Mom, Marcus and I will head over there and make sure Mel is okay."

"You will? Oh, Maggie, that's a huge load off my mind. Thank you, honey!" Wow, I actually got a thank you? A rare thing. "Margot has Jenna and Courtney at her place tonight, thank goodness. At least I don't have to worry about them, too. Oh, there's the doorbell. I have to go." And with that she abruptly hung up. It was also a rare thing to escape my mom with so little fanfare. That made two things to be thankful for.

It wouldn't do for me to descend upon Mel's home wearing nothing more than a big, fluffy bathrobe, so Marcus brought me some clothes from the bag Steff had dropped off on the porch. Jeans were completely out since they wouldn't fit over my cast, so I selected a pair of stretchy yoga pants and a light cami. Undergarments and a single flip-flop rounded out my casual look.

"Ready?"

I looked up at Marcus and nodded. "Ready."

He would have carried me out to the truck, but I insisted on the crutches—no point in wearing my welcome out too soon. We barely spoke on the quick blitz over to Mel's subdivision, but I couldn't help noticing that he stopped and looked as we passed the gates to the subdivision that the Watkinses lived in, that we had only just left a few short hours ago. I knew we were both thinking about the same things. Wondering . . . were we right?

How Mel had gotten home, I didn't know, but home she was. The front door stood open and there were lights on all over the house. Occasional movement beyond the curtains proved it.

"Well," I said, gazing over at Marcus, "I guess I'd better go in."

"Not without me," he said, already halfway out his door. He opened mine for me and helped me down, reaching into the back for my crutches. "Come on, Hopalong."

We opened the storm door and stepped inside. "Melanie?" I called out.

From the rear of the house I heard a thud and a bump. A moment later, Mel peeked her head out of a room down the hall from the kitchen. "Oh, it's you. What are you doing here? Never mind, don't tell me, let me guess. Mom sent you."

She turned back into the room she'd peered out of without another word. Exchanging a concerned glance with Marcus, the two of us moved to follow.

The room was Greg's home office, one I had been in only once right after the young married couple had signed on the dotted line for the house five years before. I'm sure the room didn't normally look the way that it looked right now: the drawers lying open and the lamp pulled over to the edge of the desk . . . all the better to see the file contents, my dear.

"Soooo," I drawled, leaning on my crutches just inside the door, "what are we doing?"

Mel didn't stop, and she didn't look up. "We," she said in a tone that was short and businesslike, "are trying to find pertinent information in Greg's files."

"Are we, now?" I clumped forward, Marcus following, until I could see into the drawer she was rifling through. "What sort of things are *we* looking for?"

"Bank statements. Insurance information. Investment portfolios. Savings account books. Credit card statements." Flip, flip, flip went her nimble little fingers. "It was too late for me to hit our bank account today, but that's okay. It was too late for him to hit it, too. But you can bet, first thing Monday morning, I'll be waiting at the doors."

I leaned a hip on the edge of the desk. "Mel, don't you think this could have waited until you were released from the hospital?"

"Hmm. No. You see, I realized today, as I stared down

into the perfect beauty of my two new baby girls and tried
to come to terms with the fact that their father found it acceptable to leave them in their first hours of life, how little I
know him. He has his job, he works long hours, he has to
entertain clients, and I am not invited along. He pays the
bills. He takes care of everything, Maggie. He always has.
He always insisted. And I let him. Stupidly, maybe. And I
realized today how easy it would be for him to have . . ."

"Have a double life?" I supplied when her voice trailed off.

"Yeah. Yeah, a double life." She sighed and leaned back in
the desk chair, pushing uncharacteristically limp blond hair
out of her eyes with trembling fingers. "Do you think I'm
crazy?"

I thought of the sense I'd had that something was not
quite right in Mel and Greg's perfect life . . . and then I
thought of Frannie Watkins and her husband and their new
baby, and secrets that refused to stay hidden. "No, I think it's
quite sensible. But Mel, you just had a baby. Two babies. By
C-section."

"And you just broke your ankle. And yet we're both here,
aren't we," she said, going back to the task at hand.

Marcus's eyebrows shot up. Good man that he was, he
smothered the smirk that threatened.

"Here, why don't you lie down on the sofa at least, and let
me do that for you," I told her. "Maybe you'd like a cup of
tea. Marcus?"

"Pop would be great," Mel said, sighing, as she shifted
over to the sofa. "With ice."

Marcus didn't seem to be fazed to be taking orders. "Back
in a sec," he told me.

When he'd gone, I slipped into the desk chair. "You're
sure you're all right?" I asked her. I didn't like her color, or
should I say lack of it? A true blond, Melanie was always
pale, but not colorless.

She groaned as she leaned back against the pillows and crossed her arms over her stomach, closing her eyes. "I'll be okay."

She would be after I took her back to the hospital. Muttering inwardly about my stupid, selfish brother-in-law and his spectacularly jackass behavior, I decided the faster I searched through his files for her, the better. "You're sure what you're looking for will be here?"

"Oh, it'll be there, all right. Greg was nothing if not meticulous about paperwork. He even kept duplicate client files here at home in the event that he needed to access something quickly."

I paused midflick through the folders. "Really . . . ?" I suddenly wondered if that would include a file for the pre-empted divorce proceedings called off between Harry Jr. and Frannie Watkins . . .

Most of the personal and home files were in this drawer, but that didn't stop me from opening the next while Mel wasn't paying attention. A quick check of the folder labels showed contents A through D. I closed the drawer and carefully slid down to the floor in order to get to the lowest one. Surreptitiously peeking around the corner of the desk to make sure that Mel had not noticed, I eased the drawer open. S through Z. Bingo.

I felt a twinge of conscience as I swiftly found the W's, and my twinge grew even worse as my fingers did the walking through to Watkins, Harold Jr. vs. Watkins, Frances C. . . . It was none of my business, no way, no how . . . but would it hurt anything, really? It's not as though I was reading through someone's personal information in order to use it against them in some way. Although, when I allowed myself to think that far, that was exactly what I was doing, wasn't it . . . assuming that all the speculation and conjecture and guesswork that Marcus and I had run through had merit. But it wasn't for personal gain, I amended in my mind. Just . . . balance in the universe.

Crossing my fingers for karmic luck, I spread the folder out on the wool carpet. The curtains were still drawn tight, leaving the room cast in shadow, and the small desk lamp wasn't doing enough to cut through the gloom, so I was forced to lean in close for a better view as I quickly began flipping through the papers. Irreconcilable differences, financial statements, blah, blah. All went unperused. That wasn't what I was looking for.

Toward the back of the file amid various legal documents and written statements, I came across a manila envelope. Quickly I scanned for a return address for some hint as to the contents. "Bartlett Investigations," I silently read in the upper left corner. That and the words "Private and Confidential" stamped on the envelope made me think I had found what I was looking for.

"What are we doing?"

Marcus's voice came from right behind me, so suddenly that I nearly leapt from my skin. I clapped my hand over my heart and gave him an accusing stare. "Criminey, you could have killed me."

He grinned and tweaked a curl that had escaped from my clips. "Sorry about that. I didn't think I needed to announce myself."

"Did you find something, Maggie?" Mel asked, straightening from her vantage point over on the leather sofa.

"Erm, not yet," I told her, pushing the folder over a bit in case she could see around the edge of the desk.

Marcus handed Mel her cold pop, but she waved a hand at it and went back to her reclining posture against the pillows, resting her head against her hand. He set a glass on the edge of the desk for me—pop again, lots of ice. "No tea that I could find."

"That's okay. It probably would have been instant, anyway," I joked.

"Here, let me help you," he said, taking my hands and pulling me up to a standing position so I could sit on the chair. Then he squatted down and started scooping the folder together.

"Oh, don't do that—" I started, but it was too late. He had already set it on the desk beneath the lamp. His eyebrows raised when his gaze caught on the contents of the folder. He lifted his to mine. All I could do was shrug, my cheeks hot with embarrassment.

Still I couldn't help but feel a *little* bit vindicated when he started flipping through the pages. Eager to help, I reached for the manila folder and drew it out on top.

Cautiously, his eyes on Melanie, he reached for a pad of paper and a pen. *Is that what I think it is?* he wrote.

I took up the pen. *PI report*, I scrawled back.

He glanced over at Mel. No response, so he carefully turned the envelope over.

It was sealed. A large label had been carefully affixed over the top of the retaped envelope, ensuring it stayed that way: "HIGHLY SENSITIVE CONTENTS. REPORT HAS *NOT* BEEN RELEASED TO CLIENTS. KEEP ON FILE UNTIL FURTHER NOTICE. NO EXCEPTIONS."

My gaze flew to his. I grabbed the pen. *Has not been released to clients??* I underscored the s. *Record definitely still sealed.*

Marcus frowned, his mind working a mile a minute. As was mine.

On paper I slashed out: *So if neither Harold Sr. nor Harry Jr. had been advised of Frannie's affair by the firm . . .*

Didn't that also mean that neither Watkins had definitive foreknowledge of the affair? Or was I jumping to conclusions? I was getting myself confused. Perhaps Harry Jr. had

had his suspicions, perhaps not . . . but at least with this unbroken seal, it was pretty much assured that he did not have the outright pictorial proof that this envelope in all likelihood contained. And without that, there went all of our conjecture about the relationship between Harry Jr. and Nunzio like so much toilet water swirling down the drain.

My head was spinning, fact and supposition and intuition no longer separable in my mind. At least I could take solace in the knowledge that Marcus didn't seem to be faring any better.

Grandma Cora always used to say, when you dropped a stitch in your knitting, the only thing to do was to unravel it . . . It was old-timey wisdom, sure, but it still applied. Go back to the beginning. Go back to basics. Get down to brass tacks. Cut your losses and start all over again fresh.

In other words, just the facts, ma'am. Because that was the problem with speculation. Sometimes the facts got lost in the dirty laundry.

Fact: Someone at the Watkins home that night phoned Nunzio. The police mentioned this, so I could only assume they had data to back it up.

Fact: The police were told that Nunzio was an intruder. Hm.

Fact: The police were also told that they, the Watkins, did not know Nunzio. Which of course had to be refuted by the phone record data, not to mention the fact that Frannie knew Nunzio very well. Even I was witness to that little tidbit.

Fact: Harold Sr. was unlikely to have been at his son's home that night, which to my mind made him an unlikely factor in Nunzio's death. Which also made his confession bogus.

Fact: I was talking myself in circles. Was I missing something? I had to be.

Think, Margaret. If it does not make sense, it cannot be true . . .

I tried again. Fact: Nunzio and Frannie had been having an affair.

Frannie and Nunzio. Nunzio and . . .

One other fact did present itself to me, but I was having a hard time going there. There *was* someone at the Watkins residence last night who definitely knew Nunzio, beyond a shadow of a doubt. Frannie. Oh, but that wouldn't make sense either, would it?

Would it?

Not once in all the conjecture and supposition had I allowed myself to explore Frannie as a possibility. Why? I don't know. Maybe it's just that as a new mother fresh from delivering her bundle of joy, she was supposed to be caught up in the heady, heartfelt throes of maternal love. Could that joyous state be put aside for something as ruthless as inviting Nunzio to her home with the intention of shooting him in cold blood? My head was spinning, trying to make the connections.

Because Frannie was the only other possibility, and she was the last one I would have suspected.

Slowly, laboriously, I opened my memory of the last few days, trying to see where my intuition had gone wrong, why I had leapt to seeing guilt where it did not lie—in the laps of Harold Sr., and then, by default, Harry Jr.

Harold Sr. had been the obvious, of course. His confession had effectively guaranteed that he was the first to come to mind, which was just what he had intended. To deflect from the truth.

That it was Frannie who had decided to eliminate the threat of her former lover; Frannie who had wielded the gun.

Marcus was writing on the pad of paper again. I glanced

over. *Frannie,* he wrote, followed by three question marks. Then, *Could it have been?* Funny, that we had both hit on her as a possibility at the same time. The universe works in mysterious ways.

The argument I had overheard . . . is that when she decided to do it? When she realized he was serious about wanting to be a part of her son's life? Was Nunzio really that much of a threat to her happy little family?

I guess the answer to that question was a resounding yes. At least in Frannie's mind.

Blood . . .

The word that Marcus had channeled floated back into my head one more time, only this time it had another meaning that I was suddenly able to perceive, a meaning my mind previously could not grasp. The word was not relevant only because Nunzio had been shot. But also because blood is thicker than water, and blood is what tied the baby to Nunzio, and blood is what Frannie was afraid might have given her secret away?

She hadn't lost the baby's bassinet card in the magazine Joyce had misplaced and my mother had inadvertently brought into Mel's hospital room. She had purposely tucked it away. That's why she had been worried about finding the magazine. That's why she had crumpled the card when we brought it to their house that day. The card listed the baby's blood type. Hadn't Harold Sr. also mentioned something about the baby's blood type being different from Harry Jr.'s? I racked my brain, thinking back. I was almost positive he had. *Another thing he must have gotten from his mother* . . . Dollars to doughnuts, I was betting that the baby's blood type didn't match Frannie's, either. My money was on the odds that it matched Nunzio's.

Blood, I wrote on the pad. *Baby's blood type? Nunzio's, not Harry's?*

Maybe? Marcus wrote back.

Only Frannie knew what really went down. But Frannie had remained silent, all the while watching her father-in-law take the blame for a death she had caused. How had she convinced Harold Sr. to do that? Why had he been willing to step in, rather than let her deal with the situation herself? Was it because he believed in her relative innocence? If he truly thought her innocent, surely he would have believed in the judicial system enough to let the police work through the details.

Or was it more likely that he recognized the true depths of her guilt?

Why else would he have stepped up to the plate?

Or maybe he thought his son was guilty. Harry would have told him the truth . . . but what if he couldn't be sure?

What exactly happened that night?

What should we do? Marcus wrote.

One thing was for sure. There was no way I was going to be finding myself in the middle of this situation. No way, no how. I was more than willing to let the police do their jobs. Except . . . what if no one told Tom and his team about Frannie's relationship with Nunzio? What if no one put those clues together? Would Harold Sr. live out his days in the county jail, waiting for a trial that would send him to prison? Was that fair to him? To Harry Jr. and Joyce? And was it any more fair that Frannie pay the piper for what she had done, thereby stripping Harry Jr. of his wife and Little Harry of his mother?

Sometimes I wished the world was just a little more black and white. It would make decision-making that much easier, wouldn't it?

"I think," I said out loud to Marcus, "we have to make sure someone knows about this."

"Make sure who knows about what?"

Mel had sat up on the sofa with a stretch that made her grimace. I jumped; I'd almost forgotten she was sitting there. There was no way I could tell her what we'd been talking about. No way, no how.

Grabbing the manila folder, I set it safely aside and stuffed the rest of the Watkins folder into Marcus's hands for refiling. "Nothing, Mel," I told her as I started grabbing Greg's personal files by the handful, pulling them out and making a neat pile on the desk. "We're just getting things together for you. I realized after I started looking at this stuff that I just don't feel comfortable knowing what I'm looking for. You'd definitely have a much better idea. Best to just grab the files and get you back to your room at the hospital safe and sound where you can sort through things in peace and still get your rest."

"Back to the hospital! Oh, but—"

I put up my hand. "No; for once, Mel, I insist. You need to get your strength back. Look at you, you're exhausted. You're emotionally at odds. You have a belly full of stitches, for God's sake. And you have four little girls who need you at your best. You need to give yourself time to heal."

She had opened her mouth halfway through my lecture, but by the end of it, she'd closed it, her expression contrite. "I guess you're right. Fine, then." She waved a hand at me, a shadow glimpse of the real Mel. "Gather the files into a box or a bag or something and we'll take them with us."

I was itching to speak with Marcus again, alone, but family always must come first. We made our way back to the hospital and took care of business, returning Mel to her room and checking in with the nurses, who promptly came to scold Mel for leaving. While they made her comfortable, I set Liss's gift for the babies down by her handbag, just a little something for her to discover later. I spoke with the nurses quietly afterward, a word or two to let them know the situation Mel found herself in, just so they would know her emotional state was stretched a bit taut at present. As we were leaving, I caught sight of the babies being wheeled down to her room. Good. Mel needed the distraction just now. Anything to take her mind off Greg.

Marcus and I were silent as we rode the elevator down to the main floor, and I couldn't help thinking, this is where it all began. Had it really been only a couple of days? So much had happened. Life—it could be surprisingly eventful.

What should we do? I asked my Guides and the universe at large. The envelope was still tucked safely away in my bag. Had I been led to it for a reason? To ensure that justice was done?

The answer came, magically enough, the moment we stepped out of the elevator.

Coming through the revolving front doors of the hospital? Frannie Watkins.

Supported between Harry Jr. and Julie Fielding, surprisingly enough, with a distraught-looking Joyce picking up the rear with the baby in her arms, Frannie did not look well. She looked . . . catatonic. Her face appeared almost paralyzed into a mask of neutrality, frighteningly vacant. Her dark hair was a tousled mess around her shoulders. Her clothes hung loose from her body as though she had lost fifty pounds, and I don't mean baby weight. Dark shadows haunted dark, unfocused eyes.

Marcus and I stopped in our tracks, transfixed by the scene unfolding before us. A word from Julie at the front desk, and a wheelchair was whisked up for Frannie, steered by a male orderly and a nurse in cheery, flower-covered scrubs in bright, happy colors.

"Let's just get you to sit down here, hon," the nurse was saying to Frannie, "and we'll get everything taken care of."

Frannie sat obediently but looked up at the nurse with a question in her eyes. "My baby can come with me?"

"No, dear," the nurse said patiently, "it will be much better for him to stay with your husband. He'll take good care of him, just like we'll be taking good care of y—"

"No. No, he can't!" Frannie said vehemently, trying to wriggle free. "He has to come with me. I'm his mother. He—"

"Help me out here, George, would you?" the nurse spoke over her. Together the two held Frannie down while they fastened her into the chair with soft straps. All the while the nurse spoke soothingly. "There we go, no harm done, dear. We'll just get you taken to a nice room, and we'll get you settled in, snug as a bug in a rug—"

"No, I don't want to be here. My baby has to come with me. He has to!"

With a quiet word from the nurse, George the orderly began to push the wheelchair toward the long hallway to the rear of the hospital. The nurse stayed behind a moment to speak with Harry.

"We'll get her processed in and get her comfortable. Don't worry, you did the right thing, bringing her in. Postpartum depression happens. Extreme cases are of course more rare, but we'll take good care of her and keep her from trying to hurt herself. Once we get her settled in, you can come back and sit with her until she falls asleep, if you like."

Harry and Joyce sat down woodenly in a matching pair of the kind of meagerly padded modern chairs found most often in hospitals and office lobbies. They looked shell-shocked. Joyce clung to the sleeping baby like a lifeline . . . and maybe he was.

Julie Fielding caught sight of us watching from our out-of-the-way corner and raised a hand in greeting. With a quiet word for Harry, she came over to say hello.

"More trauma for the Watkins family," she said with a rueful shake of her head. "My cousin Frannie is having a hard time dealing with everything. Harry thought it best to bring her in."

"Now," the voice of Grandma Cora intoned in my ear.

Now? I asked back, my eyebrows raised. *Here? Her?!*

"Now, Margaret . . ."

I put my hand on Marcus's arm. He glanced down at me, but I had the feeling he already knew what I needed to tell him.

"Julie," he said, "do you have a minute where we could go someplace quiet and talk? The three of us?"

Surprised, she hesitated only a moment before she said, "Um, sure. Just give me a sec while I let them know I'm going to get a cup of coffee."

With the everyday bustling noises of the cafeteria surrounding us and keeping our conversation safe, Marcus and I explained everything to Julie over cups of really bad coffee. Everything I had overheard, everything I had experienced, everything I had witnessed, and as a final bit of information I slid the sealed report across the table.

"I see. And what's this?" she asked, her eyes neutral in a way that completely hid her thoughts or emotions from being given away.

"A private investigator's report relating to Frannie."

"Ah. Hm. And you came across this . . . how?"

"We'd rather not say," Marcus interjected. "But we think you should have it nonetheless. It may be important to the Nunzio guy's death."

Between the two of us, we managed to convey the main ideas of our "case" based on hearsay, speculation, and intuition, the evil banes of police investigations the world over.

"You know this is all speculation, right? An arrest cannot be made with only speculation to back it up."

"We are fully aware of that. But speculation can lead to thinking in the right direction, which can then, in turn, lead to the discovery of the truth. And that is why we think you should have this."

Julie looked at us. "And why me?"

Marcus allowed the first hint of a smile to quirk at the corner of his mouth. "Providence chose you for us. Consider it being in the wrong place at the wrong time. Lucky you."

If Tom was a known stickler for playing by the rules, his ex Julie proved far less driven by such stringent personal convictions. My Guides had been right to lead our paths to cross again in the way that they did.

Frannie's arrest, and Harold Sr.'s subsequent release, was quietly reported in the *Stony Mill Gazette* less than a week later. A very beneficial "anonymous tip" led to the discovery of the truth of the matter, as stated by Special Task Force Investigator Tom Fielding. Further details of the investigation were still pending, but the sheriff's department and the prosecutor's office were certain they had the right man. Or woman, as this case had proven out.

Not that Frannie would be going to jail. Her spring, already tightly wound, had seemingly sprung as her psyche seemed incapable of dealing with the enormity of what she had done. Temporary insanity in the throes of postpartum depression might be her best defense . . . assuming she ever snapped out of it.

Sometimes, telling the truth can be freeing. I wondered if that was what Harry Jr. felt as he described what had happened leading up to that night at the Watkins residence.

Tony Nunzio had been carrying on an affair with Frannie during a time when the Watkinses' marriage had been going through difficulties. Harry Jr. found out about the affair in the course of pursuing divorce proceedings—*without* the private investigator's report, which he knew nothing about— but he'd never let on to anyone but his father. But when Frannie came to him and told him she was pregnant, Harry chose there and then to look the other way. He was getting what he'd wanted after all—a family—and the baby *could* have been his, he reasoned.

Nunzio had other plans. Not that he'd wanted the child, not at the beginning at least. Frannie had actually approached him about the baby once she had found herself pregnant. No, Nunzio had wanted to be paid off to leave the little family to themselves. Harry had agreed, because he wanted desperately to keep the illusion alive. No man likes to appear the cuckolded husband. Especially not in a small town. That should have been the end of it, and maybe it would have been, if Jordan Everett hadn't died as a result of the drugs Nunzio had been supplying to him. Nunzio knew he needed to leave town and hole up for a while, until things blew over. Who knew how long that would take? Suddenly the cash Harry had paid him didn't seem like near enough to last. Nunzio was a businessman. He needed to keep his options open.

But Nunzio had what for him was likely a rare attack of conscience or a change of heart when he went to the hospital to warn Frannie that her husband knew about her little indiscretion. Or was he just trying to make trouble on both ends? It didn't seem to matter; at the time, she didn't believe him. But Harry had seen Nunzio skulking around the Labor and Delivery floor that night. He had seen him, and he was afraid of what it meant for his little family.

That night Harry called Nunzio to have it out with him one last time. He knew Frannie would be sleeping, and he knew he himself wouldn't, not with this threat hanging over his head. He'd intended to scare Nunzio, to threaten him, to let him know in no uncertain terms that he wouldn't see another dime. That if he exposed the family secret—because after seeing the baby Harry had been certain that he was in fact Nunzio's child—Harry would in turn see to it that Nunzio went to jail for extortion. The two men argued. Nunzio took off; Harry followed, pursuing on foot even as Nunzio tore off on his motorcycle. Eventually he gave up and just kept walking to cool his temper and try to come up with a plan to keep his world from falling apart.

And that was it.

He didn't know how long he had walked, or how far, but in the end he had to call his father to come pick him up in his pickup truck.

When they got to the house, Frannie was hiding under the covers in bed, the baby was sleeping . . . and Nunzio was lying dead on the floor in the living room.

The two of them hauled Frannie out of bed, whereupon she tearfully claimed that she had been awakened by a noise downstairs and couldn't find Harry. Taking his gun out of his nightstand drawer, she had gone downstairs to investigate and saw Nunzio as only a dark threatening shadow in the living room. She told them she knew it wasn't Harry Jr. because he was far taller and broader, and she was so terrified that she had shot first and asked questions later.

And by that time it was far too late. The bullet had buried itself deep in Nunzio's chest. He was dead before she could reach him.

She was so afraid that she didn't know what to do. So she went back to bed and pretended to herself that it had never happened and simply . . . waited for Harry to come home.

It was Harold who decided that he should take the fall. Harold who loved his son so much that he couldn't bear seeing his whole world torn apart after finally having the family he so desperately wanted. Harold who made them all promise to go along with his confession. The two men summoned Joyce, who brought doughnuts, blissfully unaware of the serious nature of the situation. When Harold met her at the porch with the news, she dropped the box as she rushed to see the truth for herself. Joyce didn't want to go through with the false confession, but Harold was adamant that their new grandchild would need both a mother and a father, so finally she tearfully agreed to do as he asked.

But in the end, the enormity of what she had done had been too much for Frannie to assimilate. Her emotional and mental retreat had been abrupt and sharp and . . . complete. Harry had called Julie for help. Julie had recommended readmitting her to the hospital, this time as a guest of the mental health facility.

No one really knew if Frannie had been telling the truth about coming upon Nunzio in the dark, but everyone was willing to accept it, because truth was subjective after all. Did it matter, really? Either way, the man was dead.

The odd truth of another matter came out later. The baby was actually the child of Harry Jr. and Frannie. The intricacies of blood typing and blood markers had proven too much for her to understand that just because the baby did not have Harry Jr.'s blood type did not mean that the baby was not his. Her worry to that end had been for naught.

Marcus had been right about one thing. A psychic—and I barely considered myself one in the first place—is never one hundred percent infallible. A case in point would be the elevator conversation I had overheard. As it turns out, it had nothing to do with Frannie Watkins or Anthony Nunzio at all. It was merely a synchronicity that worked on various levels of my consciousness and was a mental heads-up to me to start paying attention. That's my story at least.

So what was the real story behind the sinister elevator conversation, and how did it connect to me and to this particular turn of Stony Mill bad luck?

I'm getting to that . . .

Epilogue

Time.

For some it was a great healer, the ultimate fixer of bad break-ups, shake-ups, and heartache. Here in Stony Mill we'd had plenty of those, and among the N.I.G.H.T.S. the general consensus was that it had only just begun. How could it ever be over, when we didn't understand what had started it?

For others, Time was an insidious stealer of all the things they want most in life, stripping it away from them by sneakily changing the rules of obtaining it. Unconscionable and completely without sympathy, like a Vegas strip dealer who gave everyone their cards, let them feel like they were in control of their hand, while secretly waiting for just the right moment to take their last dollar. For all the joyful wishes and hopeful desires held near and dear to our hearts, Time was the one element most likely to keep it from our reach.

To me, Time was all of these, and none. Time simply is.

It's the framework in which we play out the games of our lives, but the secret is not to control it. It is not to master it. It is simply to learn to exist fully within the moment, to be aware of every facet of our being, and to wring every ounce of joy from it. Perhaps we were our own thieves, lamenting the absence of even a spare moment to enjoy life, when all it really takes is to stop the complaints, take the moment firmly in hand, and make it our own. Because the secret is that Time passes, and if you let it, it will leave you in its wake, aching with every beat of your heart and in every fiber of your being for what you have missed.

It was with all of that in mind that Marcus and I planned a backyard get-together two weeks later. Well, Marcus did the planning—it was to celebrate my thirtieth birthday, an event I could probably have lived without calling an over-abundance of attention to, were it up to me. But when he sweetly proposed a gathering of our friends, how could I say no? The summer had been a long one. Celebrating the end of it meant giving thanks that we had made it through unscathed.

Well, I thought as I gazed ruefully down at my plaster-laden ankle, *relatively* unscathed.

Marcus took care of everything, stringing the backyard with white Christmas bulbs that stretched from house to tree to old carriage barn and back again, hanging paper Japanese lanterns from the tree at varying heights, and covering the picnic tables with green and white gingham tablecloths. The gas grill stood at the ready with a selection of steaks and chicken marinating in the fridge, mouthwatering summer veggies on kebab skewers awaited attention on the counter, and homemade strawberry ice cream was electrically churning in the garage. But best of all was the pièce de résistance: a chocolate ganache triple-layer cake, the ganache a delectably shiny drizzle over the top and sides, while in between peeked layers of cream cheese and raspberry preserves . . . all compliments of Annie Miller, kitchen goddess extraordinaire. My mouth watered every time I looked in that direction.

Everything looked perfect. Everything *was* perfect. And if I had anything to say about it, we were going to have a witchin' good time.

And so it was on the Saturday before my birthday that I reclined on a backyard lounger beneath the shade of his giant oak tree with my lemon-fabulous cast plopped comfortably on a cushy pillow and a giganto glass of lavender-infused sun tea by my right arm as my best friends in the whole world gathered around me. Marcus, Liss, Steff, Annie, Tara, Evie, Devon McAllister, Gen Valmont, Joe Aames, Eli Yoder (who had brought Hester, who seemed to have blossomed into life in the five months since I'd first met her . . . *hmm* . . .), and even Mel and the four girls, who with their nonstop chatter and infectious good humor immediately stole the show right out from under me.

Not that I minded.

At least not until Annie and Steff broke out the sparkle paint, faery glitter, and crystal doodads, and encouraged— nay, outright *instigated*—a new and improved version of pin-the-tail-on-the-donkey.

I was the hapless donkey. Or at least the sparkly guinea pig.

Which was why as a peaceful, heart-full lull settled over the gathering I had to raise my former lemon-fabulous cast to the nearest sunbeam to admire my now bedazzled purple/peacock blue/neon green glitter cast that had more bling factor than a Hollyweird starlet's beaded designer gown.

"Do you like it, Auntie Maggie?" Jenna, the oldest of my four nieces at five, raised her excited and proud face to mine.

Courtie chimed in, beaming, "Pretty, i'n'it?"

I put my arms around their chubby bodies and hugged them tight, then planted a resounding kiss on their foreheads. "It's the most beautiful and sparkly and perfect cast I've ever seen. In fact, I told the doctors I wanted one just like this, but"—I shook my head sadly—"they couldn't figure out how to do it. But you two knew just how!"

Courtie nodded, but Jenna tilted her head thoughtfully and looked at me askance. "Didn't they know you can get art supplies at Walmart? That's where Mommy always buys 'em."

"I guess not."

Mel was currently sitting at the other end of the picnic table. She looked tired, but then with two new babies and a husband that had gone off the deep end, I was of the mind that she had a right to be. Greg had showed up again on Mel's first "official" day home from the hospital . . . but it was only long enough to pack a bag, kiss the girls, and tell Mel that he'd been doing a lot of thinking, and what he kept thinking was that it would be better that they end things now, before there was a lot of hate and bitterness between them. He could have chosen a better time to turn Mel's world upside down, rather than hitting her with a sneak attack when she was most vulnerable. So while I couldn't say I was surprised, it didn't improve my views of him, and I was determined that my sister would learn from the experience and make a better life for herself, without him.

Steff, too, was a little down in the mouth that day and trying hard not to show it. But as her lifelong best friend, I saw the signs. I knew. Whatever was going on between her and Dr. Dan, it was serious, and my heart ached for her. Still, in true Steff fashion, she brushed all that aside now because once the cast was sufficiently nontacky from the girls' artistic endeavors, Annie had decided to break out the body-art-quality henna to further enhance my birthday experience, and Steff evidently thought that was the coolest thing in the world. Soon I had beautiful, semipermanent (*oy!*) henna designs staining the exposed toes on my right foot . . . but the two of them decided that would leave an imbalance in my energy field and so proceeded to henna my left foot and ankle, too. The results were so intriguing to Jenna and Courtie that they hounded their mom to let them be hennaed, too. Kudos to Mel for her relaxed approach to it all: a pretty shrug and, "It'll wear off."

The girls managed to sit still through the entire session, thrilled with their swirling, swishing swoops and scallops. To reward them, we broke into the cake.

It really was a lovely, lovely afternoon. Witchin', even.

And then . . .

Two SUVs pulled up in front of the house.

"I think someone's here," I told Marcus.

"Oh?" was his vague response. I saw the slight smile, too, before he hid it away. What was he up to?

My suspicion turned into surprise and bewilderment as from around the corner of the house strode Dr. Dan, wearing his full doctorly regalia of white lab coat, casual khakis, button-down shirt, and stethoscope.

Steff froze in obvious confusion. "Dan. What are you— But I thought you—"

Without a word he took her by the hand and led her over to a lawn chair that had magically (as opposed to *magickally*) appeared on a bit of lawn set apart from all the others. I glanced over at Marcus. He was humming to himself, smirking and gazing skyward. Guilty. As. Could. Be.

At Dan's urging, Steff sat down, completely and utterly bemused.

Still without uttering a single word, Dan snapped his fingers. All of a sudden a number of other doctors of assorted ages and sizes, each outfitted in lab coat and stethoscope of their choosing, appeared out of nowhere. Or at least from the front yard.

Ever the dutiful host, Marcus shook their hands and greeted each by name:

"Dr. Carmichael."

"Dr. Darcy."

"Dr. Murray."

"Dr. Crandall."

"Dr. White."

"Dr. Brooks."

"Dr. Osterman."

Only Marcus and the good doctors seemed to have a clue as to what was going on, and they weren't giving anything away.

Dr. Dan paced back and forth for a few moments while Steff's consternation and worry grew. Finally she could take it no more.

"For heaven's sake, Dan, what on earth is all this about?"

Dan turned his back on her and faced his doctor friends. "Gentlemen?"

The very professional, very dignified doctors formed a half circle behind him.

All my hairs were standing on end. Whatever was going on, it was going to be good.

Dan stuck his arm out and pointed a finger at Marcus: "Hit it."

Grinning like the loopiest of loons, Marcus pushed a button on the MP3 player. Lead-in music—horns, drums, and even a fiddle—began to blare out through the speakers. And as we all watched with mouths that had fallen open in amazement, the doctors began to sway in time to the music, some twirling their stethoscopes around like a burlesque diva's feather boa, others snapping their fingers in time to the music in a raucous parody of the climactic chapel scene in *Mamma Mia!*

Dan clasped his hand to his chest and sang:

"Steff, I love you dearly. It's been a year, or at least nearly . . ."

The doctors stopped in place and sang their parts:

"Say I do! I do, I do, I do, I do love you . . ."

And then it was Dan's turn again. He got down on one knee and took her hand:

"Marry me, baby! You love me, and I don't mean maybe . . ."

Steff's mouth had fallen open. Before the docs could launch into their group entreaties, Steff squealed, "Yes! Yes, yes, yes, yes . . ." and did a little launching of her own—straight into Dan's waiting arms. So hard, in fact, that they both fell backward into the grass, doing a fair amount of damage to Dan's pristine white lab coat.

Honestly? I don't think he minded.

The rest of us threw up huzzahs and cheers all around. But I had to laugh when Jenna tsked, a frown drawing her brows together, and shook her head. "They're getting all dirty. Bet their moms are gonna be *real* mad."

And when Steff, in between the thousands of kisses she was pressing all over his face, pulled away just for a moment and exclaimed, "I didn't even know you liked *Mamma Mia!*" Dan laughed and kissed her. Properly.

Caught up in the excitement and delight of the moment, I grinned over at Marcus, and he grinned back. "You knew all about this," I accused.

"Yup."

"And you didn't say a word!"

He bent over and kissed me on the nose. "I know how the two of you are."

When Dan came up for air at last, he stood holding a blissful, if dazed, Steff in his arms and told me, "Sorry for interrupting your birthday party, Maggie, but I had to know where Steff was going to be in advance in order to pull this off, and this was the best way I could think of. I just really wanted to make it special for her."

Mission accomplished, methinks.

"When you overheard me and Dr. Crandall hashing out our plans at the hospital—and I still don't know how you managed to do that—and then spilled the beans to Steff that someone was planning *something* . . . well, I guess I just panicked. I probably came off a little harsh, but I didn't want Steff or you digging into anything at the hospital, just in case someone accidentally let something slip."

Now it was my turn for my mouth to fall open. "So it was you I overheard? Not a Machiavellian plot at all?"

Dan laughed. "Well, I wouldn't go that far. We did have to do a fair bit of scheming and conniving."

I glanced at Steff and giggled. She was staring at her left hand, oblivious to all, perhaps blinded by the rock on her ring finger. "Well, I think *she* at least forgives you."

And so the wheel turned. Another notch forward on the gears of the history of this small town. Stony Mill doings may be provincial to some, insignificant to others . . . but I think we've all proven one thing at least:

Deadly, Stony Mill might be; but lifeless we are not.